THE DESIGN IS
MURDER

Previously published Worldwide Mystery titles by
JEAN HARRINGTON

DESIGNED FOR DEATH
THE MONET MURDERS
KILLER KITCHENS
ROOMS TO DIE FOR

Acknowledgments

To my legal guide and friend Attorney Carolyn Alden; to handwriting analysts Andrea McNichol and M. N. Bunker, who was the founder of the International Graphoanalysis Society. To the *Naples Daily News* for its ongoing coverage of the python infestation now attacking the Florida Everglades; to Naples Detective Mike Haburjak of the Collier County Sheriff's Office, Financial Crimes Bureau; to my steady and insightful critique partners and fellow writers, Brenda Pierce and Joyce Wells. And of course, to super editor Deborah Nemeth, who improves my manuscripts with unfailing patience and skill.

Also, although the State of Florida prison system does not provide a furniture construction program for inmates, other prison systems in the United States do, and this book borrows on that fact.

THE DESIGN IS MURDER

JEAN HARRINGTON

The design is murder / Jean Harrington

WORLDWIDE.

TORONTO • NEW YORK • LONDON
AMSTERDAM • PARIS • SYDNEY • HAMBURG
STOCKHOLM • ATHENS • TOKYO • MILAN
MADRID • WARSAW • BUDAPEST • AUCKLAND

To each and every friend of Deva Dunne, whoever you are and wherever you may be.

PLEASE RECYCLE
THIS PRODUCT IS RECYCLABLE

Recycling programs
for this product may
not exist in your area.

The Design Is Murder

A Worldwide Mystery/June 2016

First published by Carina Press.

ISBN-13: 978-0-373-26996-9

Copyright © 2014 by Jean Harrington

Printed in U.S.A.

ONE

I SLIT THE envelope with my Colonial pewter-handled letter opener, slid out a thin sheet of lined paper and read,

To Mrs. Deva Dunne,
My name is Number 24601. I'm also known as Mike Hammerjack, a guest of Florida State Prison. I'm in for embezzlement, 10 to 20, with time off for good behavior. After a few detours you don't want to hear about, I'm trying to do my best. That's why I'm writing to ask a favor, not for me, for my fellow inmates. Like me, most of these guys don't belong behind bars, but that's another story.

As a reward for cooperation, some of us work in the carpenter shop, making custom-designed furniture—chairs, benches, tables, desks—mostly out of pine, in different finishes.

Here's where you come in. Everything we make is up for sale at very reasonable prices, with the money going to prisoners' families. Little kids, exes, etc. I read an article about you in Design Magazine and hope you can use our pieces in some of your projects.

If you're interested, contact Warden Bill Finney

*here at Florida State, and he'll send you pictures
and info about our products.*
    You won't be sorry.
Sincerely yours,
Mike Hammerjack, President
Help-a-Con Program

Written in a tight, crabbed hand with fancy flourishes, the letter wasn't easy to read, and I had to wade
through the squiggles twice to understand it. Despite the
poor handwriting, the letter was obviously the work of a
focused person and, for some reason, I believed Number
24601 was sincere in writing to me. Then again, I tend
to root for the underdog. I'm from Boston originally,
and the Red Sox are my beleaguered team. Though they
seldom make it to the Series, I love them anyway. As
for a guy in prison reaching out to help his fellow cons,
he deserved a break, didn't he?

"Of course, he does, darlin'," echoed in my head.
Dear Nana again, though she'd been gone for fifteen
years now. "Help the lad, if you can." Gone but not silent.

I put the letter on my desk with a sigh. God only
knew what prison-made furniture looked like. Clumsy
most likely. Knocked together by big, rough hands.
Still…

The Yarmouthport sleigh bells on the entrance of
my interior design shop suddenly did their job, jangling
like mad as the door opened, admitting a distinguished
middle-aged gentleman. What else would you call a
silver-haired man cradling a Maltese puppy in his arms,
and wearing a silk suit and cravat on a hot July day in
Southwest Florida?

I rose from behind my desk to greet him.

"Are you Ms. Dunne?" he asked without preamble.

"Yes, I'm Deva Dunne. How may I help you?"

He took a step forward and said, "Do forgive me for not offering my hand, but Charlotte won't let me put her down." He caressed the dog's head. "Will you, dearest?"

The dog licked his fingers. I guess that was a no.

"She's adorable," I said, sort of meaning it. A tiny white scrap of a pooch, Charlotte didn't look like she'd ever heard of "paws on the floor," or "stay" or, perish the thought, "roll over."

"I'm sure she's easy to indulge, Mr...."

"Stahlman. James Stahlman."

I gulped. Hard. His name wasn't one easily forgotten, not after being plastered all over the *Naples Daily News* for days on end. That had been some months ago, yet the cloud hovering over him then still lingered. Had he, or had he not, killed his wife?

TWO

"I'M ABOUT TO be married," James Stahlman said. "As a surprise for my bride, I'm planning to give my house a fresh new look."

"The entire house?"

"I don't believe in half measures, Ms. Dunne."

"I see." Standing straighter—when I don't slump, I'm five-six—I said, "May I ask where your property is located?" A rhetorical question. I knew. Whiskey Lane.

"I'm at 590 Whiskey Lane," he said, stroking Charlotte softly. "I want you to see the house, and after that we can discuss any changes you deem appropriate. By the way, it may please you to know you come highly recommended."

Well, you don't, I wanted to retort, but there I went again, jumping to conclusions. Mr. Stahlman hadn't been convicted of murder, or if so, only in the court of public opinion. The official conclusion was that his wife, Marilyn, had accidentally drowned while cruising the barrier islands on her husband's yacht.

"Thank you," I said, keeping my voice politely noncommittal.

He seemed innocuous enough, standing in the middle of the shop, patting Charlotte's topknot and taking care not to disturb her perky pink bow.

At the time of Marilyn Stahlman's death, how such a champion swimmer could drown so mysteriously in the middle of the night had been the cause of much speculation. It still was and no wonder. Her body had never been found.

Anyway, I hoped what I was thinking didn't show on my face.

Apparently not, for he said, "So shall we make an appointment for you to tour the house? How does tomorrow at two strike you?"

For the second time that morning, the sleigh bells jangled, and I glanced past Mr. Stahlman toward the front door. An unshaven teenager lurched in, his knees popping out of his jeans, his eyes popping out of his head.

I froze. A Beretta aimed at your face would do that to a person.

Finger shaking, I pointed toward the doorway. "Look!"

Mr. Stahlman swiveled around, spotted Bug Eyes and in his shock dropped Charlotte—*boom!*—to the floor, probably for the first time in her fluffy little life.

"Don't move," our intruder said. As if we could.

"What do you want?" I asked, my voice as shaky as my knees. "I just opened up. There's no money in here."

"Quiet." He waved the gun at Mr. Stahlman. "Drop your wallet on the floor. Then slide it over to me. No fast moves."

James Stahlman reached inside his breast pocket and slowly withdrew a leather billfold. Bending down, he placed it on the floor, and with the toe of his polished loafer sent it sliding across the room.

To Charlotte, that meant party time. As the wallet skittered across the floorboards, she pounced, grabbed the leather in her teeth and, happy with her new toy, scampered around the shop, dodging between chair legs and swooping under the round table skirts.

The mugger followed the dog with his doped-up eyes and the muzzle of his gun. "Get the damned wallet, fast, or I'll kill that mutt."

"Mutt!" The word tore from James Stahlman's lips. Finding the insult too grievous to ignore, he drew himself erect. "She came in second in the Westminster Dog Show."

"Who gives a shit?"

As the Beretta ominously followed Charlotte's every move, the morning sun glanced off the dull barrel. *Dull? Ah!* The gun was a plastic fake. Mr. Tough Guy Mugger was playing Cops and Robbers. He wasn't even armed. I was sure of it—well, pretty darned sure. My father had been one of Boston's finest and taught me everything he knew about weaponry. But the price of a mistake could be fatal. While I tried to decide what to do, Charlotte did the deciding for me.

The mugger approached her, gun cocked and aimed. She took one look at him and dropped the wallet. A five-pound ball of fluff with the body of a crumpet and the heart of a lion, she leaped for his hand and sank her perfect little teeth into it.

He howled, and with Charlotte clinging to his flesh, he raised his arm. Swinging her around like a furry slingshot, he flung her through the air. She sailed across the shop, landing with a squeal on the zebra settee, a dazed expression on her face, her bow at a nutty angle.

Forgetting all danger to himself or to me either, Stahlman rushed to his darling and picked her up, murmuring sweet nothings into her ears.

Our mugger grabbed the wallet where the dog had

dropped it, flipped it open and removed what looked like a hefty wad of cash. He threw the raided billfold on the floor, and with a final menacing wave of his pistol, yanked open the front door and disappeared down the alley to a rousing chorus of sleigh bells.

"My brave girl," Stahlman said. "My dear, brave girl."

He sure wasn't speaking to me, but that was all right. Charlotte had been terrific and deserved the praise. All I'd done was stand frozen in uncertainty. Now that the danger was over, I thawed and sprang into action.

"I'm calling the police."

"No! No police."

Cell phone in hand, I stared at him, dismayed. "You're kidding me."

"Not at all, Ms. Dunne."

"Actually it's Mrs., but after what we've just been through together, do call me Deva."

"Of course." He stroked Charlotte's fur and kissed her yet again. "And I'm James. But no police, Deva."

The phone clutched in my sweaty palm, I said, "Why not, for heaven sake? You've been robbed."

Cradling Charlotte in one hand, he bent over to pick up his wallet.

"Don't touch that," I yelled. "Fingerprints!"

Despite my warning, he pocketed the billfold.

"You shouldn't have done that," I said. You've just destroyed evidence."

"The money is negligible. My important papers are intact. That's what matters."

"But—"

He held up a single finger for silence, so I put the

phone down on the sales desk, and without saying any more, waited for his reasoning.

He cleared his throat. "I'm assuming you read the local newspaper."

"Every day. As a small business owner, I have to. It keeps me informed as to what's going on locally."

"Then you probably know of my wife's unfortunate accident. It happened nearly a year ago…the publicity was relentless."

"Yes, I remember."

"The problem, Mrs….ah, Deva…is that *everyone* remembers. The last thing I want is more adverse publicity."

"But you were the victim here."

"No matter. The story will read badly in the media. I don't want that spotlight trained on me ever again." He shuddered and straightened Charlotte's bow. Gave her back her dignity. Then with a frown, he glanced up at me. "Do you understand how I feel?"

"I do," I said, trying not to sigh. *There goes a plum client.* "Your wishes are important to me, James, but in this I'm afraid I can't please you." I waved an arm at the door. "That's open to the general public every day. Suppose the thief returns?"

"Hmm." James sniffed. "I see your point. Very well, do what you must, but I won't stay to be interrogated. If need be, the police will know where to find me."

He was so clearly distressed, I semi-caved. "Tell you what. A friend of mine, Lieutenant Rossi, is a Naples detective. I'll call him first. If he can keep this incident out of the media, he will."

James smiled, revealing teeth that were long and yellowed but in excellent repair. "I appreciate that." He reached into his breast pocket and, fumbling past his raped wallet, he retrieved a business card and held it out to me. "Until tomorrow then. As I said earlier, before our, ah…adventure…I'm getting married soon. My first wife would have wanted a new life for me. Marilyn would have as well. I'm certain of it."

I must have forgotten some of the details in the newspaper reports, but with his reminder, they flowed back like a tsunami. Marilyn Stahlman, who disappeared at sea a year ago, wasn't James's first wife. But like the first one, she too had died an untimely death under mysterious circumstances.

THREE

"WHY DIDN'T YOU insist on calling the police immediately?" Rossi asked an hour later after he sent out an APB with a description of the thief. His face was exasperation red—somewhere between beet and burgundy. "Or insist that he leave the billfold untouched? The thief's prints could have been all over it. If he's in our database, we might have nailed him by now."

I sat slumped on the zebra settee without even bothering to cross my legs, though they look better that way, longer, curvier, sexier. Regardless, I didn't bother. Too demoralized. At least I was until Rossi squeezed in beside me and took my hands in his.

"Sorry to sound so harsh, sweetheart, but I worry about you and these scrapes you keep getting into."

"But that's not—"

"Fair," he finished. "I know. The creep who robbed your client just wandered in. You said Stahlman drove off in a new Mercedes sedan. The robber must have spotted him coming into the shop and pounced. He was probably cruising the Fifth Avenue area looking for a mark."

Rossi kissed me, but only a careful peck on the cheek. Though he'd put the Closed sign in the shop window, two women had already rattled the door handle, wanting to get in. I won't say we were in a goldfish

bowl exactly, but seated hip-to-hip on the narrow settee, we were a lot like two tropical exotics on display.

"I really should reopen, Rossi. I have nothing more
to report. As soon as James left with Charlotte, I called
to—"

Rossi reared upright. "Another woman was involved?
You didn't mention that."

"Well, Charlotte's not a woman, but she is quite a
girl."

"Want to clarify that?"

"Charlotte's a Maltese."

"A *what?*"

"She's a dog. A lap dog."

"Oh."

"And she takes her work very seriously."

"Whatever that means." He eased back beside me
and wrapped an arm around my shoulders. "Despite
Mr. Stahlman's wishes, I have to file a report, though
an unshaven, glassy-eyed teen isn't a lot to go on. Even
holey jeans doesn't add much to the picture. And you
didn't get a look at a fleeing vehicle or a plate number."

"I'm sorry—"

He stopped me with a kiss. Under the circumstances,
not one of his best, but even his non-best was very,
very good.

"Nothing to be sorry about," he said, when he lifted
his lips from mine. "It is what it is. And there's a chance
one of the cruiser teams will spot somebody fitting the
description. But it's a long shot. Unless he tries something again. If that happens, would you be able to identify him?"

"Of course, but you don't think—"

Rossi gave my shoulder a reassuring squeeze. "He

probably won't return here. But he might try something similar in another store." He brushed a tendril of hair from my forehead. "I don't want to scare you. Or maybe just enough so you'll be careful. Should you ever see him lurking around here again, call me immediately." Rossi took my hand in his and stroked it.

I loved his touch. I loved his warm peppermint breath fanning my cheek, and I absolutely adored his smolder-ing deep-set eyes. He could light fires with those eyes and had—in me. And I haven't even mentioned his big white smile. He doesn't flash it very often, but when he does, it's well worth the wait.

On the other hand, he wears hideous Hawaiian shirts and leaves the tails hanging out over his white pants. Today he had on his favorite shirt, orange linen scat-tered with red plumeria blossoms. He claimed his casual appearance helped suspects relax during interrogations. At least that was his theory. What scared me was that I had started buying into his look. Actually I'd bought into a lot more than that, but not kissing on display. I wriggled out of his embrace, turned the Closed sign to Open and unlocked the door.

"Duty calls," I said without returning to the settee.

"I should go anyway. I have desk work waiting at the station." He stood. "Tonight? Your place?"

I nodded. "Please."

A spark flashed in his eyes, igniting that same old fire in me. "You begging, Deva?"

A leading question, but asking provocative ques-tions was Rossi's stock in trade. He arched an eyebrow, waiting.

"Absolutely," I said, and after a quick glance down Fern Alley to make sure no one was coming, I gave him a farewell kiss that shot his plumeria blossoms into outer space.

Two could play head games, right?

FOUR

THE NEXT MORNING the shop phone rang up a storm before I could yank the key out of the front door. I dropped my bag on a chair and sprinted over to the sales desk.

A voice like a file rasped through the line. "My name's Hawkins. Stewart Hawkins, and I've got a house that needs some TLC. Or whatever the word is that you dames use."

"I beg your pardon, Mr....ah...Hawkins."

"No need to apologize. My bride wants the place done over. Doesn't like the colors, doesn't like the furniture. You know how that goes. I heard you're good at this stuff, so that's why I'm calling." He paused to cough and take a breath, or maybe puff on a stogie. "You want to come over now and take a look?"

"Now? Well, I don't know—"

"You don't need the business?"

"Mr. Hawkins—"

"That's right. You got it right. People at the Port Royal Club have been raving about your work. So my bride hears this and doesn't want anybody else." He lowered his voice to a whisper. "Just so you'll know what to expect when you get here, her name's Connie Rae. She's from Eureka Springs, Arkansas, and has fake red fingernails." A slight pause. "Everything else is the real deal, I can vouch for that."

"Delighted to hear that, Mr. Hawkins, but—"

"She usually hangs out by the pool, so you can come over anytime today."

"Today I have other—"

"You'll need the address," he said, butting in as if I hadn't spoken. "It's 595 Whiskey Lane. Just ring the bell and walk in. I'll be home all day too. Hey, I'm on my honeymoon. Got enough work cut out for me here, if you know what I mean. You got that address? Five ninety-five. See you later."

He hung up, and a dial tone replaced his take-charge voice. I lowered the receiver slowly, intrigued that he apparently belonged to the Port Royal Club, Naples's most prestigious private enclave. The address he gave me was intriguing too. A quick computer check of MapQuest proved what I suspected. Mr. Stewart Hawkins lived directly across the street from James Stahlman. A coincidence? Hmm. Maybe, or a little neighborly competition perhaps. Two families vying for the same designer. That kind of one-upmanship went on all the time.

On the other hand, I was probably giving myself too much credit. Mr. Hawkins most likely had no idea James had already contacted me. Well, at this point, neither project was a done deal, so in the interest of keeping my business alive, I'd check out both possibilities. If they both came through, I'd make two things clear. One, their interiors would not copycat each other, and two, my dealings with each would be kept completely private. To do otherwise would be totally unprofessional.

Despite the complication, I couldn't help but feel excited. Two clients on the same street, imagine! And two initial tours of their houses on the same day. Well, why not? Like a true Red Sox fan, I've always enjoyed a double header.

FIVE

THOUGH I DISLIKED doing it, for two hot potential clients I locked up the shop once more. While interior design firms like mine didn't thrive on walk-in sales of pillows and lamps and aromatherapy candles, turning off casual shoppers wasn't a good move. You just didn't know if today's browser would become tomorrow's major player.

But with my friend and assistant, Lee St. James, on a second honeymoon, I had no choice. So reluctantly, I posted the Closed sign in the front window where it couldn't be missed, right next to a bergère I'd found at my favorite antiques-collectibles source. The chair's wooden arms and legs had the kind of worn gilt finish I loved, and I'd had my workroom reupholster the cushions in a cheetah-print velvet. King Louis would have died at the mix, but that unexpected pairing made the old piece a knockout. Against one of the chair legs, I'd propped a white cardboard square that said,

> *From throwaway*
> *To throwaway chic.*
> *It can be done!*

The little tableau had garnered quite a bit of interest and a few good clients. It was doubtful a prison-made chair would have the same oomph as the old Louis, but that remained to be seen. Anyway, the shop secured, I hurried out to my Audi and drove down Fifth Avenue South, Naples's equivalent of L.A.'s Rodeo Drive.

Located on Fern Alley off Fifth, Deva Dunne Interiors was close enough to the high-rent district to make the shop seem like a part of the glamour. And to make me feel like I was one of the beautiful people, a little self-delusion that didn't do any harm and lifted my spirits.

I passed the street's major gem, the Sugden Theater, its palm tree-studded square a delightful green oasis in the heart of town, and continued on past planters spilling color and fragrance all along the way. For the length of time it took to drive the avenue, it was easy to believe all was well with the world. Another delusion.

But at least for the moment, everything *was* well in my world, and I took time as I drove to glory in that. If only everything could stay the same, the hot July sunshine, the flowers, the salty Gulf breeze, and Rossi and me just as we were last night. He had been amazing, tender and warm, passionate and…demanding. My face warmed thinking about him, or maybe the July sun shining in through the windshield caused my cheeks to heat up.

A truck's horn blared, yanking me out of my reverie. I pressed on the gas and turned left onto palatial Gordon Drive. For once I didn't rubberneck at the mega-mansions fronting the Gulf of Mexico. A working woman and glad to be one, I ignored the over-the-top opulence and concentrated on my driving. On Whiskey Lane, magnificent banyan trees lined both sides of the street, their lush crowns arching over the roadway. Behind the trees, stately homes peeked through the mature foliage like beautiful faces from behind a veil.

House number 595 turned out to be a steep-roofed structure that from the sidewalk looked quite modest. A deceptive view, I guessed, for the house probably reached deep into the lot.

I pulled onto the driveway and climbed out of the Audi. A panel truck with Tony's Tiles & More painted on the side in big red letters sat in front of me, its two rear doors open wide. A man in grout-stained coveralls was lifting pails and tools into the opening.

I smoothed down my green mini and grabbed my tote and clipboard. "Hello," I called.

I must have startled him, for he slammed the truck doors and swiveled around, his eyes narrowing.

"Are you leaving soon?" I asked. "My car's blocking you."

"That's okay, lady," he said, turning back for a moment to lock up. "I'll be on the job a few more hours."

"Fine then. I'll leave the Audi where it is. If you need me, I'll be inside."

"No problem."

I turned and walked away, but feeling his gaze hot on my back, I glanced over a shoulder. Sure enough, both hands stuffed in his overall pockets, he was watching me intently. Tall and bald and mountain-man skinny, he appeared to be somewhere in his mid-thirties. Caught staring, he forced out a smile and sent me a two-fingered salute. I returned it with a flourish and followed the yellow brick path up to the front door.

As Stewart Hawkins had directed, I rang the bell, and then again, but no one answered.

Ring the bell and walk in, Hawkins had said, so I

twisted the knob and opened the door. Calling "Hello," I stepped into a foyer paved with Mexican tiles. Directly ahead lay the living room and, beyond, a screened-in terrace and pool. To the left ran a short corridor that probably led to a bedroom wing, and to the right an interesting architectural feature, a small rotunda with several doors opening onto…what? There had to be a kitchen somewhere, and a…

"You the decorator?"

I whirled around. Coming from the direction of the terrace, a fifty-something man strode toward me wearing a swimsuit, a cigar and nothing else. At least the swimsuit wasn't skimpy. Thank God.

Though he was of medium height, everything else about him was writ large, very large—belly, thighs, biceps, neck—everything.

As he came closer, I backed up a step. "Mr. Hawkins?"

"Of course. Who else hangs out around here?"

Who else, indeed?

"You didn't answer the question," he said. "You the decorator?"

God, I hated the word *decorator*. "Yes, I'm Deva Dunne," I said coolly.

"Classy name."

"Really?" No one had ever told me that before, and I looked at him—well, at his hairy chest—with a freshly minted admiration. "Actually my first name is Devalera. After Eamon DeValera, my father's political hero."

"That right? No wonder you shortened it."

"Exactly."

Cigar clamped in his teeth, he yanked a shirt off the back of a chair and slid into it, leaving it open and unbuttoned. I guess he didn't want to obstruct my view of his chest hair.

He upped his chin in the direction of the terrace. "I was just going for a dip, but it'll wait. Unless you want to join me?"

I gestured at my green skirt and cropped white jacket. "I'm not dressed for the occasion."

"Oh, yeah." He grinned suddenly. "There's always skinny-dipping."

"Well—"

"Never mind. Some other time." He rested the cigar on an ashtray, where it smoldered sullenly, and stuck out his hand. "Stewart Hawkins. Call me Stew."

I let him prove his machismo by crunching the bones in my fingers. After flexing my hand to restore the blood flow, I handed him a business card. "How may I help you, Mr....Stew?"

"I bought this place a month ago. Before I met the little lady...the bride...so nothing's been done in here. Except for some chairs and stuff that I already had, this is the way the previous owner left it. The bride and me both want to make some changes. I've got my ideas about what that means, and Connie Rae's got hers." He pointed a thick forefinger at me. "Your job is to figure out whose ideas are good and whose stink."

My turn to point a finger. One tipped with Tropical Tangerine nail polish and aimed straight at his nose. "Hold everything right there, Stew. I can't get in the middle of a marital dispute."

He picked up his cigar, took a deep drag and exhaled a lung-clogging cloud of smoke.

I coughed, a hint to put out the Tampa-Havana or the stogie or whatever that noxious thing was, but my cough meant nothing. He took another puff and said, "Of course, you can. You deal with couples all the time, so handling family disputes is part of your job description. I know that for a fact. So you got a choice here, take my offer or leave it. But before you leave it, let me tell you this." He stepped forward, poking the air with his cigar and giving me a better view of his chest hair than I wanted. "I'm the one with the money. Not Connie Rae. Got that?"

"You're bribing me."

"Exactly. Now, you want a tour of the place?"

"Will Mrs. Stew be joining us?"

"Doubt it. She's still in bed. Last I looked, she was out like a light. So it'll just be you and me. Come on." Crooking a finger, he beckoned me toward the fascinating rotunda. "Over here's the kitchen. Let's start there."

No harm in taking a look now that I was here, so I tamped down the moral dilemma and followed my unlikely Pied Piper into the heart of the home. After all, what did I have to lose?

SIX

An "Ahhh" escaped me as I trailed Stew into a stunning high-ceilinged space that combined a compact kitchen-in-a corner with a soaring great room.

"Look at this." He waved his arms at a bank of windows overlooking the pool. "No privacy at all."

Through the wall of glass, I could see the man from the panel truck busy on his hands and knees, chipping away at some loose pool tiles.

"Every time I throw an arm around the bride, Tony's in on it," Stew said.

So that *was* Tony I'd spoken to in the driveway.

"And me a shutter manufacturer. It doesn't seem right, you know what I mean?"

"You run a shutter business?"

"Yeah. Florida Shutters. Couples come in, and nine times out of ten they each want something different. That's how I know you settle marital disputes. Me too. It's part of the game. Too bad I couldn't solve some of my own."

He dropped the spent stogie in the sink and ran a little water over it. Lovely.

He looked up quickly, caught my frown and ignored it. "You've done business with us. I checked the books."

"Yes, several times. Your product is excellent."

"That's the other reason I called you. One local business should help another."

"You're hardly local, Stew." I knew Florida Shutters shipped all over the southeast, and possibly beyond. If Stew was the CEO and driving force behind the company, he was undoubtedly a wealthy man. Having Deva Dunne Interiors lumped together with him gave me a momentary high, but I came back to reality fast. "Strange we never met before now."

"I leave most local floor sales to my staff. Spend my time out back in the plant. I'm a hands-on kind of guy."

"I can see that," I said, eyeing his beefy fingers, each one sprouting a little crop of black hair. "I take it you'll want shutters on all these windows."

"You got that right. On every damned one."

I dropped my tote on a chair, picked up the clipboard and made some notes. The scope of the room already had my creative juices flowing. "Do you mind if I photograph the interiors as we go through? For reference?"

He nodded. "Do what you have to."

I turned to get a shot of the kitchen corner and gasped. Where had she come from?

A short, voluptuous woman in a white nylon uniform stood rinsing the sink, a pained expression on her face. *See*, I wanted to say to Stew. *I'm not the only one who's disgusted.* But of course, I did no such thing.

"Oh, hey, Deva, this here's Teresa. The best chef Puerto Rico ever produced. Isn't that right, Teresa?"

Teresa smiled and nodded but said nothing.

"She makes the best paella you ever tasted. Only thing is she's deaf as a post. Can't hear much at all." He flexed his fingers. "Good thing I got talented hands."

My jaw must have sagged, for he chuckled and said, "I'm talking about signing. Watch me."

With a series of gestures that even an orangutan

could interpret—puckering his lips, twisting his wrist back and forth as if pouring something into his mouth, and then blowing out short puffs of air over an imaginary cup, he told Teresa he wanted a drink. A hot drink.

"Coffee, Mr. Stew?" she asked, her voice loud and clear.

Triumphant, Stew turned to me. "See! Works every time."

It was obvious that Teresa was toying with his need to believe she couldn't hear a thing. A weird little game to play, if nothing else.

Stew didn't give me any time to dwell on the matter. "Come on. While she makes the coffee, I'll show you the rest of the place."

We toured every room, from the formal dining room to a wonderful walk-in pantry that would hold multiple sets of china and glassware—what a dream—and on to his klieg-lit master bath. I took notes as we strolled but not many. An overall impression is what I was after, and so far the house showed well, though a bit too pastel for Stew's over-the-top personality. What it mainly needed was an infusion of color pops and some comfortable seating. And maybe some of Hammerjack's rough-hewn prison furniture in the study.

Finally we came to a set of closed double doors. "Showtime," Stew said. "I have to get the bride out of the sack." He winked. "I don't say that often."

"No, let's not disturb her," I whispered. "I've seen most of the rooms. The bedroom can wait for another time."

"No time like the present," he said, opening the doors and barging in. He pressed a wall switch next to the door, sending floor-to-ceiling draperies swishing open, flooding the pink-hued room with sunshine.

Sprawled on her back in the center of an ultra-king lay a naked blonde, her hair fanned across a pillow, her legs spread apart in open invitation. I wanted to leave and give her some privacy but, fascinated, I stood and stared as Stew strode over to the bed and grabbed a handful of sheet.

"Look at that," he said, gazing at the girl, whether in admiration or disapproval, I couldn't tell. He draped the sheet over her and, bending down, shook her shoulder.

"Come on, babe, rise and shine."

Connie Rae didn't move.

"Is everybody around here deaf?" he asked of no one in particular. He patted Connie Rae's cheek, and no doubt would have patted more than that except for the designer looking on from the foot of the bed.

Pale all of a sudden, he glanced up, stricken. His eyes wide, he said, "You know something? She's cold. Ice cold. And she's a funny color too. Kind of blue looking. I think she's—"

He never did finish what he started to say, for without any warning at all, he passed out, falling belly first, right on top of Connie Rae's breasts.

I screamed and ran out of the bedroom toward the great room. I'd left my tote there with the cell phone inside, and I needed the phone. *I needed the phone.*

Teresa collided with me in the rotunda. "I heard a scream. What's wrong?"

"Stew. His wife. We have to call 9-1-1."

She grasped my arm, staying me. "Where are they?"

"On their bed. Out cold, both of them."

She raced past me. I grabbed the phone out of my

purse and chased after her. Not wasting another second, I pressed 9-1-1. "A medical emergency," I said to the dispatcher. "At 595 Whiskey Lane."

"Is the person breathing?" In other words, dead or alive.

"I don't know for certain. But I don't think so."

SEVEN

By THE TIME I reached the master suite with the phone still glued to my ear, all three of them were on the bed, and Teresa was trying to peel Stew off Connie Rae's supine form. On her knees on the mattress, she tugged at his arm and called to him. "Mr. Stew, Mr. Stew. Wake up. We need help. Wake up."

Without looking over at me—she'd obviously heard me come in—she said, "A glass of water. Hurry. In the bathroom."

I flung the phone on the bed and dashed into the bath, filled a water tumbler from the sink, and hurried back to press it into Teresa's hand.

She took the glass from me and, without a moment's hesitation, flung the contents in Stew's face…well, he *was* wearing a swimsuit. The cold splash roused him, and sputtering and gasping, he came to.

"Oh my God," he said. "She's dead. My Connie Rae's dead."

"Hello? Hello?"

I grabbed my cell. "Sorry, I had to put the phone down."

"Any change in the patient?"

I glanced across the bed. Stew and Teresa were both busy trying to coax Connie Rae back to life and, from what I could tell, not having much luck.

"Her husband's trying to revive her, but I don't think she's responding."

Stew looked up. "Tell them to hurry."

The dispatcher must have heard him. "Someone will be there within three minutes," she said.

"Help's on the way," I said to Stew, but he wasn't listening. Teresa had straddled Connie Rae and started CPR.

"I'll wait outside for the ambulance," I said, and hurried from the bedroom, but not before Stew whispered to Teresa. "I'm dead meat after this. The cops'll say I killed her."

Why would he think that? Without waiting to ask, I dashed out to the front lawn. True to the dispatcher's promise, in a minute or so, an ambulance roared along quiet Whiskey Lane. I flagged it down, thanked the dispatcher and hung up.

"This way," I said, leading the two paramedics into the master bedroom with its pink satin-topped bed and deep-piled shag rug. Teresa climbed off the bed, and together we helped Stew stumble out of the room.

After spending several frantic minutes trying to revive Connie Rae, the medics pronounced her dead. As was standard procedure in a case of unexpected death, they remained on the premises and notified the police.

While we waited, Teresa served Stew his coffee, which he raised to his lips with a shaking hand. "I can't believe this," he kept muttering. "I can't believe it. Poor Connie Rae. Poor little rich girl." At that he snorted and sent coffee spray spewing across his chest. Absentmindedly, he wiped it off with a palm and sat staring, coffee forgotten, out to the pool where Tony, ignoring all the drama, was still on his hands and knees working the tiles.

Car doors slammed, and Stew stiffened in his easy chair. "They're here. Oh God."

Teresa hurried to the front door. A moment later two Naples Police Department officers strode into the great room. Some things never change, and once again big, beefy Sergeant Batano accompanied by his partner, petite, no-nonsense Officer Hughes were the first responders.

They'd been first on the scene last fall when I found the body of my old friend, José Vega. But from their behavior today, you'd think they had never clamped eyes on me before now. A curt nod of Batano's crewcut head was his only greeting. And as for Hughes, no change there either. She was the same pretty poker face. I returned Batano's stingy nod and let it go at that. For once I decided to keep quiet until I was asked to speak. Not exactly a new thing for me, but not easy either.

After telling us to remain where we were, they followed the medics into the master suite. When they returned a few minutes later, Batano stood, legs apart, in front of Stew's chair. It forced the bereaved husband—always a person of interest in a spouse's unexpected death—to look up at him, deliberately creating an uneven playing field, so to speak.

In between sips of his now lukewarm coffee, the pale, shaken bridegroom gave his initial testimony. "My wife's name is…was…Connie Rae Freitas Hawkins."

"How old was she?"

"Twenty-two."

"Her place of employment?"

A brief, humorless laugh. "Bartender at the Port Royal Club. That's how we met."

"How long were you married?"

"Three weeks." Stew's voice broke. "Three great weeks."

"What do you think happened to her?"

"I don't know. I just found her like that." As he spoke, his hand shook so badly that what was left of his coffee slopped over the rim of the cup.

"Had she been sick?"

Stew shook his head. "Not to my knowledge. You saw her body. She look sick to you?"

As he answered Batano's questions, irritation began to intensify Stew's natural testiness, but though he didn't know it yet, he had only begun to fight. Wait till Rossi interrogated him. It could go on for hours. Poor Stew. His grief seemed genuine, but then I'd been wrong about people before.

"That'll do it for now," Batano finally said to him. He pointed out to the pool where Tony stood surveying his work. "Get him in here," he said to Hughes. "I have to call Lieutenant Rossi."

While Hughes went outside to fetch Tony, Batano hauled out his cell phone and with fingers poised over the pad, said, "You can be assured, Mr. Hawkins, that your wife's death will be thoroughly investigated. The county coroner and a homicide detective will be here shortly."

Stew let out a soft groan and slumped back in his chair. Even his chest hair drooped.

EIGHT

THAT EVENING, TOO agitated to sit, Rossi paced my living room. A study in frustration, he waved his arms in the air as he wove a path back and forth in front of me.

"I could not believe, I absolutely could not believe you were there in that room when I walked in."

"After what happened, you know I couldn't leave, and besides Stew wanted me there."

That stopped him dead in his tracks. "Oh? Stew, is it? How long have you known this guy? His wife dies suddenly under mysterious circumstances, you're on the scene and now you're calling him Stew like you're old friends."

"Are you jealous, Rossi?"

"Jealous? Jealous! I'm worried, for God's sake. Worried. About you."

I patted the sofa cushion. "Come sit beside me, please. I don't like to see you so upset."

He heaved one of those sighs that start deep in the belly, but after a few more passes on the carpet, he sank down next to me and placed a hand on my thigh. "My intention is not to be difficult."

"Or juvenile," I added, trying to inject a little humor into the evening.

"That either, but you do have a penchant for being on a crime scene before the police, before the medics, before the coroner, and—"

"Before you."

"Bingo!"

"It's simply coincidence. Every time."

"Say I buy that," he said, stroking my knee, my thigh, my arm. "That doesn't mean I like what I bought. This Hawkins character, for instance, is nobody you want to get too close to. We've been checking into his background, and so far what I've read I don't like."

I sat up straighter. "What?"

"Okay, for your own safety, I'll tell you this. He has a record of domestic violence."

I drew in a shocked breath. "Against Connie Rae? They were only married three weeks ago."

"No, against his former wife, Kay Hawkins. On several occasions in the past couple of years she called the station for help. Said she was afraid of him. He was drinking and out of control. One report states that the officer found her with a black eye."

"He beat her?"

"That time she said she'd gotten up at night and walked into an open closet door." He shrugged. "Who knows?" His hand on my knee tightened. "But I do know you need to stay clear of this guy."

I slumped back against the cushions. "Not to worry. He called me this morning, said he and his bride wanted to redecorate their house, but after this, I doubt I'll hear from him again. Poor little Connie Rae. I wonder why she married him."

"I can think of a few million reasons," Rossi said sounding cynical and looking irritated. "Only twenty-two years old, and Hawkins is fifty if he's a day."

"A May and December romance I guess."

"Or maybe a beauty and the beast romance, but in

fairness to all, that remains to be seen. In the meantime, please be careful."

"I will. Though tomorrow I'm due back on Whiskey Lane. I have an appointment at 590, the house directly across the street from Stew's. But I won't go near 595. I promise."

"Good." Leaning in closer, he treated me to one of his famous smiles and to what was morphing into a really beautiful, soothing, sexy massage.

THE MOMENT I rang the chimes at 590 Whiskey Lane, James Stahlman, with Charlotte in tow, opened the front door of his stately two-story house.

"Deva! Come in," he said. "Do come in."

"Happy to." I held out a hand. "Thank you for allowing me to reschedule."

His well-manicured fingers briefly touched mine. "Not a problem."

He had dressed down this time, in linen shorts and a starched white shirt. He struck me as older and more nervous than I remembered. On the other hand, Charlotte looked exactly the same, frisky and relaxed, the pink bow still riding the crest of her topknot.

Curious as to what I'd find, I entered the foyer and glanced around. Spacious but nondescript rooms opened off both sides of a central hall, and at the end of the hall James ushered me into a glass-walled living room that extended across the back of the house. A typical Florida layout would feature a pool outside that rear glass wall, but from the look of the terrace and garden area, there wasn't one. Strange. James's last wife had been a champion swimmer. She'd have wanted a pool, wouldn't she?

"I've arranged for tea," he said, stroking Charlotte

as if her life depended on it. "But first I thought you'd like a tour."

"Yes, by all means."

"Though before we tour, we must talk. So please sit down."

No question about it, James was tense. If he kept patting Charlotte so vigorously, she soon wouldn't have a topknot left to love.

He waited politely until I took a seat on a living room wing chair before sitting across from me with Charlotte on his lap. He'd been right about the interior needing a redo. One quick look around the room revealed that it was stuck in a time warp. Somewhere in the late eighties. That faded blue wallpaper would have to—

"Imagine how I felt," he began, his voice throbbing with emotion. "Just imagine. I've never been so shocked in my life."

"I'm not following you, James."

"I'm referring to the circus that went on across the lane yesterday. You were there. You know all about it. Although possibly not everything."

In his distress, he dumped Charlotte onto the floor. "Go play, sweetheart," he ordered in a tone I doubt sweetheart was accustomed to.

"I know Mrs. Hawkins passed away at a tragically young age."

"Mrs. Hawkins!" James actually snorted. "My fiancée is Mrs. Hawkins. At least for the time being."

"You're confusing me, but that's easy to do," I fibbed, striving for some levity. Actually I'm not easily fooled—at least not all the time.

"My fiancée, Kay Hawkins, is that man's former wife."

Startled by his unexpected revelation, all I could think to say was, "Oh my."

"Exactly. Now why, I ask you, *why* did he choose to buy a house directly across the street from mine?"

"I have no idea."

"Well, I do. Surveillance, Deva, surveillance. He wants to spy on us. On our comings and goings, to be a constant presence and threat to Kay every day of her life."

"Surely you're exaggerating, James."

"No, I am not." His emphatic tone left no room for argument. "The police are aware of how he treated Kay. The many calls she made for help. Her black eye. It's all on record."

True. Rossi had told me about Kay's marital woes, but I don't think Rossi was aware that she would be living across the street from Stewart Hawkins, her former husband and the very cause of those marital woes.

"I knew 595 had been sold," James was saying, "but I was too busy with my own interests to inquire as to the buyer. A mistake. Had I known, I would have purchased the property myself and resold it to someone suitable. Someone less *lethal*."

At the venom in his voice, I stiffened. What on earth had I gotten myself into? In an attempt to defuse his anger, I said, "Stewart Hawkins hasn't been accused of any wrongdoing. Not in his wife's…that is, Connie Rae's…death."

"Mark my words, he will be. It's just a question of time."

Charlotte was whining at his feet. He scooped her up. "Am I neglecting you, darling?" he asked.

She licked his face. *Yes*.

"What worries me the most," he continued, "is that Kay is terrified. Positively terrified."

Under the circumstances, who wouldn't be? "Would you consider selling and moving?"

"Kay asked me the same thing. Begged me, in fact. But I had to refuse her. What kind of man allows himself to be forced from his home? A home, I might add, that I've lived in since the late eighties."

Thought so! I experienced a moment of professional triumph, then forgot about it when James went on, "I was almost equally shocked when you called yesterday from the Hawkins house. I couldn't believe it, in fact. Had you really considered taking on both Hawkins and me as clients?"

"Of course. There was no reason not to. Though when Stew contacted me, I had no idea of your past... shall we say history together." I paused for emphasis. "I trust you understand that I never work exclusively for any one person."

"Perhaps not." He sniffed. "But I would prefer you work either for me or for him, not for the both of us."

"I can't promise you that, Mr. Stahlman," I said and stood. "Naples has several excellent designers. I'm sure you can find one to suit your wishes."

As I bent to pick up my purse, James put Charlotte back on the floor, a sure sign he was upset. "Please don't take that attitude, Deva. There's no need. You're my designer of choice, and I will not be deterred by Hawkins or anyone else. I simply needed to state my preference. That's all it was, a preference. Apparently Hawkins and I are already sharing a tile repair service. I saw the truck in his driveway yesterday. So why not share a designer?" He nodded at the chair I'd just vacated. "Do be seated. I'll ring for tea. I think we both need a little refreshment before we tour the house."

While I sorted out my reaction to being lumped in with Tony the Tile Guy, James raised a small silver bell from the table beside his sofa and rang it. Like wind chimes caught in a breeze, its tinkle echoed throughout the room.

A moment later, a stocky middle-aged woman with sturdy, no-nonsense legs appeared from what I guessed was the kitchen. She wore her hair in a bun, and like Teresa was dressed in a white uniform. As if acting in an English farce or something, she said—so help me God—"You rang, sir?"

"Yes, Eileen. Our tea please."

"Very good, sir."

Stunned, I sat back as far as the wing chair allowed. *This should be interesting.*

Our repast must have been ready and waiting, for in the short time it took to boil a kettle of water, Eileen reappeared, pushing a tea wagon laden with a silver service, blue and gold porcelain cups and saucers and a mouthwatering array of luscious-looking morsels.

In years past, I'd enjoyed one or two formal teas at the Copley Hotel in Boston, and the Copley, I decided, perusing the tea wagon, had nothing on Eileen.

"Would you do the honors, Deva," James asked as Eileen pushed the cart up to my chair and quietly left.

The challenge was awesome. This was dowager stuff, pouring tea. *You can do it,* I told myself, and gripping the silver pot by its curvy handle, I poured James's tea into an exquisite Limoges cup.

With the devil urging me on, I asked, "One lump or two?"

James, however, didn't get the humor in that. "Just lemon, please."

The tension over, I poured tea for myself and passed a dish of precisely cut finger sandwiches to my host. Getting prison-made furniture in here sure was going to be tough.

As we munched and sipped, he asked, "What do you make of the house so far?

I put down my cup and cleared my throat. "Its bones are wonderful, and it's aging well, but if you'll pardon my saying so, it could benefit from a facelift."

He fed Charlotte a nibble from his plate. Unsatisfied, she sat in front of him and gazed up expectantly, her big brown eyes wide and waiting.

"No more," he said.

Ha!

And to me, "Would you explain what you mean by facelift?"

If I were reading him correctly he was annoyed at the analogy. What a shame that tact and truth were such poor bedfellows.

"Let me answer that with a question." I pointed at the living room walls. "How long has this paper been here?"

"Oh, since…" he fed Charlotte another bite—*I knew he'd cave*, "…1990 perhaps."

"And the upholstery on the chairs and sofa?"

"The same."

"The draperies?"

He held up a palm for silence. "I see your point."

I believe he did, but to nail it in firmly, I said, "Are you aware that colors in home décor wax and wane in popularity, much like colors in the clothes we wear? Oh, some classics—the little black dress, the tailored white shirt—remain eternally in vogue. But many do not, and those date us. Do you recall tie-dyed T-shirts and neon orange minis?"

"Hardly. But I understand what you're saying. The colors in here are dated."

"I'm afraid so. And badly faded. If the rest of the house is the same, then what you need, James, is a clean sweep, and that calls for a master plan."

"I like the way you think, Deva. Let's finish our tea and then complete the tour."

"Fine." Now that James and I had an initial meeting of minds, I was enjoying my cucumber sandwich when the front door opened and a pair of stiletto heels clicked briskly along the hall.

Alarmed, James glanced up. "Oh dear," he said, absent-mindedly popping a morsel meant for Charlotte into his own mouth. "We've been caught red-handed. I think that's Kay."

NINE

As James and I watched—with bated breath, for some reason—Kay Hawkins strode into the living room. Tall, lithe and late thirties, she had streaked brown hair falling to her shoulders, and though not beautiful like poor Connie Rae, she was nonetheless stunning. And in her purple dress, carrying a lime-green straw bag, she was clearly a woman who wasn't afraid of color.

At the sight of us she stopped short. "Tea for two. How charming," she said in a bitchy tone that meant exactly the opposite.

James scrambled to his feet and held out his arms. "Darling," he said in the same voice he used on Charlotte. "What a surprise."

"Indeed," she said, eying me without moving into his outstretched arms. "One doesn't know whether to leave or to stay."

Oh heavens. Time to jump in. I stood and held out a hand. "I'm interior designer Deva Dunne, Mrs. Hawkins. Your fiancé—" I might as well establish the correct pecking order, "—is planning a surprise for you. And I seem to be it."

We shook briefly, fingertip to fingertip. Then I rummaged in my bag for my card case, removed one and gave it to her. With a show-me frown on her face, she took the card and glanced at it. Tapping it on a thumbnail, she turned to James. "You're planning to redo the house for me?"

"Yes, darling," he replied, his voice loaded with relief.

"How lovely, Jimmy, but did it not occur to you that I might like to be part of any changes?"

His face fell. "But that would negate the surprise."

"Precisely," she said.

"I thought while we were on our wedding trip, Deva here could sweep in with her crew and give the rooms a…a facelift. Then when we returned, you'd have a wonderful new look awaiting you."

"But, Jimmy," she said, pointing a cerise fingernail at the house across the lane, "haven't we had enough surprises? And besides, how do I know Deva's changes would suit me? We may have totally different taste."

"That would not be a problem," James said. "I intended to direct the project from the get-go." He waved a rather thin arm around the living room. "As I did years ago when I purchased the property and redid the interior." He flicked an imaginary fleck of lint from his shorts. "Pardon me for boasting, but I do have a gift for this sort of thing."

Kay shot a quick glance my way, and our eyes locked. We were on the same page. I knew in that moment we'd work around Jimmy—I mean James—and that together Kay and I would make a good team.

I fake-checked my watch. "I do have another appointment this afternoon," I lied. "So if it's convenient, shall we begin our tour?"

AFTERWARD, I DROVE back to the shop, delighted with the Stahlman meeting. Decisive and direct, Kay had wasted no time informing both her fiancé and me about her color preferences. As a concession to James, she would include cobalt blue as an accent, and loved my idea of combining that with coral and white and adding touches of black for sheer drama. Recently I'd seen a gorgeous Thibaut paper in coral with silvery birds that would make a sensational dining room, especially with James's silver pieces polished and on display, perhaps on a mirrored sideboard. We'd agreed to retire two of his brown dining chairs and replace them with upholstered host and hostess seating, and re-cushion the others. And that was just for openers.

I was actually humming when I opened the shop and took down the Closed sign. At my desk, I sorted through the mail, tossing circulars and opening bills and a few checks. An envelope with a familiar crabbed handwriting embellished with fancy flourishes caught my attention. I slit it open, removed a thin sheet of lined paper:

Good news, Mrs. Dunne,
The parole board finally came through and granted my release. Thought you'd want to know in case you need to contact me about the Help-a-Con Program.

Not to worry. I have brochures and price lists for all the prison furniture and will stop by your shop and drop them off. That might not be for a few days, though.

Once I'm sprung, I'm getting in on the last week of the Python Challenge, so I'll be in the Everglades by the time this reaches you.

See you soon. Wish me luck with the snakes.
Yours truly,
Mike Hammerjack

TEN

EGADS, THE PYTHON CHALLENGE. I shuddered, unable to believe people actually went into the Everglades—the biggest swamp in the world—and searched for Burmese pythons. Just the thought made my skin crawl.

According to the *Naples Daily News*, the pythons were decimating the Everglades' native wildlife. In an attempt at control, the state was sponsoring a month-long hunt for the critters. Some were seventeen feet long and strong enough to kill an ox or a deer or a grown man, slowly by constriction.

As an incentive, the hunter who caught the most snakes would win a prize of fifteen hundred dollars. Not nearly enough in my opinion. To up the challenge, the pythons had to be killed or captured humanely by snare or net, not by blowing their heads off with a pistol or stabbing them in the throat.

Anyway, since no guns were allowed in the hunt, I guess the fun had been okayed by Hammerjack's parole officer. Then fresh from tangling with the snakes, Hammerjack would pay a visit to Deva Dunne Interiors. Terrific. Rossi had been so upset about the Hawkins case last night, I wouldn't mention receiving letters from Florida State Prison. Why upset him further?

On the other hand, Hammerjack didn't necessarily mean trouble. He could simply be a reformed man wanting to reach out and help others. Wasn't it a well-known fact that people with the least were the first to offer assistance to those in need? They understood from personal experience what being in harm's way really meant.

I folded the letter with the prison return address and put it in a desk drawer with the first one. Yesterday, Kay had mentioned she'd like to turn one of the guest bedrooms into a personal study. That would mean installing a computer station, a desk, bookcases. Maybe I could put the Help-a-Con Program to use in there after all.

Pythons. Funny, I'd lived in Naples for several years now, and the only snake I ever saw was a little black garden runner. The diameter of my pinkie finger, it was maybe seven inches long, but when I spotted it on the lawn I'd screamed like I was in mortal danger and jumped onto a patio chair.

Snakes that were seventeen feet long boggled my mind and raised goose bumps on my arms. I shook my head, relieved when the Yarmouthport bells on the shop door jangled.

A woman who looked strangely familiar stepped in and gave me a radiant oh-there-you-are-again smile. Had we met before? I got up from behind my desk to greet her and realized—no, she couldn't be—yes, she was—Teresa in the flesh and looking spectacular.

Fluffed-out Big Hair cascaded past her shoulders, and red-tipped nails matched her movie star lipstick. Hugging her curves, a mini sheath careened to a stop just above her knees, and platform stilettos added inches to her height. At her throat a rhinestone leaf sparkled like a Broadway sign at midnight. Va va va voom! A filled up Brassy de Bra in the exuberant flesh. So long, white nylon uniform and sensible oxfords.

"Teresa," I said, extending a hand as I strolled toward her. "Is this really you?"

She laughed, pleased, I think, at my confusion. "Yes. This is me all right."

"You're not deaf, are you?"

She shook her head. "No. I never was."

"Then why pretend to be?"

"Oh, it's a game Stew and I...I mean Mr. Stew and I play."

"Really?"

At my question, or maybe my quizzical tone, the confidence a tight skirt and stilettos can give a girl wavered for an instant. An instant only, then her mouth turned down at the corners. Way down. "I pretended to be deaf when Stew...Mr. Stew was married to that Kay woman."

That Kay woman. I recognized female animus when I heard it. Teresa clearly hadn't liked Kay.

"I don't understand," I said.

"They fought so much, shouting matches night after night...oh, it was awful...so I began acting as if I couldn't hear a thing. It made life easier for all of us. Mr. Stew—" she got it right that time, "—liked me for pretending and kind of made a joke out of it."

The stilettos must have been killing her. She shifted from one foot to the other then back again as she dug around in her shoulder bag. "I have something for you. From him."

She rummaged in the purse a while longer, searching for whatever it was. "I can never find a thing in this bag."

Two women could bond over that alone.

"I know the feeling. Do come and sit down."

She teetered after me and perched on the Eames chair in front of my desk. After a few more seconds of poking, she produced a white envelope and handed it across to me.

"For you. A retainer from Mr. Stew. He wants you to work on his house, but not until this, this...*mess* is over."

"Mess?" I asked, knowing full well what she meant. Who *was* this woman, really?

She nodded. 'Yes, his new wife's death. The police are questioning him, acting as if he caused it. He can't sleep. He can't eat. Not even when I cook him his favorites. It's not fair."

I tossed the pewter letter opener onto my desktop. "A woman is dead, Teresa. A very young woman. The police want to find out why. For that they have to get at the truth."

"The truth?" She actually scoffed. "The truth is Stew should never have married that bimbo in the first place."

Stew. Interesting. The word *Mr.* was apparently a frill she'd decided to abandon.

While she looked on, I slit open the envelope she'd given me and gasped. Sight unseen, without even hearing a single one of my design ideas, Stew had sent me a check for ten thousand dollars. What a show of confidence. Frankly I was thrilled and wrote him a receipt on the spot.

"Please give this to Mr. Hawkins with my thanks," I said, handing it to Teresa. "I'll be awaiting his call after the funeral is over and he's recovered from his grief."

"I don't think there'll be a funeral. Stew needs to forget all this and get on with his life." She dropped the receipt into her bag and stood, smoothing the mini over her thighs.

Hmm. Where did she come off displaying an attitude like that? I didn't like it. I didn't like it one bit and indulged in something I despised, a nasty female barb.

"When Stew gets on with his life, as you put it, you think he might get married again? With you as his new bride?"

She looked me straight in the eye. "That's exactly how I see it."

To that I had no response. Her brass-plated nerve took my breath away. Plus her recklessness. If the autopsy showed Mrs. Connie Rae Hawkins was the victim of foul play, then Teresa had just revealed a perfect motive for murder.

ELEVEN

AT CLOSING TIME I was at the computer logging in initial design ideas for the two Whiskey Lane houses when the Yarmouthport bells swung into their happy dance.

I glanced at the door. "Rossi!" I leaped up from my chair and hurried over to him.

He turned the lock in the shop door and took me in his arms right in front of the plate glass window. After kissing me breathless, he said, "I have a surprise for you. So get your purse and close up for the night. We need to leave while there's still plenty of daylight."

"This time of year, the sun doesn't set until about eight o'clock. So what on earth is your hurry?"

"If I tell you, there's no surprise."

"You know something? You sound like James Stahlman."

His hand on the light switch, Rossi frowned. "The guy whose wife disappeared a year ago? The accidental drowning?" His frown deepened. "Accidental until proven otherwise."

"He's the one."

"You know him?"

"We met the other day. He's my other client on Whiskey Lane."

"Your *other* client? You mean you've taken on Stew Hawkins after I warned you to stay away from him?"

"I hate to be crass, Rossi, but a ten-thousand-dollar

retainer trumped your warning. The business needs the cash infusion. I simply can't afford to turn him down. Besides, Stew hasn't been accused of a crime, has he?"

Rossi pressed the off switch for the overheads with more force than necessary. "No, I haven't received the autopsy report yet. But Hawkins's rep with women is pretty unsavory."

"He has a housekeeper." *Boy, did he have a house-keeper.* "She'll be there whenever I am. And except for the first one or two planning sessions, I'll be meeting tradespeople on the property. I won't be alone with him."

"Good. That's something anyway. Now all I have to worry about is this other guy. This Stahlman." Rossi held the door open for me. "You know his last wife's disappearance is still an unsolved case, but are you aware his first wife died of an overdose?"

"No." I shook my head. "I never heard that."

"Well now you have. So don't go swimming with the guy and don't take any pills from him."

"Very funny, Rossi. For your information, he's a consummate gentleman. Even served me tea, for Pete's sake. From a silver pot."

Well, technically *I* had served him, but that was beside the point.

I locked up and, tucking my arm in his, Rossi escorted me down Fern Alley to Fifth Avenue where he had parked his party wheels. Usually for everyday events like work or picking up a pizza and a bottle of Chianti, he drove his old, deliberately unwashed Mustang. Like his Hawaiian shirt theory, his dirty car theory aimed at disarming suspects into thinking he was an inept flatfoot. For special occasions though, like this apparently was, he rolled out his vintage Maserati. Sleek, silver and shined to the max, the car had been a gift from his late Uncle Beppe and Rossi loved it. No wonder. It was a special vehicle for a special guy and made me feel special too each time I slid onto the red leather passenger seat beside him. Like now.

So he did have a big surprise in mind, and I was aware of a rising excitement. What could it be?

We drove to his secret destination with the car windows open. Through some miracle of Mother Nature, humidity didn't clog the air. Instead, a dry Gulf breeze with a hint of jasmine and oleander wafted over us and riffled my red Irish curls. But I had terminal frizzies anyway, and Rossi actually liked my hair on the wild side.

I tried to compensate for it by wearing rather conservative clothes—no super minis, no sky-high platforms, no XS sweaters. After all, I *was* in the taste business, although I've been known to tell my clients that style begins where the rules end, at least as far as interior design is concerned. But I digress.

From Fifth Avenue we headed north on the Tamiami Trail, past the street leading to the Naples Beach Hotel, then past the Community Hospital and through two stop lights until we reached a set of stone markers that read Calista Sands. Rossi turned in between the markers and drove slowly along a lush, curvy street lined on either side with gracious, low-roofed houses of a comfortable but not ostentatious size.

Quietly residential yet near enough to Fifth Avenue and Old Naples to be centrally located, Calista Sands was one of the neighborhoods in town I most admired. Too bad I couldn't afford to live there.

In fact, driving by one well-groomed property after the other, with their manicured lawns that even in the torrid midsummer heat were as green as if it were early May, I was drooling mentally.

"Look at that one, Rossi," I said, pointing to a house I especially liked. "And that one. It's beautiful in here."

"I know," he said, taking his attention from the road for a second to glance across the front seat and treat me to a big, white Chiclets grin.

He was happy about something. That much was plain. But *what?*

Rossi never drove fast, always five miles under the speed limit, never five miles over it. Tonight he was outdoing himself, driving the Maserati as slowly as if it were a sightseeing bus loaded with tourists. For some reason, he didn't want me to miss a thing.

We kept heading west, toward the setting sun, or more precisely, toward a wide finger of water, an inlet that marked the end of Calista Sands and the beginning of the Gulf of Mexico. At an empty waterfront lot covered with stubbly sawgrass and sprouting a For Sale sign, he stopped and turned off the motor.

"What do you think?" he asked, turning to me. "Do you like it?"

Though a light bulb had popped on in my head, I said, "Like what?"

"The lot. It's empty."

"I can see that."

A frown replaced his grin. "You're not making this easy for me."

"Rossi." I took his hand in mine. "Are you saying you want to buy this lot?"

"Yes."

"And build a house on it?"

"Yes."

"Am I in the picture?"

"Triple yes. You're the reason I've been looking."

"You *have?* I didn't know that."

"The surprise," he said.

"Oh. Right. How long?"

"Three hundred feet deep by one fifty wide."

"No, I mean how long have you been looking for land?"

"Since the day you proposed." The grin was back.

I had to smile, remembering how the duvet cover had slipped and… "I *did* propose to you, didn't I?"

"Positively, and I accepted. So don't try to wiggle out of anything." His grip on my hand tightened. "You're mine, and I want you. I've wanted you since the day we met. I think it was those little green shorts you had on that did it. And your sorrow over losing Jack. I knew in that moment you were a woman for a lifetime and…" his voice faltered, "…I've never told you this, but I envied Jack that day. And there's something else, too…I was grateful to him for dying and leaving you free for me." He let go of my hand and stared into my eyes as if he could still look but had lost the right to touch. "Do you hate me for that?"

Tears sprang into my eyes. I swiped at them with the back of my hand. "No. Never. I love you for your honesty." And I did. Life had taken Jack, my first love, but had given me a second chance at happiness. I'd be a fool to let it slip away. I retook Rossi's hand and squeezed hard, letting my fingers tell him what I was too soggy to say. We spent the next several minutes acting like teenagers in love before he said, "Shall we get out and look around?"

"Yes, let's."

We made our way over coarse patches of scrub grass. On both sides of the lot, well-cared-for houses faced the shimmering blue Gulf, their screened-in lanais taking advantage of the view. In front of the one on the left, a glistening Chris-Craft was moored to a small wooden dock.

"The inlet has Gulf access," Rossi said, pride of place already clear on his face.

"It's wonderful. The view, the neighborhood, the surrounding houses. Only one thing is bothering me."

"What's that?" he asked, sounding faintly alarmed as if I had noticed something he hadn't.

"It's so perfect, it has to be expensive."

He shook his head, visibly relieved that I had no other objection. "No, not really. It's been on the market since the beginning of the housing crisis. The owner is eager to sell."

"May I ask the price?"

"No."

"Or how you intend to pay for it?"

"No, ma'am."

Like the Cheshire cat's, his grin reached both ears. He was enjoying himself. On the other hand, I was getting ticked. Halfway back to the car, I stopped midstride. "If you trusted me, you'd answer my question."

"Of course I trust you. Implicitly. But—"

"Nothing matters until you reach the 'but.' So why won't you answer the question?"

"As you pointed out, this location is perfect for us,

and I have no intention of risking a 'No, Rossi, it's too expensive.'"

He took my arm. Though I tried to shrug away, he held on tight and together we wended our way over the rough grass back to the Maserati.

Once inside the car, he said, "Let's watch the sunset for a while."

"Fine." I stared straight ahead at a frieze of palm trees lining the shore and beyond at the blue Gulf water.

"You asked if I trusted you," Rossi said softly.

"It was a logical question." Ice frosted my tone.

"Now I'm asking you the same question."

I half turned to face him. "You're very good at interrogation. I'll have to remember that."

"You're not going to give an inch, are you?"

"All I want to hear, Rossi, is what the damn lot costs. What's wrong with that? You said you're buying it with me in mind."

"Even in Dorchester I'll bet people don't ask the price of a gift."

"Oh." I put my hands on my hips, letting my left elbow jab him in the ribs. "So now you're insulting my background."

He laughed. Out loud. "God, you're impossible."

At his laughter, my anger fizzled out like a wet firecracker. "I think we're having a lover's quarrel."

"Those are the best kind, the aftermath is so great. This parcel of land is my gift to you. Your name will be on the deed. And on the house I want to build here." His gaze left the view to focus on me. "You spend your life creating beautiful houses for other people. Isn't it time you had one of your own?"

"And for you?"

"Yes, for the both of us."

I exhaled and nodded, partly satisfied and partly not. Rossi's gesture was beautiful. How could I not love him for it? But dammit, I did want to know how much the lot cost.

I eyeballed the For Sale sign. I could call the listing agent and ask the price. That would be sneaky, though, and I couldn't cheapen Rossi's gift that way, but I did huff out a sigh.

Like Kay Hawkins, I wasn't sure how I felt about being surprised and wondered, suddenly, if James Stahlman had any more in store for Kay. And if Rossi had any more for me. I didn't know how Kay might feel about that, but I knew secret surprises weren't easy for a redhead from Dorchester.

TWELVE

TANNED AND TERRIFIC in a new butter-yellow sundress and matching espadrilles that wrapped around her ankles, Lee St. James waltzed into work the next morning. All smiles, she caught me in a bear hug and said, "I want y'all to know I've been on the best second honeymoon ever."

I believed her. Always beautiful, today she radiated happiness.

"So Hilton Head is a good vacation destination?"

"I can't rightly say, Deva. I didn't see much of the town."

"No?" I smiled but tried to hide it.

"Uh-uh. Just the little bitty beach in front of our hotel and the dining room. Though we mostly ordered in room service."

"And how was the room service?" I arched an eyebrow.

She perched on the Chiavari chair behind the bureau plat. "I wish I could say, but if my momma were alive, she'd be shocked if I did."

"That good?"

"Yes, ma'am." She blushed and changed the subject. "When we got home, though, we had some bad news waiting for us."

"Oh? Sounds serious."

She nodded, frowning. "It is, even if Paulo says it's a first-world problem."

I sank onto the zebra settee across from her. "Lee, explain, please."

Her lips trembled ever so slightly. "We're being evicted."

"From your apartment?"

"Yes. And the owner didn't tell us why. Just wants us out as soon as our lease is up—at the end of the month. It's not fair. We thought the lease was being renewed, and we've taken such good care of—"

"I know you have." I blew out a breath. "Now what?"

"Well, we'll look for a temporary place if we have to. But what we really want to do is buy a house. Paolo says we can afford a condo to start. Something like yours at Surfside, with two bedrooms and a lanai and a pool, would be just about perfect."

"Funny you should say that. My place is going up for sale as soon as I get around to putting it on the market."

"Really?" Her eyes widened into two blue pools. "Wait till Paulo hears that. Do y'all mean it?"

"Absolutely," I said, deciding in that instant.

Though I hadn't a clue as to how much Rossi would pay for the Calista lot, I did have an idea of what a lieutenant in the Naples P.D. earned. So unless he had more surprises in store, we'd need the equity from both my condo and his house in Countryside to build our new dream home.

"My goodness," Lee said. "I leave for a week and come back to all kinds of changes."

"True." I laughed. "There's been a lot of excitement around here in the last few days."

We spent the next couple of hours straightening merchandise and greeting drop-in browsers. We were catching up on girl talk when a tall, statuesque brunette with excellent carriage strode past the front window. A moment later, James Stahlman's fiancée, Kay Hawkins, pushed open the shop door, sending the bells into their usual frenzy.

Holding her shoulders as square as a sergeant-at-arms, she smiled a small smile at the sight of me. "Deva, I was hoping you'd be here. We need to talk."

"Kay, how stunning you look." And she did, in a smart black sheath and leopard print pumps.

After I introduced Lee, Kay checked her watch. I could have told her it wasn't quite eleven.

"Is lunch possible?" she asked. "My treat. I know it's early, but I was hoping you might have some free time. We really need to talk."

"Of course. I'm sure Lee can spare me for an hour or so."

I reached underneath the sales counter for my purse, wondering what this emergency visit was all about. I thought we'd nailed the color scheme for James's house—basically an ivory envelope with flashes of cobalt and coral. There hadn't been time to select fabric for his sofas and chairs, or to shop for lamps and other accessories. In interior design, hurry wasn't the path to a polished effect, and I hoped Kay understood that. More than a little concerned she would insist on a rush job, I accompanied her along Fifth Avenue to the Magnolia Café, too preoccupied to enjoy the breeze or the sunshine or the flowers along the way.

As we settled into a booth, she dealt me another surprise. Raising her chin, she flung her chestnut hair from her face and said, "I'm going to be honest here,

Deva. If it were up to me, I wouldn't have hired you to redo James's house."

A challenge. Okay. I raised my chin, but no point in trying to fling back my hair. I have the kind that doesn't fling. My chin had to do double duty. "Why not, Kay?"

My tone must have been super cool, for she flushed and reached across the table to give my hand a quick squeeze. "Sorry. I didn't mean that the way it sounded."

"Good. Because it sounded shitty." Not a professional response but one straight from the heart.

To her credit, Kay laughed just as a waiter with the bearing of an ambassador to Great Britain approached and placed menus in front of us. Before he said a thing, she waved him away with, "Just water for now."

She turned back to me. "Your reputation around town is marvelous. Several people at the club have been singing your praises."

Somewhat mollified, I picked up my menu. "I'm glad to hear that."

Our waiter returned with goblets of water and a basket of rolls. This time he hovered.

"Give us a few more minutes," Kay said, dismissing him.

Obviously we weren't going to eat anytime soon. But that was fine. All I really wanted was to hear the reason for this meeting.

"What has me concerned, Deva, isn't your lack of designing skill. It's Stew Hawkins."

"Stew?" I leaned forward and forgot all about the menu. "Why is he the problem?"

"You know we used to be married?"

"Yes. James mentioned that."

"Our divorce—our whole marriage—was a nightmare." She frowned but for a moment, only then her dark eyes took on a shine. "The ending settlement, however, was almost worth what I went through with that—"

"Ladies, we have several specials today." The ambassador had returned.

"No recitals," Kay declared, picking up the menu with an exasperated sigh. "I'll have the grilled chicken Caesar, with a side of fresh fruit."

"Make that two," I said.

When we were alone again, she said, "As they say, all's well that ends well. But the end isn't in sight yet. Not completely. That bastard—" she finished the sentence this time, "—bought the house across from James."

"I know. James told me."

"Can you believe it? The nerve of him." She plucked a roll out of the bread basket, buttered it and bit off a chunk.

Having her ex living across the street sure hadn't affected her appetite.

"No need to worry," I said. "I'll be careful not to create parallel designs."

She stopped chewing and swallowed. "Parallel designs? What does that mean?"

"One house copying the look of another."

As if swatting away flies, she waved a hand in the air. "I'm not worried about that. I intend never to step foot in Stew's place. Do whatever you like. Make the interiors twins, for all I care." She forgot about the bread and, leaning over the table, lowered her voice. "But you do have to promise me, Deva, that you will never talk to Stew about me, not even so much as mention my name."

"I assure you, I—"

She raised a palm for silence. "And never, under any circumstances are you to tell him what James and I are doing or planning or saying. Nothing. Absolutely nothing."

Annoyance stiffening my spine, I sat up soldier straight. "I have no intention of doing any such thing," I said, for emphasis leaving a little space between each word.

"Excellent. Because he bought the house on Whiskey Lane for one reason only. To torment me."

Too irritated with the woman to simply agree, I said, "Isn't that rather bizarre, Kay? I mean your divorce is final, and he remarried and all, though I will admit Connie Rae's...Mrs. Hawkins's death was an unexpected blow."

"He probably killed her," Kay said smoothly, breaking off a piece of roll and popping it in her mouth.

"That's quite an accusation." And this was quite a conversation. I was an interior designer, not a shrink. Or a homicide detective, though Rossi would laugh to hear me admit that.

"You think so?" Kay said. "He's capable of it. What kind of husband locks his wife out of the house in the middle of the night? When she's stark naked?"

"No, you don't mean to tell me...no, he didn't." I forgot all about eating. This stuff was better than food.

"Yes, I didn't have a thing on. Not even jewelry."

Not wanting to miss a word, I bent in closer. "What happened?"

"Stew and I were arguing. As usual. He didn't like something I said, so he grabbed my arm and threw me out onto the front lawn, and me without a stitch on. And the mosquitoes! Omigod."

With a flourish, the waiter placed our salads in front of us. "Enjoy, ladies."

Kay dug in immediately, but more curious than hungry, I asked, "What on earth did you do?"

"I found a beach towel thrown over a patio chair and wrapped myself in it. Then I sat on the back terrace all night shivering and fighting the bugs. While Stew was sleeping it off the next morning, Teresa let me in."

"Yes, she mentioned that she'd worked for you."

Kay stopped chewing long enough to laugh. "Not really for me. Always for Stew…at times I wondered what went on between them. Especially after she refused to testify against him during the divorce."

"I see," I replied, really beginning to.

"Do you understand why I needed to talk to you? I don't trust Stew's motives in buying the house at 595, and I don't trust Teresa, either. In fact, I'm surprised he didn't marry her instead of that Connie Rae person." Kay looked up from her salad. "You met Connie Rae, didn't you?"

I shook my head. "No, she was already dead when I saw her."

"Too bad," Kay said, too casually to be believed. "I remember her from the club. She was a bartender there, though barely of drinking age herself. That must have been the lure—youth. Teresa's forty if she's a day." Kay shrugged. "Oh well, now that I have your promise not to gossip, I don't have anything to worry about, do I?"

I picked up my fork and took a bite of chicken, hoping it wouldn't choke me. Whether Kay knew it or not, her warning not to carry tales from her house to Stew's was frigging insulting. To spread gossip about clients was not only totally unprofessional, but on a practical level, a sure way to kill a business.

Instead of wondering if I would betray her daily comings and goings, she might be better off wondering about how James Stahlman's first two wives had died. If I were about to become wife number three, I'd sure wonder. And worry.

THIRTEEN

OUTSIDE THE MAGNOLIA CAFÉ, Kay and I hugged good-bye, best-friend style. Why not? We weren't friends, but we were both women who had experienced life and its, well…surprises.

I strolled leisurely back to the shop, breathing in salty Gulf air that showed a definite tendency to succumb to summer humidity. But no complaints. The breeze was still balmy, the sky blue, and the flowers perfuming Fifth Avenue spilled exuberantly from their planters.

With high season over, traffic had thinned, and mir-acle of miracles, empty parking slots lined both sides of the street. Our town slowed down for the summer, and that was good as long as it didn't slow to a crawl. After all, people like me had businesses to run.

I turned off the avenue onto Fern Alley, and as I passed the window of Off Shoots, the ladies boutique next to my shop, I waved at Irma, one of the leggy young twins who ran it. Farther along the alley, a white panel truck sat parked outside Deva Dunne Interiors. Big, bold red letters on the truck's side announced To-ny's Tiles & More. This same truck had been parked in the Hawkins's driveway the day Connie Rae died. And if I wasn't mistaken, that was Tony sitting behind the wheel with the motor running. Strange. Why would he be lingering in the alley?

I was about to step into the shop when the truck's

passenger side door opened and a man jumped out. He had a manila envelope in his hand and the most perfect physique I'd ever laid eyes on. No wonder I noticed. In a muscle shirt and shorts that revealed his tattoos and every toned line of his body, he'd be hard to miss.

I had my hand on the shop door handle—and probably my mouth hanging open—when he sprang forward. "Allow me, ma'am."

I tore my gaze from his pecs long enough to murmur, "Thank you," and walked inside. He followed me in, took one look at Lee and zoomed right over to her.

"I'm looking for a Mrs. Deva Dunne," he said. "Are you the lady, by any chance?"

"No, sir, I'm not. She's standing there beside you."

He swiveled on those toned legs of his and treated me to an eye swipe. Head to toe. A tattooed Adonis with a shaved head, he was here for something other than interior design services or my name wasn't Devalera Agnes Kennedy Dunne.

Using my Boston voice, the one I hauled out for occasions calling for cool and smooth, I said, "I'm Deva Dunne."

"I'm Mike. Mike Hammerjack."

My jaw fell open. This time no question about it. It unhinged. "Mr. Hammerjack from Florida State Prison?"

He grinned as if I had paid him a compliment. "You remembered. That's nice, coming from a beautiful redhead."

Really? So who was the smoothie here?

I wasn't anxious to make physical contact with this guy but good manners dictated that I extend my hand. So I did, holding it to the fire so to speak.

He tucked the manila envelope under his arm and took my hand in both of his, sandwiching it between his palms. "At last," he said, gazing into my eyes with the intensity of a lover. I swear, a lover.

Perspiring, I slipped my fingers free and found what I hoped was my off-putting Back Bay tone. "How may I help you, Mr. Hammerjack?"

"Mike."

I just nodded.

"I would love to hear you say my name."

I cleared my throat and glanced over at Lee. She winked. That did it. "Let's just get to the reason for this visit, Mr. Hammerjack."

Unfazed, he handed me the manila envelope that had been pressed to his armpit. It was dry, thank God.

"This is the Help-a-Con information I wrote to you about. With pictures of the prison-made furniture. Price lists, too." He cleared his throat. "I added Warden Finney's private phone number. Cost me two packs of cigarettes, but it was worth it. Thought I might get you through to him faster, in case you had a question or something."

"That was very considerate of you."

"Not a problem. I hope you can use some of the stuff the boys made. It's for a good cause."

"Yes, I know. I'll try. I have a project, possibly two, that may need office furniture. If the prison pieces are suitable, I don't see why they wouldn't work."

"Terrific!" He grabbed my hand and pumped it up and down. This time I was aware of the calluses on his fingers.

Outside, a horn honked. Mike Hammerjack glanced

out the window. "That's Tony. I'd better go. He's chomping at the bit."

"You know Tony well?" I asked out of idle curiosity.

"Yeah, we go way back. He's a good guy, I can tell you that. We went to high school together. Difference is, Tone stayed on the straight and narrow, know what I mean? He's a great guy all right, even gave me a job. I'd rather work with wood, but that's okay. I can lay tile with the best of them."

He turned to leave then stopped as a thought hit him. "Hey, you want to see a piece of the prison furniture? Tony's got one in the truck. It'll give you an idea of the quality."

I nodded. "Good idea."

"Tony bought a table for his mother's place. Like I said, he's a good guy. A good snakeman too."

"A good *what?*"

"Professional snake trapper. One of the best in the business. He ferrets out those wigglers like nobody else. Caught a fifteen footer opening day of the Python Challenge. The only snakeman who did."

"I'm impressed." *And horrified.*

"So's everybody else. I wish I'd been there, but that was a couple of weeks ago, before I got out of Florida State," he said, making the slammer sound like a four-year college. "But as soon as I got sprung he took me into the 'Glades for a couple of days. We had good luck too. If I didn't have to meet my parole officer tomorrow, we'd still be out there. You have to love that swamp."

Talking nonstop, he led me slowly to the back of the truck. He unlatched the rear doors, flung them wide, and stepped aside so I could peer inside.

"Hey, Tony, the lady wants to take a look at—"

Tony never heard him. A scream of pure panic rose up from my lungs, ripped into my throat and burst out of my mouth, shattering the quiet calm of Fern Alley.

Frozen with fear, I stood there shaking, a cold chill raising goose bumps on my skin. I wanted to run but shock had me rooted to the spot—the back of the truck was full of snakes.

"Hey, the table's not that bad," Mike joked. He put one of his callused hands on my arm, for reassurance, I guess, but I recoiled as if one of the snakes had wrapped itself around me.

My scream had brought a cluster of people on the run. They stood in a rapt semicircle behind us—Lee, Irma, and several women wearing outfits with boutique tags dangling from their sleeves. Repelled and yet fascinated, when they spotted the snakes, they screamed too, but like me, they couldn't look away either.

A truck door opened and slammed shut.

"What's going on back here?" Tony asked.

Nobody answered him. Then Mike said, "I was showing the little lady the table you bought. Guess I forgot about the snakes."

"You'd forget your head if wasn't screwed on," Tony said.

"I didn't think they'd scare her so bad. They're in cages."

"You don't think, that's right," Tony retorted.

"See that big one over there?" Mike asked me. I saw it all right and shuddered. "He's thirteen feet long. Been measured. Tony caught him, the first day of the Challenge, the same day he caught the fifteen footer. It's a record, hey, Tone?"

"You know what? You need to shut up. You talk too

much," Tony said, slamming the rear doors shut. "Come on, let's go. We got work to do."

Mike nodded and turned to me. "It's been a pleasure, ma'am." His eyes sparkled as he spoke. Had he enjoyed scaring the daylights out of me? And worse, had he done so on purpose?

I couldn't be sure, but when he extended his hand, I didn't take it. He shrugged and hopped into the truck. As they drove off, he rolled down his side window. "Hey, Mrs. Dunne," he called. "I forgot to ask. What did you think of the table?"

FOURTEEN

AFTER MY ADVENTURE with the snakes, I was ready for some relaxation and could hardly wait for closing time and my dinner date with Rossi.

I wore a new outfit today, a short shift in mustard, summer's hottest shade—sounded bad, looked good, especially with my hair. Being a redhead, I could only wear a limited color palette, so I was always pleased to find something that was fresh and chic and suited me. And even made my one pair of Jimmy Choos look new again.

I was in the shop's tiny bathroom, refreshing my makeup, when Beethoven's Fifth chimed out. Da da da DA. I dropped the lip gloss, rummaged in my bag, and grabbed the cell phone on the second ring.

Rossi. Was he working late and calling to cancel our date? An all-too-common occurrence in a detective's life. And to be honest, one I'd probably never get used to.

I pressed Talk with my pulse spurting up a bit. "Rossi."

"Deva, we're celebrating tonight. I made reservations at Sully's."

Our favorite steakhouse? Sounded like an occasion. "How nice," I said. "What are we celebrating?"

"Tell you when I see you. One hitch, though, I have

a little car problem at the moment. Would you mind picking me up?"

"Of course not. Where are you?"

"At the station. Can't wait to see you."

"For a man with no wheels, you sound very cheerful."

He laughed. "I am. I'll explain later. See you soon?"

"A half hour."

"Perfect," he said and rang off.

I think I could guess what Rossi wanted to celebrate. He'd bought the Calista Sands house lot. With a spark of excitement pulsing in my veins, I finished my makeup, brushed out my hair and waved goodbye to Lee. Tonight, she'd close up and make the daily bank deposit.

Parked in the small lot behind the shop, the Audi didn't look in shape for an evening on the town. At the very least, it needed a wash. No time for that, but how about gas? I checked. Less than a quarter full. Why was I always running on low? Truth was, my loyal little buggy was a gas guzzler. Long in the tooth with a hundred and ninety thou on the odometer, it needed to be traded for a newer model. Maybe a different color this time, a muted green with tan leather seats.

I sighed and turned on the ignition. Truth was I couldn't afford a new car. The old bomber would have to last for another year or two.

After stopping for gas, I drove directly to the station. Constructed of gray granite, with weathered Bermuda shutters tilted over its windows, the building looked more like a resort hotel than the local headquarters for crime busting. But that was Naples for you.

Outside in a patch of shade, Rossi was waiting with a smile on his lips. One of those small ones that didn't reach the eyes, but I'd learned to read him. The smile spoke volumes. He was delighted about something.

He slid onto the passenger seat and gave me a discreet kiss on the cheek. "Let's go, sweetheart. Party time." His glance swept over me. "Hot dress."

From long experience, I knew it wouldn't do any good to ask what he was so elated about. Rossi kept his secrets well. Super well, darn it. When he was ready, he'd tell me. For now, I was happy driving along the Tamiami Trail with his hand on my right knee.

At the restaurant, he said, "Let's valet park tonight,"

"But the car's such a heap. I'll be embarrassed."

His hand on my knee tightened. "Looking the way you do, once the valet lamps you, he won't even know what he's driving. Besides, I can't wait to get the full effect when you stand up on those gorgeous pins of yours."

Who could argue with that?

Anyway, we strolled through Sully's well-designed foyer with its white marble floor and intimate groupings of blue-and-white-striped sofas.

The dark, woody bar was located off the foyer to the right. After making a margarita stop there, we followed the hostess to a small table for two in a quiet corner of the restaurant. I loved the way Sully's décor played with opposing elements: rustic wood walls punctuated with black-and-white sports photographs in elaborate gilt frames.

Once we were seated, Rossi reached across the table for my hand. "I'd order a bottle of champagne, but we don't have a designated driver. Unfortunately." He grinned, "Or fortunately. I'd much rather be alone with you. A glass of merlot instead?"

"That would be lovely. So would knowing the reason for this dinner. It's story time, Rossi."

He tried for nonchalance and failed. "I bought the Calista lot today."

Ah, I knew it. "Is that what this is all about?"

He nodded somewhat gravely. "It is."

"Wonderful! I love the location, the neighborhood, the view, the whole idea of living there some day. But—"

"You want to know what it cost."

"Well, yes. If we're going to share a life and a house there, don't I deserve to know?"

"There's no need to worry. It's paid for." He cleared his throat. "I sold the Maserati."

"What!" I reared back in my chair. "Your pride and joy? Uncle Beppe's bequest to you? How could you do such a thing? You love that car."

"I love you more. I want you to have a house of your own. I want you to design it and decorate it and be happy in it. With me. What's a set of wheels compared to all that?"

Our waiter approached with menus. I did a good imitation of Kay Hawkins and waved him away.

"The car paid for the lot free and clear," Rossi added. "It was an excellent decision, one I'll never regret."

He held my glance with his, daring me to contradict him. How could I? The Maserati was his to do with as he wished. And what he wished was to make me happy.

The waiter returned just as I burst into tears.

"I'm sorry," he murmured, "I'll come back later."

"No," Rossi said, "that's not necessary. The lady's too happy to order right now, so I'll do the honors. Shrimp cocktails to start?" he asked me.

I nodded.

"And a filet for the lady, medium well. A T-bone for me. Medium rare. Chop salads. That should do it. Oh, and two merlots. You choose the vintner."

"Very good, sir."

I found a tissue in my handbag and mopped my face.

"You *are* happy, right?" Rossi asked, his eyes on me warm but worried.

"You know I am." I sent him a watery smile. "But I'm practical too. What will you use for a car?"

"You forgetting the Mustang?"

"No, but—"

"Don't let the dinged body fool you. Under the dusty hood purrs a world-class engine. Besides, for occasions calling for a touch of class, like tonight, we can use the Audi."

That did it. I laughed out loud, startling the waiter as he was about to serve our shrimp.

"Enjoy," he said, placing the appetizers in front of us and hurrying off.

"He's running scared," Rossi said with a smile, picking up his fork and digging in.

"This has been a rollercoaster of a day," I said. "Up, down. Up, down."

"What do you mean? Exactly."

"Well, first Kay Hawkins came into the shop to tell me not to spread gossip around Whiskey Lane."

"Was that an up or a down?"

"Very funny. Then there were the snakes and—"

Rossi's fork struck the tabletop. Hard. "The snakes?"

"Yes, in the back of the truck. Pythons. Cages full of them."

"You've lost me, Deva. Would you please start over again? From the beginning."

"Like an investigation, you mean?"

"Deva."

In between delicious bites of cold Gulf shrimp, I related my adventure. Rossi didn't think a truck full of pythons was a big deal. After all, he pointed out, they *were* in cages. But he was intensely curious about Mr. Mike Hammerjack and said, "An ex-con might be the biggest snake of all."

"He's fulfilled his debt to society, and now he's out on parole. That's a good sign, isn't it?"

"Perhaps." Rossi shrugged. "He may be rehabilitated. On the other hand, he may just be good at following rules. Bottom line, he's a convicted criminal. An embezzler. You said ten to twenty in the state penitentiary? And he's somebody you're thinking of doing business with? Not good, Deva, not good at all."

Experienced in law enforcement, Rossi understood the criminal mind. I'd be foolish not to listen to him. "Well, our business would be for a good cause, but I have wondered exactly what he did."

"Why don't we find out?" Pushing his shrimp cocktail aside, he removed his cell phone from a pocket and pressed the station's call number. "This is Lieutenant Rossi. Connect me with criminal investigation."

FIFTEEN

TWO DAYS LATER I stood uneasily in the foyer of 595 Whiskey Lane, holding a portfolio containing color boards, paint chips and fabric samples.

Only a few days had passed since…well, since Connie Rae had passed, and despite the phone call summoning me there today, I was uncertain about how I'd find the bereaved husband.

I needn't have worried. Stew Hawkins strode out of his bedroom wing with a smile on his face and no sign whatsoever of grief.

"Glad you could make it, Deva. I want to get the place fixed up as soon as possible. No point in letting what happened keep us waiting."

Wow. That gave new meaning to the word *cold.* Did Stew have no regret? No sorrow?

I cleared my throat before answering. "My schedule is slower in the summer, so that won't be a problem, but ah, wouldn't you prefer to wait until after the funeral?"

He shook his head. "No funeral. Connie Rae's family in Arkansas wants a funeral, that's up to them. I can send her ashes. But there won't be a funeral on this end."

So Teresa had been right. "I see," I murmured.

"No, you don't. I can tell by your voice." He cocked a finger, beckoning me forward. He led the way through the dining room and rotunda and into the great room. "The truth is, I hardly knew the kid. Married her on a spree...shouldn't have happened." A pause. "We were in Vegas. I was drunk. You do stupid things when you're under the influence."

He'd have no argument from me there. But it still didn't explain what had caused the death of an apparently healthy twenty-two-year-old girl. Much as I wanted to know, I didn't have the nerve to ask. Turned out I didn't have to.

With his next breath, Stew blurted, "She had a bad heart condition. Real bad. Never told me a thing about it. So that's how much I knew about her. Nothing, when you come right down to it."

I ventured a question. "Her heart failed? Is that how she died?"

"Yeah, natural causes, the coroner said. Guess I should be glad they didn't find something to hang on me. Especially after Kay...she's my ex...got through bad-mouthing me to the cops. That was a while back, but the cops got memories like elephants. The slightest slip, they'll nail me."

He shrugged. "What can I say? Life goes on. Come on in, have a seat. Teresa'll make us some coffee, and you can show me what you brought."

So much for the grieving process. Poor little Connie Rae, whoever she was. With Teresa hovering in the background, pretending to be busy in the kitchen but listening to every word, I sat on the couch beside Stew so we could go over my schematics together.

As I unzipped the portfolio, I glanced out at the back garden. The hibiscus were a riot of orange blooms, a color that would harmonize beautifully with the design plan I had in mind. Out of the corner of my eye, I saw a man in coveralls pushing a loaded wheelbarrow toward

the far end of the pool surround. Tony the tile guy back
on the job. Since they were so tight, no doubt he knew
his good friend Mike Hammerjack was a master forger,
with two convictions for grand larceny under his belt.

I'd almost emptied the portfolio when Mike himself
rounded the corner of the house, boxes of tiles cradled
in his buff arms. So I guess he'd been honest about one
thing—Tony *had* hired him. Despite his love for snake
hunting, Tony was a nice guy then, the type of man who
helped out a friend in need.

"Ah, here we go," Stew said, pulling me back into the
moment as Teresa, in red Capri pants and a flowered
jersey top, placed steaming mugs on the coffee table.
I guessed she'd probably ditched her shapeless white
nylon uniforms for good, and who could blame her? No
woman wants to look like she's wearing a parachute.

I rested my computer-generated CAD drawings and
the color boards on the coffee table. "Shall we start with
the overall philosophy?"

"You're the boss." Stew settled back with his coffee.

"All right." I picked up the first drawing. "What I
see for you is a masculine environment. One with big
bones. In fact, you're already moving in that direction
with the Mexican tiles and the wooden shutters you're
planning to install. Those design elements establish a
strong tone, and the tone is male. So let's take advantage of what's already been decided." *Time for a little
sugar.* "Besides, a masculine setting is a perfect fit for
your personality."

He nodded. No argument there.

"So no small statements. We'll write large."

Stew took a sip of coffee then put down his mug. "I

get the masculine drift," he said, "but I'm not following the rest of it. You're talking in decorator speak."

"Design speak."

Stew shrugged. "What's the dif?"

I sighed. "They're mostly the same." Something I'd never conceded before, but we had a lot to discuss, and you have to pick your battles. A semantic skirmish with Stew was the last thing I wanted.

"What I see emerging is a desert palette," I went on. "A warm Arizona sand tone on the walls." I pointed to a paint swatch on the color board. "Distressed beams overhead. As for furniture, unstructured butter-soft couches and chairs in leather." I handed him several leather samples to finger for texture. "These are colors that would work." *Now for a little more sugar.* "We'll make the seating large enough so a big guy like you will be comfortable."

"Yeah, I like that idea," Stew said, nodding.

I sent him a smile. "I was hoping you would. Some hand-loomed textiles for visual warmth and a few area rugs to soften things underfoot." I gave him several catalog photographs to look over. "I've marked the pages with possibilities."

He'd listened intently so far, but no point in barraging him with detail on our first run-through. "That's it for openers. If we nail the basics, we can move on from there to accessories. The room jewelry—lamps, pillows, artwork."

"Excellent. I like your plan. Only thing—you didn't mention the bedroom. The master where Connie Rae…"

I nodded. "Yes?"

"I want you to start in there. Today if possible. Change everything. I mean everything. That includes getting rid of all her stuff. Once it's boxed up, I'll mail it to Arkansas. Otherwise Teresa and I can't…otherwise, I'll never get a good night's sleep in there again."

"I'll be happy to start in your bedroom, but most people like to begin with the public rooms."

"Yeah. Well, I'm not most people." He gulped the rest of his coffee and stood. "I trust your ideas, so do what you want in the bedroom. Just make it look different. Get rid of the pink. Now if you ladies—" a slight nod to Teresa, "—will excuse me, I have to see what Tony's up to."

Left alone with Teresa, I repacked the portfolio, picked it up and said, "Well, let's have a look at the master suite, shall we?"

She stopped her fake task at the sink, dried her hands and led me through the house to Stew's bedroom. Unlike the day Connie Rae died, this time the draperies over the French doors were parted. In the bright afternoon light, the room was relentlessly pink, its focal point a king-sized bed in French provincial, all white curves and gold edging.

With the insight of a rocket scientist, I said, "Stew didn't choose that bed, did he?"

Teresa chuckled. "No, it was in the house when he bought it. The rest of the things in here were also. Not the clothes, of course. Those were hers."

"Hers?" I asked just to make Teresa say the name.

"That Connie Rae's."

"Oh, I see." I pointed to the cardboard boxes on top of the satin bedspread. "You're packing up Connie Rae's things?"

"Yes, as I was asked to do," Teresa replied with a prim sniff.

As you were dying to do.

"Well, don't let me hold you up," I said, glancing around. "I really can't make changes in here until it's cleaned out. Do you think Mr. Hawkins would switch to another bedroom while the renovation's going on?"

She held up a skimpy black lace teddy that was more lurid holes than fabric. Three holes in particular. "Look at this. What decent woman would—"

"Well, what do you think?"

"It's a disgrace, that's what I think."

"I mean about Stew moving into another bedroom temporarily." I glanced out the French doors. He was standing in the blazing sun, discussing tile repairs with Tony and Mike.

"Oh not a problem. He's already decided to sleep across the hall. I brought his clothes to a guest room this morning." She folded the black lace teddy and laid it on top of a pile of sweaters.

"That going to Connie Rae's mother?" I asked.

She looked up. "Everything is. Stew's orders."

"Maybe you should leave out the teddy."

Teresa shook her head. "No, that wouldn't be honest. Her mother should know what her daughter was like."

"She was a sick girl who died at twenty-two. Her mother must be heartbroken." I held out a hand. "Let me take care of it."

For a minute, I thought she'd refuse, but after hesitating for a moment, she reluctantly plucked the teddy off the pile and slapped it onto my palm. I slipped it into the portfolio and made a mental note to tell Stew I had it. Who knows, maybe he could make good use of it again sometime. Anyway, while Teresa continued packing, I took some measurements, then studied my color chips. I needed a shade that would tie in with the main rooms, be masculine enough to suit Stew yet soft enough to create a relaxing atmosphere. Engrossed in my work, I forgot about Teresa until she came out of the walk-in closet with an armload of shoes and dumped them on the bed. One fell off and rolled under the pink dust ruffle.

"Oh, for heaven sake," she muttered, bending over to grope under the ruffle. "Where did that darn thing go?"

The groping didn't help, so she dropped to her knees and peered under the bed. That was all it took, one look, and she let out a wild scream—the kind that peels paint off walls—and scuttled backward on all fours. A safe distance from the bed, she leaped to her feet and yelled, "Get out of here. Run for your life." Little more than a red blur, she disappeared down the hall.

Her cries must have reached the men outside. Startled, they stood frozen for an instant, then Stew dashed from the pool and sprinted for the great room door.

Whatever was hidden under the bed hadn't hurt Teresa, just scared her. As she ran screaming through the house, my curiosity became stronger than my fear—or my common sense—and, heart pounding, I got down on my hands and knees, raised the dust ruffle and peered under the bed.

A pair of slanted eyes looked straight into mine, a jaw gaped wide and a long tongue flickered out.

"Argggh!"

I leaped up, faster than Teresa had, I swear, and raced over to the French doors. I flung them open and yelled at the top of my lungs, "Tony, get in here fast!"

SIXTEEN

TONY DROPPED HIS TROWEL, and with Mike hot on his tail, he rushed to the French doors.

"Under the bed," I whispered.

He didn't need any further instructions. Something in my voice must have told him everything he had to know. He knelt beside the bed, tossed the ruffle out of his way and, peering underneath the mattress, he reached for the snake.

Slowly, without hurry, he grasped the creature as I stood, horrified, next to the open door, ready to beat a retreat if need be.

With one hand behind the python's head and one on its body, he pulled. And pulled and pulled. A cold sweat trickled down my back. *Was there no end to the thing?*

Finally, grunting with effort, he said, "Mike, give us a hand here. Take his head."

Mike knelt and grabbed the snake's front end. Flat on his belly now, Tony reached farther in and said, "Okay, I got him good." Together, they dragged the python out to the center of the room where it writhed in their hands, ready to wrap itself around one of them and squeeze....

"This your fifteen footer?" Mike asked. "The one that escaped?"

Tony flashed him a warning glance to shut up. But impervious to hints, Mike glanced over at me, his hands full of snake, and said, "Isn't this guy something? You don't see one like this very often. His skin's worth big bucks. You know how many pairs of shoes he'll make?"

Hurried footsteps pounded along the hall. A moment later Stew hovered in the doorway. "Had to calm the housekeeper down. She was half nuts. What's going…?" He took one look at the python stretching across his bedroom and all color drained from his face. "Where did you find it?"

"Under your bed," I told him.

He pointed to his chest. "Under my…" His eyes widened and if anything he grew more ashen, and then like the day he discovered Connie Rae's body, he passed out cold, toppling over like an axed redwood right across the struggling python.

"The snake! Get him off the snake," Tony yelled. Mike dropped the python's front end and, grabbing Stew's feet, yanked him across the carpeting.

The movement woke Stew, who came to with a shudder. He sat up and aimed a shaky finger at the python writhing in Tony's grasp. "You telling me I slept with that thing under my bed?"

"Looks that way," Mike said cheerfully, picking up the python about a foot down from the head.

"How long?"

"When did he escape on you, Tone?" Mike asked.

"You ought to know," Tony retorted, disgust clear in his tone. "You let him loose."

"I didn't let him loose. The boys in Jake's Diner wanted to see him. I just forgot to relock his cage is all."

"How long was it out?" Stew asked. "How long?"

"He got loose two days ago," Tony said. "Thanks to this bonehead. It never should have happened. You've got my apology, Mr. Hawkins."

"Hmmph," was all Stew could muster, and from his position on the floor, he watched in silence as Tony and Mike hustled the snake out to a cage in the truck.

I spent the rest of the afternoon on damage control. Back in the great room, stretched out on the couch with a damp dish towel on her forehead, Teresa let me play nursemaid. Ditto for Stew, collapsed on a club chair. He refused a dish towel but gulped down a double scotch on the rocks.

Even though Tony vowed the fifteen footer was the only one missing, Stew had him search every room in the house to make certain no other pythons lurked in dark corners. In less than an hour, Tony declared the property snake free, and after all, he ought to know, he was the best snakeman in the business. Too bad he'd let Mike so carelessly manhandle the fifteen footer.

Once the house was again safe, Stew insisted that Tony and Mike drive "the damn snake off my property." The two men left for the day with promises to return tomorrow.

Stew waved them off with a weary hand, and when Tony's Tiles backed out of the driveway, he said, "I'd tell them to get lost for good, but I want that pool job finished. A couple more days should do it."

With my two patients resting comfortably, I felt free to leave as well. Before I could, and as much as I didn't want to, I had to return to the master bedroom to retrieve my portfolio. My car keys and wallet were in one of the side pockets.

For all the earlier excitement, the bedroom was now a calm if somewhat gaudy pink retreat, the dust ruffle still tossed over the mattress like a skirt hiked waist high. I flipped it down and made a mental note to dispense with a ruffle on Stew's redo. His new bed would be platform style with no space underneath where critters could hide. I think Stew would appreciate that. At the very least, it would save him—or Teresa—from checking under the mattress every night before they went to sleep.

The pile of Connie Rae's clothes covered the bedspread, ready to be packed into the shipping boxes. Topping the pile was a pretty lilac-flowered notebook, the kind a young girl might scribble in. Connie Rae's journal? I picked it up and skimmed through a few pages. Had Connie Rae confided all of her secrets to this book, secrets she wouldn't want her momma to know? For some reason—pity for her untimely end, perhaps—I wanted to protect the girl's memory and her family from further hurt.

Not to be hypocritical about it, I was curious too. What *had* Connie Rae confided to this pretty flowered notebook?

Nothing much. Disappointed, I glanced through several pages, reading girlish confidences about manicures and haircuts and how she hated her boss, all told in loopy, unformed letters.

And then, pay dirt. Three weeks ago, right after her impulsive marriage, she wrote,

Tonight...afterwards...I told Stew all about my <3. He swears he won't let me die. He said there are doctors in Naples who can treat a bad <3 like mine. Isn't that wonderful?

Yes, indeed. I snapped the notebook shut and dropped it in the portfolio. This wasn't a crime scene, so technically I wasn't tampering with evidence, though technically...actually...I *was* stealing someone else's property.

I fully intended to return the notebook, but only after Rossi had a chance to read it.

Stew had pretended to know nothing about Connie Rae's heart condition, and yet he had known. Why had he lied, not only to me, but to the police? Clearly he was trying to hide something.

SEVENTEEN

WITH THE TEDDY and the lilac notebook tucked in my portfolio like contraband goods, I left Chez Hawkins for home but didn't get far.

No sooner had I tossed the portfolio in the Audi's backseat than a voice called, "Deva Dunne! I want to see you."

I turned from the car and glanced over a shoulder.

James Stahlman stood on his front lawn holding Charlotte's leash in one hand and a wineglass in the other. "Don't drive off," he warned. "We need to talk."

Maybe *he* did, but what I needed was to get home to Surfside and cook a simple dinner for two.

Reminding myself that James was a valued client, I pasted a big glad-to-see-you smile on my face, closed the Audi door and strolled across Whiskey Lane. For I suspected James wouldn't cross the road to Stew's property if his life depended on it.

"How are you?" I asked, stooping to pat Charlotte's topknot. She must have visited the groomer since I last saw her. Today she sported a kelly-green bow.

"We're fine if somewhat offended," James replied.

"Oh?" I asked as if I didn't know why.

"I have to say I'm disappointed, Deva." In true James fashion, he left off the accusatory "in you."

"Why?" This wasn't going to be easy.

"Your car has been parked in Hawkins's drive the

entire afternoon and not once did you call or ring my bell. And if I'm not mistaken, I secured your services before Hawkins did."

He drew himself upright and, ignoring Charlotte's tug on the leash, took a sip of his wine.

"A cabernet?" I asked, tilting my chin at his glass.

"Yes, a 1997. A good year for reds. But let's not change the subject. I can't linger, much as I'd like to. Charlotte and I are on our evening cocktail dog walk, and she's eager to meet her friends."

"What's a cocktail dog walk?" I asked, really wanting to know

"Exactly what the name implies," James replied coolly, as if miffed that I should have to ask. "It's an evening ritual Charlotte wouldn't miss for the world. Would you, sweetheart?"

Woof!

A few doors down the lane, a schnauzer strained on a leash. An elderly woman with a glass in her hand struggled to restrain him.

"There's Max," James said to Charlotte. Judging from her taut leash, I figured she already knew.

"Do join us for a bit, Deva. As you can see, Charlotte can't wait any longer."

The schnauzer, his hind leg raised, was anointing a banyan trunk while his mistress sipped something clear and icy from a tall glass.

"I don't wish to sound petulant," James said as we approached the pair, "but why have you seen fit to work with Hawkins and let my project languish?"

"I've done no such thing," I said, striving for a tone somewhere between indignation and conciliation. "We've already decided on classic white for your major color, and I've made several selections for your accent pieces and fabrics. Once you let me know when you want the painters to begin, I'll contact Tom Kruse at Oceanside Finishes."

Having completed his business, the schnauzer lowered his leg and sniffed around the base of the banyan for a few moments. Then apparently finding Charlotte more alluring than whatever he'd been sniffing, he bounded toward us. His sudden lurch caught his mistress off guard, and some of her drink sloshed onto the sidewalk. Max sniffed that too, but not for as long as the banyan trunk. Well, some odors *are* more fascinating than others.

Returning my attention to James, I said, "You do understand that your rooms will be in disarray for a while. We'll have to remove the window treatments, send your seating to the upholsterer, and painters' drop cloths will be everywhere. Though I realize the surprise is over, I thought you still preferred to wait until you and Kay left on your honeymoon."

A shadow of annoyance crossed James's face. "I prefer the expression 'wedding trip.'"

Charlotte preferred to hurry, and after exchanging lip licks with schnauzer Max, the instant she caught sight of a chocolate lab, she tugged on her leash

"Oh, there's Moose," James told her as if she didn't know. Moose's owner, a portly man in a white shirt and tie and the bottom half of a business suit, held a drink that looked dark enough to be medicinal.

Charlotte barked out a hello and Moose woofed back. An adorable Lhasa Apso who had the same beauty-queen potential as Charlotte scampered down a driveway with a striking blonde—a white wine girl—racing to keep up.

"There's Stella," James told Charlotte. No need, her tail wagged like a metronome.

I placed a hand on James's arm. "Could we stop for a moment? Without a dog on a leash, I feel terribly underdressed for this party."

He frowned and pointed to Charlotte's tail. "A moment only…"

"I know. When are you planning to leave on your… ah…wedding trip, so I can tell the contractor to begin?"

"We're not leaving. At least not before the house is refurbished."

"No?"

"No. Kay wants to be here to supervise the renovation."

Oh, really?

Charlotte's tail wagged overtime, but screw it, this was serious. It was design over dog. "Kay's input will be welcome, of course. But let's make one thing clear before we begin. The success of the project depends on me. That makes me the decider. And the decider is the supervisor. Also, not to be crass but practical, one half of the estimated costs are payable before we begin."

Moose, Stella and Max were bearing down on us fast. Giddy with excitement, Charlotte did so much yipping and sniffing and leaping up and down that James had difficulty keeping his cabernet from spilling. My day had me so frazzled, I wanted to yank the glass out of his hand and drain it, but instead I quietly waited to be fired.

James surprised me. He smiled. "I like your spirit, Deva. Rest assured, as soon as I receive your proposal, a check will be in the mail. Now if you'll excuse me, I must find out how Moose fared at his chiropractor's."

My jaw dropped. "You're kidding me?"

James's eyes widened. "Certainly not. Moose suffers from a bad back. The chiropractor has done wonders for him."

Speechless, shaking my head, I turned and headed back to the Audi. Wait till Rossi heard about the cocktail dog walk. No question he'd believe every word. You just couldn't make up stuff like this.

I also wondered what he'd think of Connie Rae's journal.

EIGHTEEN

WHEN I DROVE onto the Surfside parking lot, my condo lights gleamed through the front window.

Rossi's home.

It had been quite a day, and I looked forward to a quiet evening. Maybe we could have dinner in the living room in front of the TV. Kick off our shoes, share a bottle of wine.

I hurried inside and dropped the portfolio on a chair. "Rossi, I'm home!"

"So am I," he said, striding out of the kitchen.

I ran to him, and holding out his arms, he enfolded me in one of those embraces that I lived for—never tiring of them, never getting too many of them, never wanting them to end.

He kissed me as if he had invented how, starting slow and soft, his lips velvet against mine, then hardening, and teasing until I opened to him, a mini opening, an opening that promised more, much more.

My neediness must have shown, for he held me at arm's length for a moment and smiled into my eyes. "That was quite a welcome. Too bad I can't stay and make the most of it."

"Oh no. Not again tonight."

"Afraid so." He stroked my bare arms, his fingers telling me what he wouldn't say—he didn't want to leave. "There was a pileup on I-75 this afternoon, and we're trying to sort out who's responsible. One of the victims is in surgery. If he's alert enough later, I need to question him." He planted a kiss on my forehead and let me go. "So I'm off to the hospital. Can't be helped."

"I know." I also knew this was what a detective's life entailed, and I was struggling with the reality of it—the danger, the uncertainty, the times when emergencies came first.

But I pasted on a smile and tried not to show my disappointment.

"I called earlier," Rossi said, "but when you didn't answer, I figured you were having a busy day. So I bought a pickup meal at Publix Market. Barbequed chicken and a Greek salad. I just stopped by to drop them off."

"That's wonderful, Rossi. Thank you. It has been a long day."

"And I left something for you to read. It's in that envelope on the desk. Why don't you take a look at it?"

"I will," I said. "Sounds important."

With a quick, two-fingered salute of farewell, he was gone.

Curious, I strolled over to the desk and, with a little sigh, picked up the envelope. I'd be the one doing the reading tonight, not Rossi.

I sat on the sofa, slid a finger under the envelope flap and lifted out what looked like an official document. It was the deed to the Calista Sands house lot, and it listed me as the paid-in-full owner.

Clipped to the deed, a note in Rossi's big bold scrawl read,

*Let's get started, Deva. You've always praised
Harlan Conway as a gifted architect. Why not
contact him ASAP and have him draw up a set
of plans?*

He'd signed the note simply R. Actually it wasn't a
note. It was a love letter, Rossi style. He wanted me to
have the house of my dreams and was doing everything
in his power to make that happen. Even to suggesting
Harlan Conway. Though I'd disliked Harlan's indiffer-
ent treatment of a former client of mine who had been
madly in love with him, as a Florida architect he had
no peer. Rossi was right. Together Harlan and I could
design a house that would fit the site perfectly and in-
corporate all my favorite features and Rossi's too.

I leaned back against the cushions and just for fun
dreamed of living in a postmodern shotgun-style house,
its sleekness softened with Old Florida motifs. Bead-
board ceilings and floors built from salvaged hardwood.
Vintage tiles in the baths and a Viking stove in the
kitchen. A deck on stilts overlooking the water with a
screened-in porch behind it for when night fell and the
mosquitoes buzzed…

Or maybe something totally different. A pillared,
neo-Classical folly, say, small in scope but exquisite
in detail. No, too formal. Rossi wouldn't care for that
approach, and he had to be happy too. Well, we could
always…

Whoa. I'd gotten way ahead of myself. First we'd
show Harlan the site and let him make suggestions. Besides, though contemplating the future might be exciting, I had to be practical too. Building costs were high,
especially for custom work, so as soon as Rossi and I

both approved a design, I'd put the condo on the market. Maybe Lee and Paulo would get their financing soon and be able to buy it. I hoped so. I knew they'd love it. And then I'd move in with Rossi in Countryside until the new house was ready, and after that...

I breathed a sigh of pure contentment and tucked the deed back in the envelope. My fantasies were wonderful, even doable, but to help make them come true, I had work to perform, clients to keep happy, and a business to run. Rossi had set our plans in motion, but building our new home was a team effort, and I wouldn't want it any other way.

That meant I'd soon be moving from Surfside. I glanced around my familiar living room. For the first time since I'd lived here, it seemed cramped to me, its muted greens and turquoise a tad dated. I had to smile at my own dissatisfaction, for to be honest, ever since I'd sold my late husband Jack's Irish antiques, I hadn't really been happy with the changed look of the place. Not with the colors, or the consignment store secretarial, or the nubby club chairs... *Designer, heal thyself.*

The portfolio with the journal inside still lay on the chair where I tossed it.

Too bad I hadn't had a chance to show it to Rossi. Though on second thought, maybe that was just as well. He'd been working twelve hours most days, sometimes even longer, and I didn't want to burden him with yet another problem. After all, no crime had been committed. Stew had lied was all...lied about Connie Rae's life-threatening illness. At least I think that was all.

Anyway, according to what I read in the journal, somebody had lied. Why would a girl claim her husband knew she was in danger of dying if he didn't know? And if Stew was aware of his wife's desperate situation, why would he deny the knowing? None of it made sense. To get at the truth in Connie Rae's journal, I needed Naomi Pierce, a handwriting expert and woman of many talents. Providing I could find her.

I had to. An urgent need to learn more about the dead girl crowded out all other thoughts. Acting on a hunch, I stowed the deed safely in a desk drawer, retrieved my cell phone from the orange tote and carried it out to the kitchen counter.

I perched on a stool, clicked on the Google icon and tapped in Handwriting Analysis. A menu of several names from around the country popped up, but no Naomi Pierce from Naples. Not under America's Handwriting Expert or Forensic Document Examiner, either. Before switching to Graphology, I'd try Signature Expert—Forged wills, contracts, forms. And there she was, with both an email address and a local phone number.

Though psyching out human behavior from how a person wielded a pen wasn't exactly a skill in high demand, on occasion the NPD had used Naomi to help crack a case. She excelled at ferreting out hidden motivation. And that was what I was after. Motivation.

I'd try the phone number first. It would be faster. But I was out of luck. A robo voice came on the line: "The number you have dialed is no longer in service." The email address then. No luck there, either. An instant after I sent a message, it was bounced back to me. Now what?

Naomi was a free spirit who moved from one rental apartment and trailer park to another. I'd never known exactly where she lived at any one time, and in the past year or so, I'd lost track of her completely.

The duty officer at the station might have her new number. But even so, he wouldn't give it to a stranger on the phone. If all else failed, I'd ask Rossi to track her down, but he was already so overworked I hated to add to his schedule.

I glanced at my watch. Nearly eight o'clock. He'd been on the job since dawn. I wondered if he'd had any dinner and hopped off the stool to check the fridge. Nope. The barbequed chicken hadn't been touched nor the Greek salad either. He'd probably feasted on a cup of stale coffee and a bag of peanuts. What he needed now was a meal and a good night's sleep, not another task.

That settled it. I had to find Naomi on my own. Naples was her home. She'd been born and raised here, and chances were good that she still lived in town. I could go to the Collier County tax assessor's office, or drop in at a local bistro she used to frequent...

Or...

Or! Wanting to slap myself up the forehead for not remembering sooner, I forgot about the chicken and the greens and scrolled through the cell again. Naomi used to do calligraphy at an art shop, the fancy kind of penmanship people used on bar mitzvah, bridal shower and wedding invitations. She once said she made more money from calligraphy than from analyzing people's handwriting. How much more was a good question. Naomi pretty much lived on the edge.

At the Art Shops listing, I ran a finger along the search results. What was the name of the last place she'd worked at? No...no...no...then there it was.

You've Been Framed.

NINETEEN

THE ACCIDENT VICTIM had died on the operating table before he could be questioned. In light of that, Rossi rose early the next morning tense and troubled and not in the mood for conversation. Seeing him so worried, I was doubly glad I hadn't added to his problems.

After he left for the station, I dressed more or less effectively in a short tomato-red skirt and a taupe cropped top that matched my cork-heeled slides. The emotional cloud that had darkened the day's opening dissolved as I drove to work under a glorious blue sky. What a stunning ceiling that sky blue would make in our new home, especially in the bedrooms.

But there I went again, getting ahead of the game. I eased my foot on the gas pedal and rolled down the windows, continuing on to Fern Alley with the scents of gardenia and jasmine floating all around me.

According to its website, You've Been Framed didn't open until ten, an hour from now. I used the time to leave a call-back message for Tom Kruse at Oceanside Finishes and made an urn of coffee that along with cookies we offered to drop-in customers. After Lee arrived, I helped her rearrange the display tables, and then at ten on the dot, my heart pulsing a bit overtime—would Naomi still be there?—I punched in the art shop's number.

"You're in luck. She's here today," owner Jane Walsh

said. Her voice trailed off. "I don't see her right now. Guess she stepped outside for a smoke. You want me to get her for you?"

"No, that isn't necessary. Would you just tell her Deva Dunne called? I'm coming right over. Please ask her not to leave until I get there."

"Sure thing. Will do."

I hung up and reached into the desk drawer where I'd stashed my bag and the journal.

Busy with our first drop-in of the day, Lee was chatting about the merits of silk pillows over polyester. When I mimed that I had to leave, she nodded and went on talking.

I flung my bag over a shoulder, opened the center desk drawer and took out the two letters Mike Hammerjack had sent from Florida State Prison. If Naomi could shed some light on the journal's mystery, why not on mystery man Mike? I already knew he'd been convicted for forgery, but what else might his handwriting reveal?

"NAOMI'S OUT BACK AGAIN," Jane told me when I arrived at You've Been Framed. "She spends more time outside than she does over there."

"Over there" was a card table set up in a corner of the shop. Samples of Naomi's calligraphy were pinned to a folding screen behind the table, and as always, the quality of her work stunned me. She made the most mundane address look like a work of art.

"You can use the back door if you like." Jane pointed in the direction of her rear workroom.

I cut through the cluttered work space and pushed open a door that led out to a concrete slab overlooking a couple of trash cans and a small parking lot.

Seated in a plastic tub chair, taking in the view, was Naomi, the familiar gray pigtail snaking down the middle of her back much as I remembered.

"Hi, Naomi," I said.

She swiveled around, cigarette in hand. "Well, hi there, girl, where you been lately?"

"Not too far. Busy, mostly." I sank onto a plastic chair next to hers, downdraft from the smoke. In her thrift store jeans and outsized T-shirt, she looked older and thinner than she had a year ago.

"You keeping well?" I asked.

"As you see," she said, inhaling the mother of all drags. She sucked the nicotine down to her toes and hung onto it for what seemed like forever before exhaling into the beautiful blue morning.

I pointed to the butt nestled between her stained fingers. "Those things will kill you yet, Naomi."

She guffawed, a hoarse smoker's laugh that ended in a rasping cough. "Your advice is a little late, Deva."

I peered at her in the clear, merciless light. Circles of fatigue rimmed her eyes, and the lips that had been pursing around drags for years were sunken in a network of wrinkles.

I took her hand, the one without the butt dangling from it. "Are you telling me you're sick?"

She glanced over at me, her eyes a fresh, startling blue in the wrinkled wreckage of her face. "I'm not telling you anything. You're asking."

"Well?"

"Well, you didn't come to discuss my health, so what does bring you here?" She took a final drag, flicked the butt onto the concrete slab and stepped on it.

Clearly she was sick and didn't want to talk about

herself. For now, I had no choice but to respect her wishes, but later, as soon as I had Jane alone, I'd ask her about Naomi's health. Though from the look of her, I feared I already had my answer.

"I have a job for you, Naomi. Some handwriting samples."

Her eyes took on a shine. "Great." She raised her arms and waved them at the ugly back lot. "This place is as good as any. So let's have a look at what you brought."

I took the journal from my bag, opened it to where Connie Rae mentioned Stew and handed the book to her. "Tell me what you see, and then I'll tell you what I'm looking for. That okay?"

"Yes," she said, already nose deep in the book.

While she perused it, I took in the view. Stare at something long enough and it starts to grow on you. I'd about decided the view really wasn't ugly but part of the urban landscape when Naomi coughed and laid the notebook on her lap.

"You want to hear it?" she asked.

"Of course, that's what I came for."

"All right." She reached for a cigarette, thought better of it, thank God, and dropped the pack back into her T-shirt pocket. "This is the writing of a young female."

"Well, the lilac ink..."

She shook her head. "Not that. See the little circles over the i's? No hetero guy does that. Mainly girls and immature women, but despite the emphasis on the middle zone, the writing is too literate to be that of a child. So I'm guessing she's in her teens or early twenties."

"What's the middle zone?" I asked.

"Everyday reality."

"You lost me, Naomi."

She shrugged. "It happens. Think of the writing in Freudian terms—the id, ego and superego. Tall reaching strokes, like d's and t's, represent the superego, the spirit. The id, or sexuality, is found in the lower loops, the y's and g's. The middle zone, the a's and o's and e's, is the ego or everyday reality. That's where children live, and this example is written mostly in the middle zone. The writer, though not a child, is naïve and very sweet."

"Where do you see sweet?"

She pointed to a word. "Look at this one. See how the letters are rounded? Almost no sharp edges, no spiky strokes, no long lower loops."

"So you're not seeing much id?"

"Right."

What about that black lace teddy with all the erotic holes? Stew's idea?

"But the weak id could be the result of illness. She's a sick girl."

"Oh, Naomi, I can't believe you see that."

Her eyes filled with tears. "Sickness always shows."

I knew she wasn't talking about Connie Rae in that moment. Reaching across, I took her hand and squeezed it. I didn't dare ask any more questions about her own health. Above all else, Naomi was a private person. Nor did I get to ask how she could tell the writer was sick, she volunteered the information. "The writing pressure is uneven. She isn't maintaining an even hand. See, here and here." Naomi touched the places where the lilac ink was lighter than elsewhere. "That's a total giveaway."

She brushed away the tear sliding down her cheek.

"But none of this is why you brought the girl's sample to me. What, exactly, are you after?"

I plucked the notebook from her lap and pointed to the place where Connie Rae mentioned her heart condition to Stew. "In here. Is she telling the truth, or is she lying?"

Naomi took the book and read where I indicated. A few seconds only and she handed it back to me. "She's not lying. Absolutely no indication of lies at all."

"How can you be sure? It's important, Naomi."

She smiled. "I won't ask why. If it is, it is. But I can tell you this—in a case of conscious lying, the writing loses spontaneity. The writer hesitates to think up the lie. That creates a longer space between words and a tensing in the strokes." She pointed to the place. "Take a look for yourself. No wide spaces, no loss of roundness. According to the rules of graphology, the girl's telling the truth." She paused, and asked softly, "What happened to her? Did she get well?"

I shook my head. "No. She wasn't given the chance."

The back door barged open, startling us. Jane poked her head out and said, "A woman in the shop needs some wedding invitations. You want to see her?"

"Tell her I'll be right in." Naomi rose out of the stiff plastic chair with difficulty. "Shucks. I wanted a smoke, but guess I can't now."

"Before you go in, I have another sample for you to look at. No hurry. It'll wait until you have some free time."

"Ha! That's most always."

I handed her the Mike Hammerjack letters. Knowing she usually sold herself short and would refuse payment if it were offered outright, I'd slipped some twenties into the envelopes while she studied the journal. "See what these yield, Naomi, and give me a buzz when you're through."

"Righto." She turned to go inside.

"Hey, girlfriend," I said. "Not so fast." I caught her in a bear hug. Underneath the loose T-shirt, Naomi Pierce was a bag of bones. I wondered if her calligraphy would reveal that she was dying. I hoped to God it wouldn't, but one sad thing that *had* been revealed today—however unprovable it might be in a court of law—Stew Hawkins had lied. He knew his wife had a life-threatening illness but denied it. The question was why. What was he hiding?

Though Naomi answered a lot of questions, she couldn't answer that one. No one could except Stew himself.

TWENTY

I'D HARDLY PULLED away from the curb in front of You've Been Framed when my cell phone rang. Da da da DA.

Caller ID said Tom Kruse. Excellent.

I pressed Talk and when he answered, I said, "Where are you? You sound like you're in an echo chamber."

His chuckle came through the line like a men's barbershop quartet. "I'm in an empty store in a strip mall. Getting it ready for the new owner."

My heart sank. "You're tied up then?"

"No just the opposite. I'm about finished here. Things are slow right now, the season and all…"

"Then the stars are in alignment. I have a question for you."

"Shoot."

"Do you have two trucks and two crews?"

"Yeah." He stretched the word out into a question.

"Marvelous. I need two trucks the same color and the same size. Two crews with the same number of men in each crew. They both have to arrive at the job at the same time each day and begin work at the same time. Oh, and they have to be dressed exactly alike."

"With all due respect, Deva, that's the daffiest request I've ever had. Even coming from you." His laugh echoed over the line.

I guess he'd never forgotten the time I gave him a rotten mango and asked him to copy the skin color for a dining room wall. He had, and the room turned out great.

"I'll explain everything when I see you," I said. "Want to meet me at Whiskey Lane tomorrow afternoon? Two o'clock?"

"That'll work. What's the number?"

I didn't know whether to say 590 or 595, or the middle of the road. But since James seemed more sensitive to slights than Stew, we'd better start at the Stahlman house. "Five ninety."

Meeting date agreed upon, we both hung up, with Tom probably shaking his head, and who could blame him?

At Fern Alley, I found Deva Dunne Interiors packed with shoppers. The minute I put a foot in the door, Lee whispered, "I'm so glad you're back. There's a convention at the Ritz. Cosmetics distributors and they love to shop. They're buying up everything in sight." She nodded at the line forming in front of the sales counter. "Y'all need to ring up those sales."

I hurried over, guilty at having ignored my business for the sake of what might well be called a wild goose chase. To make up for my neglect, I treated each and every customer as if she were a friend who'd just dropped in for a social visit and packed every purchase extra carefully in tissue paper, even tied big wired-ribbon bows on the handles of every gift bag. Guilt is a powerful instrument. Besides, the day's tally would be terrific after this unexpected bonanza, but what I had to keep in mind was these drop-in purchases, though nice, didn't keep the business viable. For that, Deva Dunne Interiors needed design customers who wanted far more than a pair of souvenir candlesticks or a sofa

pillow from Florida. In short, I needed customers like
James Stahlman and Stew Hawkins.

While trying to fathom whatever mystery surrounded the deaths of both their wives wasn't part of
my job description, redoing their houses definitely was.
So as soon as the crowd thinned out and Lee could handle the sales alone, I called first James then Stew and
firmed up tomorrow's appointments with the painter.

WHEN I DROVE up to 590 the next afternoon, Tom Kruse
was waiting for me in his truck. We strolled up the brick
walk together and rang the chimes.

"You're in luck," I told him. "You get to meet Charlotte."

"Oh really? A cutie?"

"Yup."

She greeted us at the door, all yips and leaps and
happy barks. Ignoring James's request to be a good
girl, she licked my ankles and sniffed the cuffs of Tom's
pants.

"Meet Charlotte," I said to him, "and not incidentally
Mr. James Stahlman."

Tom's face fell at the sight of the cutie, but he recovered fast and shook hands with James who scooped up
Charlotte for the grand tour.

I was somewhat surprised to see James at home. Not
young, but not of retirement age either, he seemed never
to be busy, never out and about, as if his main occupation were keeping Charlotte entertained. According to
the newspaper account of his wife Marilyn's drowning, he had been a well-to-do stockbroker at the time
of her death and was presumed to be the likely heir of

her considerable fortune. Which could well be the reason he lived a life of leisure.

I huffed out a sigh. There I went again, venturing into what was none of my business. So giving Charlotte a topknot pat—her bow was purple today—I accompanied James and Tom, who with his clipboard at the ready took notes as we moved from room to room.

"Flat white on all the ceilings," I said. "Classic semigloss white on the woodwork throughout, except for the kitchen—Mr. Stahlman and I haven't yet discussed what he wants done in there—and linen white on most of the walls." Tom nodded. We had worked together on several projects, and he was familiar with my preferences. "For a color jolt, vivid coral behind the living room bookcases and in the foyer. I'll give you the manufacturer's number for that."

"Excuse me, Deva," James said. "You are aware that blue is my favorite color?"

"Absolutely. I wouldn't forget anything so important, but blue is a cool shade and if not used carefully can make an interior appear…well, cold. To avoid that, we'll introduce blue in your upholstered pieces and pillows and in some porcelains. Little blue islands, if you will. I found a gorgeous blue-and-ivory-striped fabric for the dining room chairs. And a silvery blue paper that will be stunning in the powder room."

James didn't object, so encouraged, I went on, "And if we bring an oriental into the dining room, we'll strive for one with a few blue tones. Faded blue for elegance." I ventured a smile and pointed to one of the drab living room walls. "Faded blue in orientals isn't the same as in wallpaper."

James placed Charlotte carefully on the floor and

clapped. Actually clapped. "Bravo, Deva! Bravo. I like everything you're suggesting."

"So do I."

We all swiveled around to the source of the voice. It was Kay in high-heeled sandals and a drop-dead bikini. The bra consisted of white stars on a blue ground and the bottom of red and white stripes. It was enough to make you want to salute. The sheer blue pareo cruising her hips didn't conceal much either.

Tom stared at her, mouth agape, and lost his grip on the tape measure he'd been extending along one of the walls. It zinged back into its metal holder with a loud *whack!* No wonder. For forty Kay looked good. For thirty she looked good. Ditto for twenty...well, twenty-five.

"Kay," James said, his tone cool with disapproval, "a cover-up?"

"Hardly necessary, Jimmy. I'm heading for the pool. Ta-ta, everyone."

So there *was* a pool on the property. I glanced outside. The terrace steps led down to a clipped lawn that ended in a carefully pruned boxwood hedge. The pool had to be discreetly hidden behind the hedge.

Anyway, Kay slipped through the sliders and started down the terrace stairs.

Carrying Charlotte, James hurried outside. "Careful, darling, those stairs are wet and—"

Too late. Whether James distracted her, or her ankle twisted, or the stairs really were slippery, Kay lost her balance and tumbled down the length of the stone steps, landing at the bottom with a thud.

"Here," James said, dumping Charlotte in my arms and hurrying to Kay, who lay unmoving.

He knelt beside her. "Darling," he murmured. "Darling."

She had landed on her side, one arm raised in an instinctive gesture to protect her head. At the sound of his voice, she stirred and attempted to sit up while tucking a breast back under the stars. James helped her with both attempts then sat holding her and murmuring into her ear.

Cradling Charlotte, I called down, "Do you need 9-1-1?"

Kay shook her head.

"No," James replied. "She's fine. Just needs a minute to rest."

I watched them for a while longer until Kay, with James's help, got to her feet and together they started up the stairs.

"I'll make this fast," Tom said to me quietly. In command of his tape again, he went back to measuring, calculating the amount of materials and man hours he'd need to transform the interior into what I intended to be a showstopper. In this opulent neighborhood, a stunning redo might result in some good word-of-mouth PR, exactly what Deva Dunne Interiors needed. Especially now, with that empty Calista lot waiting for its new house.

I gave Charlotte's bow a pat. "How about I put you down?"

Woof.

"Is that a yes or a no? Help me out here. I don't speak your language too well."

I bent down and set her on the floor. The instant her paws touched wood, she barked out several woofs in a row and stood on her hind legs. Crisis or no crisis, she needed attention, so I picked her up again. I guess I did understand Maltese speak. Besides, James had enough to deal with at the moment. With Kay in tow, he'd nearly reached the living room sliders.

Once inside, leaning heavily on his arm, Kay limped over to the sofa and stretched out. Alert but somewhat pale, she appeared shaken by the experience. No wonder, a fall like that could kill a person. She'd been lucky, the only damage appeared to be a rapidly swelling left ankle.

"Deva," James said, taking Charlotte from me and looking as pale as Kay. "Would you please go into the kitchen and tell Eileen we need an ice pack?"

"Of course." I hurried to the back wing and pushed open the swinging door to a kitchen that could be called retro or mid-twentieth century or just plain shabby. Whatever. It was slated for a redo, but for now I had a more pressing task. I was on an errand of mercy.

Standing at the sink, as sturdy and reliable as I remembered, Eileen glanced over at me and managed a little smile. "I saw Mrs. Hawkins take that tumble and thought she might be needing this." She held out an ice pack nestled in a soft white towel. "I wish Mr. Stahlman would do something about those stairs. They're treacherous."

"I'll mention it to him." I took the ice pack from her and hurried back to the living room. James tenderly draped it over Kay's ankle as Tom, looking a little goofy with Charlotte in his arms, tried not to stare at the bikini.

As soon as Tom's measurements were complete, we said goodbye and crossed Whiskey Lane to number 595. Teresa, in a cheetah-print jumpsuit cinched with a wide black belt, let us in. "Stew…Mr. Stew…is at work," she said. "He wants you to go ahead and do what you have to do."

Good. Without Stew's heavy presence, the task would go faster, and Tom would only have Teresa's jumpsuit to interfere with his concentration. It had *pow* appeal, no doubt about that, but wasn't in the same league as a flag bikini. After seeing Kay's effect on staid, solidly married Tom Kruse, well, I was beginning to wonder if James had been right about Stew's motivation in moving across the street. Maybe he *was* still in love with Kay and really *was* running a one-man surveillance operation.

Anyway, Tom and I went through the house, discussing the parameters of the job and the effect I was looking for.

"I want the rooms to have personality," I told him. "Not just be color coordinated."

"Right. Personality." He sent me a glance that said, *There you go again, Deva, just like that time with the mango,* and calmly wrote down what I asked. In short, Tom was a consummate professional and a joy to work with.

Teresa followed us as we worked. I guess she was making sure we didn't steal the family silver, for halfway through she said, "By the way, I told Stew about the teddy you took."

"Oh? That's fine."

"Yeah. He said you can keep it."

"How sweet. I hope you told him I took it for safekeeping. That I was concerned it might accidentally be sent to Connie Rae's mother."

She shrugged. "No, it never occurred to me to tell him that."

Of course it had. She'd deliberately let him think I was a thief. I gave an internal sigh. Well, technically I was. "I'll explain my reasoning to Mr. Hawkins when I see him."

"Good idea."

I was relieved that she hadn't mentioned the notebook. Maybe Stew didn't care that I took the teddy, but for sure he'd care about the notebook. At the moment, it was in the handbag slung over my shoulder, but I had no intention of relinquishing it before Rossi had a chance to read what it said.

As Teresa went to walk away, I said, "Do thank Mr. Hawkins for me, but I have no use for the teddy, so I'll bring it back. It'll be perfect on you."

TWENTY-ONE

OKAY, I HAD a brief moment of satisfaction telling Teresa that basically she was a slut. And I'd lied too. She wasn't getting the teddy. I'd already thrown it in the trash. I was wrong on both counts. Nana Kennedy would be furious if she found out. Though I missed her terribly, maybe it was just as well she had passed away fifteen years ago.

"Say what you mean," she'd once told me, "but always be kind. Nasty remarks are not worthy of God's children. Unless," she'd added, eyes atwinkle, "you're pressed to the wall. Then let 'er rip." She'd held up a warning finger. "Now don't be goin' out of your way to find trouble, but when it finds you, stand up for yourself. Remember, you're a Kennedy." Well, a Dunne soon to be a Rossi.

Whatever my name, that exchange with Teresa didn't make the cut as trouble. Bottom line, I was ashamed of myself and vowed to be extra kind the next time we met. I fretted over it all the way to Fern Alley where a surprise awaited—Rossi. He leaped up from the zebra settee and gave me a kiss on the cheek.

"Glad you're back. Though the wait gave me a chance to visit with Lee." He winked at her. "Don't tell your husband."

"I most certainly will," she said with mock indignation.

I laughed, enjoying their banter. As Rossi had said once, Lee was the daughter he'd never had—yet.

"We have an appointment," he informed me, checking his watch. "In one hour."

"We do?"

"Uh-huh. I made an executive decision. We're meeting an architect at the house lot. Harlan Conway, to be exact."

"Wonderful! I meant to call him earlier but I—"

"Got busy. I had a feeling that would happen, so I went ahead. You okay with that?"

"Love it." He really wanted this new house, one I would help design and furnish and decorate to my heart's content, and the knowledge of that swept through me, leaving a warm glow in its wake.

I turned to Lee, who was listening and smiling at us. I guess in some ways, we were like the parents she no longer had. Leaving her to lock up, we left for Calista Sands. Early for our meeting, we sat companionably in the Mustang waiting for Harlan, enjoying the view.

Rossi had recovered from his worries of the morning and leaned back in his seat with a sigh of content. "Look at the sky. It's as blue as the water. And look at those palm trees over there."

"They're beautiful, I agree completely."

"And look at—"

"This."

He sat up straight and tore his gaze from the palms to glance over at me. "What's that?"

"Connie Rae Hawkins's journal."

"The girl who died?"

I nodded.

"What are you doing with it?"

"I, ah, borrowed it."

He frowned. "No euphemisms, Deva. You swiped it."

"Temporarily," I said, my tone all oily. "There's something in it I think you should see." Ignoring his disapproval, I opened to the page where Stew learned about Connie Rae's heart and handed the notebook to him. "Read this."

He did, snapped the book closed and gave it back to me. "Poor kid, but what's your point in showing me this?"

"Stew Hawkins knew she needed heart surgery."

"So?"

"He told me he never knew she was ill. Not until the coroner's report."

Rossi's brow knitted together. "Even if you did catch him in a lie, what does that prove? The ME verified the cause of death. The girl succumbed to natural causes."

"Stew had a reason for lying, and the reason wasn't a good one. He was hiding something."

Rossi nodded in that infuriating, look-at-all-angles-before-you-leap nod. "Say he did lie, this book proves nothing. Need I remind you no crime has been committed?"

"What makes you so sure, Rossi? What makes you so sure?"

He never did get to reply. A sleek black Infiniti pulled onto the lot behind us, and a handsome, blond Viking stepped out from behind the wheel.

Harlan Conway in the gorgeous flesh. I'd kind of forgotten how beautiful he was, then his opening salvo brought everything back.

He nodded at us by way of greeting and pointed to Rossi's beat-up Mustang.

"Your car?"

Rossi nodded, his eyes wary.

"How old is it?"

"Let me put it this way," Rossi said. "It can vote. That answer your question?"

Harlan shrugged. "The neighbors…"

"What about them?"

"Oh nothing, I just wondered."

Some things, and some people, never change, but before our meeting deteriorated any further, I asked, "What do you think of the lot, Harlan?"

He glanced around, his keen professional eye not missing a detail. "Narrow. You'll be limited in what you can build, size-wise, but for something compact, I think it'll work."

"I know it will," Rossi said, leaving no doubt for argument.

I couldn't speak for Harlan, but as for me, I was totally on the same page as Rossi. He wanted a house here so badly I was determined we would make the lot work. And work supremely well.

"Compact has many meanings, Harlan," I said, not even attempting to hide the annoyance in my voice. "Let's discuss that concept before we go any further."

TWENTY-TWO

WE STOOD BY the Mustang and watched Harlan back his Infiniti off the lot. Rossi's happy anticipation had dimmed to a scowl. "You sure the guy's as good as you thought?"

Deflated, too, by Harlan's supercilious airs, I nodded grudgingly. "Check out his website. He's posted some awesome projects. You'll see. He does brilliant work."

"I've already checked out the site," Rossi said. "That's why I called him. But he's a pain in the butt to deal with." He peered at me. "Is having him design a house worth putting up with his attitude?"

"Yes and yes. Let me put it this way…did a producer ever fire Marilyn Monroe for being difficult?"

Rossi's lips curled up. "As an analogy that one has flaws. She *was* fired from her last film, just before her death. But I get your drift. Okay, you're the designer; I'll bow to your wisdom in this. With one caveat. Conway deals with the designer, not the detective."

"Done. I'll shake on that. But you could help me out with a list of what you want in the house, and what you don't want. Kind of a guide."

"I want you in the house, and I don't want to live in it without you."

That was even more beautiful than the view. Disregarding any neighbors who might be looking, I flung my arms around him and kissed him until we were both breathless. Finally, reluctantly, we pulled apart. "What do you say we get back in the car?" Rossi said.

"Your legs are wobbly, huh?"

He laughed. "So's my reputation in the 'hood."

We settled onto the Mustang's front seat and watched the orange sun sink slowly into the horizon. When the light show ended, I said, "Seriously, Rossi, I really do need to know your preferences. What you like in colors and furnishings and that kind of thing."

He shook his head. "You know my house in Countryside is Beige City. I have no preferences."

"None?"

"Well, one. A king-sized bed and dark shades for when we want to sleep late. Maybe one of those thick covers. The kind that's full of feathers."

"A duvet?"

"That's it, and extra pillows." He smiled a dreamy smile. "A little radio for night music would be nice."

"How about a central sound system instead?"

His eyes brightened. "That would be great. But only if the controls are on my side of the bed so I can turn it down. And up." He grinned wickedly.

"I'll be certain to include every one of those ideas. What about the kitchen?"

"I want one."

"How many baths?"

"One a day. Sometimes two."

"All right, you win. I give up. Let's go home to Surfside and have something to eat."

"Umm."

Rossi plainly hadn't given up, and though I wasn't overly concerned about the neighbors, nor was he—at least not in the same sense Harlan seemed to be—I figured we needed to do our teenage necking behind closed doors. That was fine with Rossi too.

The next morning he'd already gone for the day and I was about to leave for work when the Tony's Tiles truck cruised onto the Surfside parking lot and stopped outside my front windows. Mike Hammerjack sat behind the wheel, staring at my door, no doubt checking out the address.

Not good. Not good at all.

He parked and jumped out of the truck dressed for God knew what in shit kickers, tight cutoffs and a black muscle shirt. Not exactly a flag bikini, but a head-swiveler, nonetheless, especially with those tattooed pecs of his.

Now what? Pretend I wasn't home, or answer the bell and let him in? Neither choice was a viable option. I had to get to work, and I didn't want him in my home. Bottom line, I didn't trust him. He'd let Tony's python loose, hadn't he? And though I tried to keep an open mind, he *was* a paroled felon.

He wasted no time strutting toward my condo, and I wasted no time grabbing my bag, dashing outside and locking the door behind me.

"Well, there you are," he said, smiling as he approached. "I wasn't sure I had the right place."

"You don't. How did you get my home address?"

My cool welcome didn't faze him a bit. "A man has his ways," he said, shrugging off my question. "Tony's over at Jake's Diner having breakfast, so I thought I'd stop by and show you some more of the Help-a-Con furniture. I've got a desk in the truck and a couple of chairs." His brows came together. "You already saw one of the tables."

Had I? All I remembered was the snakes.

While I wasn't happy to see Mike at my doorstep, I did need to take a good, hard look at the prison-made pieces before ordering any for my clients. So I followed him over to the pickup without any further protest.

Before he unlocked the back panel doors, I said, "Any surprises in there today?"

A grin cracked his face wide open.

Oh? Scaring me with a truck full of snakes had been funny, had it? Fuming that he might have set me up that day, I examined the furniture in silence. But I soon got over my snit. The cons had done a marvelous job. The joints on each chair fit smoothly, the mitered desk drawers slid in and out without a single squeak, and best of all, I loved the finishes. No high shine, no glare, just a nice polished effect.

"They're terrific," I said. "If everything is this good, I'll definitely place an order."

"Now?"

I shook my head. "The answer to that is no."

"Too bad. I got a message from one of the boys. They've been wondering. They don't like waiting. They wait enough, you know what I mean?"

The hot summer air, heavy with sea salt and humidity, did nothing to cool my irritation and a lot to frizz my hair. Steaming hot and getting hotter by the minute, I lost it and threw caution to the winds.

"Let's get the record straight," I said, shifting my bag from one shoulder to the other. "No pun intended, of course."

He laughed anyway. An accommodating guy, Mike Hammerjack.

"The furniture's great. No problem there, but I have

a place of business, and this isn't it. So in the future, please remember I do not...*not*...see clients in my home. My phone is unlisted largely for that reason. That means you are trespassing on my privacy. And I don't like that."

"Oh, come on—"

"Secondly, I cannot guarantee anything to the men in prison. If possible I'll be glad to help, but if you've made promises—" he looked so taken aback at that, I knew he had, "—I can't help it. The next time..." He went to speak, but I held up a finger and he stopped. "The next time you need to contact me, call the shop."

"I hate to see a beautiful lady like you so mad." He put a hand on my arm.

As if scalded, I jerked it away. "Our acquaintance is strictly business, and that will end if this scene is ever repeated."

"You've got the wrong idea, Mrs. Dunne."

"No, you have." I walked away, heart pounding, fully expecting him to do something nasty—leap on my back, knock me to the ground, hit me over the head. But I reached the Audi unscathed and slipped behind the wheel.

Breathing a sigh of relief, I backed out of my slot in the carport, put the car in drive and headed out of the parking lot. Or so I thought. I'd only gone a few feet when coming fast was the panel truck with Tony's Tiles on the side and Mike Hammerjack at the controls.

With an ear-shattering crash, the truck struck the Audi head-on. The impact whiplashed me backward and then forward. My head struck the windshield with a *crunch*, and out I went like the proverbial light.

THE NEXT THING I knew, a man sitting beside me on the passenger seat was patting my cheeks and cooing my name. When his hand slid down my arm, I opened my lids to a narrow slit.

A few inches away, Mike, his jaw tight, gazed at me with big, blue eyes.

"Mrs. Dunne, are you all right?"

"I don't know," I whispered. I fingered my forehead. A lump the size of Mt. Rushmore had popped out above my left temple. And my right knee hurt more than my head.

Excited voices floated in the air. The crash must have brought out the neighbors. Someone knocked on the driver's side window. Chip, my next-door neighbor to the rescue. He yanked the door open and peered in, his round face a moon of anxiety.

"Deva, you all right?"

I gave him a cautious nod—even so, the earth tilted on its axis. "Everybody's asking me that," I said, trying to convince myself that the world wasn't spinning overtime.

Chip bent down and glanced across the front seat. "Who are you?" he asked Mike.

"Hammerjack's the name."

"You the driver of that truck?"

"Unfortunately, yes."

"Well, you did a number on Deva's car. This is a private lot, not a speedway. How fast were you going?"

"I'm not sure. My foot slipped off the brake. I guess my driving's a little rusty."

"That so?" Chip didn't sound convinced. I might have moaned, for Chip snapped his attention from Mike back to me. "I'm calling 9-1-1."

"No, please." I grasped his wrist.

"From the size of that lump, you have a head injury. You need to get to the hospital and have it looked at."

"Okay, but no ambulance, please. Let's not turn this into a big deal."

Chip frowned, then nodded. "It'll be faster if I don't argue, so fine, we'll do it your way. But first I'm calling the NPD and asking for the lieutenant."

I definitely moaned that time. Not too thrilled about my association with Mike Hammerjack to begin with, Rossi would be less than thrilled over this accident. The last thing I'd wanted to do was add to his worries, but no way around it, I'd done exactly that.

Mike stirred on the seat next to me. "I better move the truck out of the way."

Too weary suddenly to talk, I leaned back on the headrest and closed my eyes, aware of a deep throbbing at my temple and a worse pain in my knee. Mike's hot breath fanned my cheek. "I'm real sorry about all this."

"I know," I said. Did I? Was he?

"Before I go, can you tell me something?" he said. "Why's the big guy calling a lieutenant? This isn't a crime scene."

I opened my eyes. Mike's usually cheerful expression had disappeared, replaced with a scared kind of tension.

"Lieutenant Rossi's my fiancé," I said.

"Oh my God." The color drained from Mike's face. He took my hand and squeezed it. For emphasis, I guess. "Be sure to tell him this was an accident, will you? Or I could end up back in State."

My eyes flared open. Mike was desperate…but why? Of course the crash was an accident. My heart skipped a beat. Or had he rammed my car on purpose?

The question was too much for my aching head. With Chip's help, I eased out of the wounded Audi and slowly limped over to the passenger seat of his Malibu.

Chip's wife, AudreyAnn, in a pink terry robe and fluffy slippers, waited alongside holding a pencil and a piece of paper.

"Get the truck driver's information," Chip told her, nodding at Mike. "License, registration and insurance. Then call a towing service for the Audi. I need to get Deva to the ER."

Chip slid behind the wheel of the Malibu. If he spoke on the drive to the hospital, I didn't hear him. I dozed—off and on—as we wove through morning traffic to the Naples Community Hospital. When he pulled up at the ER entrance, Rossi stood waiting with a wheelchair, as grim-faced as I'd ever seen him.

As soon as Chip hit the brake, Rossi yanked open the passenger side door.

"You're conscious," he said. No hello. No smile.

"Of course." I left off "barely."

He leaned farther into the car. "Chip, you took a chance. Why didn't you call 9-1-1?"

"This was faster," Chip replied. "It cut out the argument."

A wry smile lifted Rossi's lips. "Say no more, my friend. And thank you. I'll take her in. The ER staff is expecting her."

"The ER staff is *expecting* me? What did you do, Rossi, pull rank?"

"You could say that," he said, helping me into the wheelchair. Chip gave me a farewell buss on the cheek and waved goodbye. Without wasting a minute, Rossi pushed my chair through the automatic doors.

Though the dizziness had settled over me like fog, I did notice the waiting room held only a single man. Satisfied that Rossi wasn't wheeling me past a roomful of dire emergencies, I relaxed a little, and once inside a curtained cubicle, I lay on the hospital bed with a sigh of gratitude. My head hurt, dammit, and my knee hurt worse. And over and above those concerns another loomed large—a growing realization that the accident should never have happened.

The ER physician, a young resident from the boyish look of him, examined me and ordered a CT scan of my head and an X-ray of my knee. The upshot, several hours later, was that I had suffered a bone bruise on the knee, but despite the blow to the occipital region of my head, no concussion.

A kind of minor miracle, the doc told me. "You have a hard head, lady," he said, a medical joke with all the freshness of a stale donut.

Still I sent him a grateful smile and went to get out of bed. The spinning started up immediately, and I fell back against the pillow.

"I suggest you go home and rest for the day. See how you feel in the morning before resuming your usual activities." He paused. "The knee will take a while. Bone bruises are slow to heal. If it bothers you unduly, I suggest you see an orthopedic specialist."

A handshake and he was gone. A moment later, the cubicle curtain parted again. "Rossi chauffeuring at your service. You've been sprung."

I sat up slowly and, to my relief, nothing spun in front of my eyes. "I'm so sorry for all this." The tears I'd been holding in leaked out onto my johnny. "You have enough to do without worrying about me."

"Worrying about you is my main occupation. The department is a poor second to that," he said, kissing my wet cheeks then handing me a fistful of tissues. "Also I do double duty as a ladies' maid." He opened the bedside stand, lifted out my clothes and held up my bra and panties. "This'll be a first, putting them on instead of taking them off."

"Rossi, give me my clothes and go find a nurse. A female one."

With a chuckle, he did, and a half hour later, I was back at Surfside, stretched out on the living room couch with an ice pack on my knee and a pillow under my head. Where I needed to be was Fern Alley, running my business but, truthfully, I couldn't have driven downtown nor functioned normally if I had to. So I lay there, outwardly calm and inwardly fuming, while Rossi went next door for the information Mike had given Audrey-Ann.

He also went to have a look at the accident site. With my car towed away for repairs and Tony's truck gone as well, I didn't see what good it would do.

I should have known Rossi wouldn't waste his time. Ten minutes later, he returned to my condo looking none too happy.

"The skid marks from that truck are facing in toward the building, not out toward the street. Where the hell did Hammerjack think he was going? There's no way out of the lot in the direction he was headed. I don't believe in accidents, Deva. I think the guy may have rammed you on purpose."

TWENTY-THREE

STILL FLAT OUT on the sofa, I answered Rossi's questions as best I could and watched his face go from grim to grimmer. After serving me a bowl of canned chicken soup, he was determined to find out exactly what had happened and left for Whiskey Lane, to pay a call on Mike at the Hawkins house. And, I suspected, to scare the daylights out of him while he was at it.

I dozed for a while and awoke with the late afternoon sun streaming through my windows. Restored by the nap, I risked getting off the couch to freshen up. My head ached, but the dizziness had disappeared. The knee was another story. It throbbed as badly as earlier. I hobbled out to the kitchen, put the thawed ice pack in the freezer and took out a bag of frozen peas—Rossi hated them anyway—to lay on the knee.

On the way back to the couch, I plucked my tote off a club chair. At least I could make a few calls and not waste the entire day.

Lee assured me all was well at the shop, which made me feel happy and obsolete at the same time. Actually gratitude quickly took over. I was lucky to have someone as reliable and capable as Lee helping me run the business. She deserved to be rewarded for all she did, and the same thought I'd had for a while popped up again: I should offer her a partnership in the business. A junior partnership to begin with and gradually as her design skills grew, make her a full partner with a client list of her own. Then we could hire someone to work on the floor and keep the shop…Dunne & St. James Interiors…open without interruption. It was a good idea, one that lifted my spirits.

They stayed elated, too, until I called You've Been Framed and spoke to Jane Walsh.

"Naomi's not in today," she said, "and I don't know whether she'll return."

"How is she, Jane, really? I'm worried about her. She didn't look well the other day."

Jane cleared her throat as if weighing what she could or couldn't tell me, then came out with a shocker: "She's been given six months."

"Oh." I slumped farther down on the sofa. The peas fell off my knee, but I didn't care. "I'm so sorry. Her lungs?"

"Yes. She said if you called to tell you she wants to talk about some letters of yours. Said it was important. Wait a minute, I have her home phone number around here somewhere." A thump as the phone hit the desk.

While she searched, I scrambled in my tote for a pen and a scrap of paper. She came back on the line, gave me the number and said, "Mum's the word on the six months, okay?"

"I won't say a thing, I promise. Thanks for trusting me with the truth."

"No problem." Except, of course, there was.

I took a deep, reinforcing gulp of air and rang Naomi's number.

Instead of a hello, she answered with a cough.

"Hi, girlfriend," I said, when she caught her breath.

"Deva?" she asked, her voice a raspy whisper.

"Yes."

"I'm glad you called. I mailed those Hammerjack letters back to you along with twenty bucks. You paid me too much."

"No, I didn't. You deserved every penny." Another racking cough. "You feel like talking about what you found? If not, it'll wait."

"No it won't. You've got quite a dude there, Deva. Oh, he's charming, all right, but not to be trusted. I wanted you to know—" she stopped to draw in a ragged breath, "—before something happened."

"Well, something has."

"Yeah? Not surprising. I saw the prison address, but that's not what alerted me. When you get his letters, look at his signature. It's a mile high in comparison with the rest of his writing. You'll see a lot of fancy swirls around the *M* in Mike. That's self-importance, or you can call it an inflated ego. Either way, nothing illegal about it. But take a look at how he writes his y's and g's. The guy uses the felon's claw."

"The felon's claw? What on earth is that?"

"It's coming from a downstroke and immediately going into a claw shape below the line. It's underhanded, goes against the norm."

I could tell she was sucking in the air trying to get a full breath.

She mustn't have succeeded, for she said, "There's more, but not today. I'm done. Gotta get to my oxygen tank."

"Thanks a million. You've helped me more than you know. And as soon as I get the letters, I'm sending back the twenty."

"Don't bother," she rasped. "If you do, I'll use it to light a cigar."

My turn to gasp. "You smoke them, too!"

"Only when forced to. *Ciao.*"

She hung up wheezing and laughing, but I hung up saddened and troubled. Saddened about Naomi and troubled about Mike Hammerjack. Now that I had some insight into his character, what in the world was I supposed to do about it?

TWENTY-FOUR

I WAS STILL mulling over the Mike Hammerjack problem when Rossi walked in. It was early evening by then, and he carried a frozen pizza and a bottle of Chianti. Dinner. Oh well, his pizza was better than his scrambled eggs, and I really wasn't hungry anyway.

"How are you feeling?" he asked, eyeing me from head to toe and frowning.

"As you see."

"I thought so. What's with the peas?"

"You freeze them and put them on your knee."

"So that's the reason people grow them?"

"Exactly."

"Seriously, you okay?"

"Well enough."

"Not true. I can see your freckles. That's never a good sign."

Freckles. Something else to worry about. "How about you put the pizza in the kitchen and then tell me what happened with Mike?"

"You got it. Be right back." He returned in a few minutes with two glasses of wine, handed me one, and settled into a club chair across from the sofa.

"So?" I said.

"So, you could say I wasted my time," he began.

"Really? That surprises me. You never do."

He raised his glass in a mock toast. "Thank you.

However, this was an exception to my otherwise perfect record. The guy's slick as they come. Claims his foot slipped off the brake, his driving's rusty, blah, blah, blah. I didn't believe a word he said, but there's no way to disprove his story, so that's that. Luckily the owner of the truck, this Tony Pavlich, carries insurance. So repairs to your car should be covered, and we can pick up a loaner in the morning."

What he wasn't saying was how much he regretted selling the Maserati. We were down to one set of wheels—the Mustang of voting age. Not good.

"Regrets?" I asked softly.

"Yes!"

About to take a sip of Chianti, I lowered my glass.

"I deeply regret your tangling with this Hammerjack character. Promise me you'll have nothing more to do with him."

"But—"

"He had no business being at your door. That alone scares me, never mind this phony accident."

"I'd love to do as you ask, Rossi, but I said I'd try to sell some of the prison furniture. Not for Mike, for people in need. I have to follow through on my word."

"You don't *have* to, you want to."

The sofa suddenly felt like a hot seat. As if my pants were on fire, I squirmed before answering. "I need to. That means I have to."

He sighed, one of those deep, I'm-annoyed-beyond-words type of sighs. "You're being incredibly naïve. You'll be selling the work of murderers, pimps, thieves, wife-beaters, addicts. The list goes on."

I took a good stiff slug of wine. "Just so you'll know, the furniture they make is excellent. Besides, my grandmother wants me to do what I can in the name of humanity."

"This the Nana Kennedy who passed fifteen years ago?"

"The very same."

"I give up," he said, throwing his hands in the air. Thank God his glass was empty. "Who can argue with logic like that?" He eased out of the club chair. "I'll put the pizza in the oven."

"That's all you have to say? You're not going to try and talk me out of it?"

"Nope. Do what you must. Besides, I told Hammerjack if he caused you any more trouble, I'd personally see that he went back to State. For good." A small smile lifted Rossi's lips. "Even if I had to invent the evidence."

I nearly dropped my glass. "You *didn't!*"

"Damn right I did. I won't act on the threat, of course, but Hammerjack doesn't know that. Not for sure." Halfway to the kitchen, he swiveled around to face me. "I'd do anything to keep you safe."

Wow. The man of integrity had lied. For me. My elation at being loved so much quickly turned to guilt. Once more I'd caused a problem for Rossi, but this time I'd placed him on the horns of a moral dilemma, and that made me feel terrible.

His evaluation of Mike Hammerjack was most likely correct, but if I told him my phone conversation with Naomi tended to verify his findings, that would only disturb him all the more. So I'd keep what I learned to myself and be extremely wary around my Help-a-Con contact. Bottom line, I didn't want to believe that when Mike crashed into the Audi, he meant to harm me. Or maybe even kill me.

TWENTY-FIVE

My CONCERN ABOUT Mike and his motives took a backseat the next day when James Stahlman dropped into the shop with Charlotte in tow. I'd just settled down behind my desk with a cushion under my sore knee when in he came.

To my delight, Charlotte wriggled out of his arms and scampered over to me, licking my ankles and woofing her head off.

"Are we friends?" I asked, picking her up. A lick on the cheek erased the question and most of my Tropic-Glo blush. I took that as a yes.

"I'm so glad we caught you in," James said. "We're on our way to Klaus and Hartmann to select a new suit for the wedding. While we're in the neighborhood, I thought I'd better stop by and alert you."

Uh-oh. "Alert me about what?" I put Charlotte down in case James's answer caused me to tense up and grip her too tightly.

"Kay and I are tired of waiting." *Just like the guys in the state pen.* "Last night we decided to stop all these postponements and set a date. It's etched in stone, Deva," he said, his voice stern of a sudden. "Two weeks from today."

"Well, congratu—"

"We're getting married in the house."

"*Your* house? The one with painters swarming all over the inside?"

His pale eyes rounded. "What other house could I be referring to?"

His question required no response, but I gave him one anyway. A groan. "I can't possibly have the house ready for a wedding. Not in two short weeks."

"Of course you can, and you will. I insist." He reached into the breast pocket of his double-breasted linen jacket, removed a check and laid it on my desk. "In anticipation of your objections," he said with a smile. A smile of supreme confidence, as if he were convinced money solved all problems.

I sighed and then my peripheral vision spotted the amount on the check face. A hefty five figures. Well, money didn't solve everything, but this money would help to swell the Rossi-Dunne building fund.

I picked up the check and, tapping it with a thumbnail, stared at James with what I hoped were steely eyes. "Say I agree to your time constraint. It will have to be with the understanding that every detail won't be in place on your wedding day. The tradespeople and workrooms have other clients to consider, other orders to complete. All I can do, with or without this check—" which I was holding onto tightly, "—is my best."

"That will more than suffice. I trust you completely," James said. "Please send any further bills to my financial advisor. This is his address." He placed a business card on my desk and then snapped his fingers at Charlotte. "Come here immediately, young lady."

Woof!

"I insist."

To her credit, Charlotte ignored him and kept right

on sniffing the table skirts, especially the one topped with a display of aromatherapy candles. Then, bored with that, tail on high, and not letting James intimidate her for a second, she disappeared around the corner to explore the back storeroom. I felt like clapping. Or making her an honorary member of NOW.

As for me, I wasn't quite so independent. I put James's check in a desk drawer for safekeeping and stood, not without difficulty, to shake his hand. After which he chased Charlotte all over the place, finally managing to nab her in a corner. "Naughty girl," he said, kissing her.

"One thing puzzles me, James," I said as he was about to leave.

"Yes?"

"Since the house is undergoing a rehab, wouldn't it be simpler for you and Kay to be married elsewhere?"

"Simpler yes, but not as satisfying."

Ah! How could I have forgotten? Having the wedding at 590 directly across the street from 595 meant that they could marry and torment Stew Hawkins at one and the same time. Not nice. Not nice at all.

After James left, I took another peek at the check. It was real, all right, with a tidy Palmer Method signature and big clear numbers. I was no Naomi when it came to handwriting, but I sure did like what I saw, especially those numbers. So why did I feel as if I were aiding and abetting a crime? All I was doing was my job. Wasn't I?

TWENTY-SIX

WHETHER OR NOT James and Kay wanted some kind of revenge against Stew Hawkins, I convinced myself their private feud had nothing to do with me or my role as interior designer. Anyway that sounded good to my conscience.

So I tamped down my guilt, and as soon as Lee returned from the bank with a supply of petty cash, I left for the Stahlman house. My knee, hugged by an ace bandage, had slowed me down but not knocked me out. Which was a good thing. For no way could I let the windfall from James slip through my fingers.

At Whiskey Lane, two identical panel trucks sat in each driveway, and without checking I knew that true to his promise, Tom Kruse would have the same number of uniformed men working in each house. About to suggest we break that rule, I walked in to 590 feeling a tad foolish.

In the living room, the odor of wet paint permeated the air, an odor many people objected to but that I loved for the way it signaled fresh, new beginnings. Rocking to whatever his iPod was pumping into his ears, a lanky young guy was busy painting the ceiling. I caught his attention and pointed to my own ear. He removed the buds. "Is Tom around?" I asked.

"He was working in the master bedroom earlier."

I found him there and greeted him with, "We have a problem."

He rested his brush across the top of a paint can. "What's wrong?"

"James and the bikini are getting married."

"That's a problem?" Tom shot me a grin. Ah, the power of a well-filled flag.

"The wedding's in two weeks."

"Umm-hmm." He bent to pick up his brush.

"In this house."

His jaw dropped and so did the brush. "Oh God, no."

"My sentiments exactly."

"Well, I'll tell you right now, I can't finish this job in two weeks." He waved an arm at the dated wall covering. "Not with all that paper to be stripped off. No telling what's underneath it. And some of the rooms need three coats of paint."

"Okay, how about this? The bedrooms stay as is until after the ceremony. The kitchen too. That leaves the living and dining rooms, the foyer, den and library."

"Even so…"

I pointed to his brush. Paint was dripping onto the floor. A first, I'd bet, for perfectionist Tom. He grabbed the brush with an oath. Another first.

"Suppose we hire a temporary crew?"

Tom shook his head. "No dice, Deva. That's how you lose quality control. I've got a reputation to protect."

"You're right. So do I." *Back to Plan A.* "How about taking your men out of 595 and putting them to work over here? Would that help?"

"It might. If we work through the weekend." He pulled a rag out of his back pocket and wiped up the drips. "That means time and a half for the men."

"I'd be willing to double their hourly rate providing they finish in twelve days. Mr. Stahlman gave us two weeks, but I'll need at least two days to put the rooms back in order after you're through."

With Tom's promise to do his valiant best to meet the timetable, I limped across the street. If Stew refused my request, I could kiss James's check goodbye, and I really couldn't afford to do that. Or to lose Stew as a client either.

My knee throbbing and my heart beating faster than normal, I rang Hawkins's bell. The moment the chimes pealed, Teresa yanked open the door, her face falling at the sight of me. Without saying hello, she peered over my shoulder as if hoping someone else might be coming along the walk. "They're late. They should be here by now."

"Who?"

"The exterminators."

Small critters were a problem in southwest Florida where everything, including *la cucaracha*, thrived in the heat and humidity. So the bug men, as exterminators were affectionately known, made regular calls at almost every building in town.

But this was different. In jeans, a washed-out T-shirt and no makeup, Teresa looked too scared to have had an encounter with a mere water bug or two.

"What's the problem?" I asked.

"A snake." She hissed out the word.

Another python? "Omigod. Where?"

"In my kitchen. Under the sink." She shuddered. "I slammed the cabinet shut and trapped him inside. Nothing can make me go back out there."

"I don't blame you. Not a bit." As she peered up

and down the street, I glanced past her, into the living room. Tom's crew was applying a coat of desert sand latex to the walls. Even partially finished, the room had taken on a masculine vibe that would suit Stew's personality to a T.

"Is Mr. Hawkins at home by any chance? I need to speak to him," I said.

Teresa shook her head, sending her ragged ponytail into a little dance. "No, he's out of town. At a convention. Of all the times, just when we're infested with snakes."

"Oh, surely not."

"What do you know? You didn't see it." She shivered. "I can't stay here, I'm too afraid. But I don't know what else to do. I have no other place to go."

"Can you reach Stew?"

"*Sí.* I mean yes. He left a number in New York. I called him there. But he hasn't called back."

"I hope he does. I have a problem too."

"Not like mine. Mine is worse."

Arguable, but I never got to debate the subject with her, for an exterminator's truck pulled onto the driveway, and two men in coveralls jumped out of the cab.

Teresa raced outside to embrace—I mean meet—them. As she was relating her woes, the living room phone rang. I did debate answering that—for a second or two—then made a dash for the receiver.

I was in luck. It was Stew.

"Who's this?" he barked.

"It's Deva Dunne."

"What the hell's wrong with Teresa? She sounded half nuts on the phone. Something about snakes."

"Well, uh, she says the house is infested with them."

"That's crazy."

"She doesn't seem to think so. She's out on the driveway right now, speaking to the exterminators."

"Dammit, I leave for a few days and all hell breaks loose."

"She's scared, Stew. Afraid to stay here in the house. Says she has no place else to go."

A sigh wove its way through the line followed by a long moment of silence. "Okay," he said finally, "I'm glad you're there, Deva. Do me a favor, will you? Stay with her while she packs some clothes. Buy her a one-way ticket to LaGuardia and give her some cab fare to my hotel. Put everything on my tab. And give the exterminators a key. Tell them to do whatever it takes. Then lock up the house."

"What about the painters?"

"Oh for crying out loud, I forgot about them." Another sigh. "Tell you what. Put a halt to all that decorating stuff until I get back. We have to get the house fumigated first. What good's a fancy redo if my girlfriend...housekeeper...won't spend a night in the place?"

TWENTY-SEVEN

EVEN WITH MY gimpy knee, I happy-danced across the street to relate the good news to Tom. He flung down his brush—on a wad of yesterday's newspaper—and wasted no time in hurrying over to 595 to inform his crew the game plan had changed, to put what they were doing on hold and transfer their equipment to 590.

Afraid to stay in the house with the snakes and the exterminators, Teresa waited outside while Tom and I went over the change in plans. Then I hurried back to 595 as fast as my knee allowed, and together Teresa and I packed a bag for her trip. That took a little longer than it should have. Afraid a snake lurked inside her walk-in closet, she refused to step foot in it. So I did the selecting, and she disapproved of half the things I brought out. Through trial and error we finally filled a carry-on with two or three outfits and collected some underwear to toss in too. When she quietly balled up a new black teddy and stuffed it in a corner of the bag, I pretended not to see a thing. A pair of spike heels went in next, and we were finished.

Luckily Southwest had a late afternoon flight to New York with a few empty seats available—one of the advantages of Florida's off season. We booked her on it, and I drove her to the Ft. Myers airport.

Once free of the house, Teresa morphed into a different woman. Actually the transformation began inside, right after Stew's phone call. While I stood on snake guard, she changed out of the ratty T-shirt and jeans into a snug print dress and red heels, and spritzed herself with Opium. She was brushing out her hair as we got into the loaner, and most of the way to the airport kept busy putting on her face. Not easy in a moving car, though I did try to control fast stops and starts, especially while she was applying the mascara. Five coats.

A mile from the airport, she screwed on some dangly earrings then added an armload of bangle bracelets and a great big I-gotcha-smile.

I tore my attention from the road for a second to glance over at her. She looked as sunny as the day.

"There wasn't any snake, was there?" I said.

She hesitated, but not for long. "No. But it's your word against mine."

"You need to get to New York so bad you cooked up a whole scheme?"

"Why not? I can't leave Stew up there all by himself—or worse, not by himself. Look what happened when he went to Vegas without me."

"You know something, Teresa? You missed your calling. You're a fabulous actress."

She shrugged off the compliment. "I've been acting my whole life. It was the only way out of my village."

"I see." And I did.

Her charade had been anything but honest, but she hadn't committed a crime. At least I didn't think so, and actually without intending to, she'd done me an enormous favor. For both reasons, I had no intention of tangling with her over this, but she didn't have to know that.

"What happens if Stew finds out what you did?"

"He won't unless you tell him."

"I won't say a word, but he's a sharp guy. He may figure things out for himself."

"Then he'll be flattered. Besides, I'm going to make him very, very glad to have me there."

Of that I had no doubt and dropped her off at the Southwest gate with something like a blessing though I couldn't quite bring myself to say, "Have a wonderful time." Maybe the thought of Connie Rae's little purple notebook full of girlish confidences stopped me. One line especially kept playing over and over in my mind— the one in her round, childish scrawl saying her husband knew that without heart surgery she would die.

Anyway, after we waved goodbye, Teresa sashayed into the terminal, and I checked my watch. Darn it. One house problem under control and another waiting to be solved. But this upcoming one I was looking forward to. I had a date with Harlan Conway to plan the new house. But I'd never make it back to town in twenty minutes, and a late arrival would be sure to irritate The Great One.

Before airport security asked me to move, I made a quick call and left a message on Harlan's voice mail, doubting if any excuse, however legitimate, would matter to his prickly ego.

Well, nothing I could do about that except drive the loaner five miles over the limit all the way back to town. Rossi would have had a fit had he known, but it did get me there only ten minutes late.

Two surprises awaited. Harlan wasn't annoyed, and his office turned out to be quite spartan, a single room in the industrial park off Pine Ridge Road. In addition to a computer desk and a couple of filing cabinets, a large drafting table faced with a pair of upright chairs were the extent of the furnishings. Though initially surprised by the modesty, I forgot all about it when I glanced up at the walls. They were breathtaking. Against a taupe background, he had hung double-matted line drawings of his architectural achievements. There were several mega-mansions, a hospital, a bank, even a small museum. All had pride of place, and I was fascinated, studying first one and then the other.

He watched me, a smile playing about his lips. "You like what you see." It wasn't a question.

"It's eye candy, Harlan. I do have one major concern though," I said, sitting across from his drafting table to rest my knee.

"Yes?" One of his eyebrows lifted as if he couldn't believe that, after viewing his work, I could have any serious concerns.

"What Rossi and I have in mind doesn't begin to compare with any of these projects." I waved my arms at his walls.

"Not a problem," he said. "I understood that the night I saw your building lot. I fit in small projects like yours around my major clients. In fact I find the change of pace refreshing."

"So for what I have in mind, a set of drawings won't take you long?"

"No. A few days at most. Now I have a question for you."

"Shoot."

"During preliminary planning sessions, I like to meet with both clients. But the lieutenant chose not to join us today?"

That one *was* a question. Time for me to take an acting lesson from Teresa.

"He's so terribly busy…he said you'd understand… one hardworking professional to another."

He frowned but nodded. "Very well. Ultimately, the lady of the house is the one I aim to please. So what do you have in mind, Mrs. Dunne?"

He leaned across the drafting table, and if I were the susceptible type, those dazzling blue eyes with their impossibly long lashes—no five coats of anything on those babies—would have had me in a flutter. But with Rossi in my life, I reacted to Harlan Conway as if I were a piece of wood. All I wanted from him was a set of house plans.

I cleared my throat and plunged right in.

TWENTY-EIGHT

LIFE WAS SELDOM perfect, and when it was—watch out.
I learned that lesson a few days later when I had:

Two major projects under control.

Plans for a jewel of a new house in the works.

An Audi dealer who promised Tony's insurance
would cover repairs to my car.

A knee that had stopped throbbing and a forehead
without a lump.

And last, but far from least, I had Rossi to love.

Then Tom Kruse called me at the shop and stole the
line I'd used on him the other day. "We have a problem."
"What's wrong now?"
"I can't tell you over the phone. I think you better
get over here. Make it fast, okay?"
Ready for high fives a moment earlier, I hung up
not wanting to slap anything except my own forehead.
Lee took one look at me and hurried over to the desk.
"Everything all right?" she asked.
I shook my head. "I thought so earlier. Now I'm not
so sure. I hate to leave you alone in the shop again today,

but the painting contractor needs me. Sounds like he has an emergency."

"Don't worry about a thing, Deva. I'll manage just fine."

"I know you will. You always do."

"Besides," she added softly. "I won't exactly be alone…"

Busy retrieving my purse from the lower desk drawer, I didn't recognize the import of her words immediately. It took a second, and when the message hit home, I let the bag flop back into the drawer and leaped to my feet. "Are you having a baby?"

Her smile beamed from ear to ear. "Yes, ma'am."

"You're having a baby! Omigod!" I caught her in a bear hug and held her tight. *Too tight?* I let go. "Did I hurt you?"

She laughed. "Paulo said the same thing this morning. I'm fine. Just fine."

She looked it too. Always lovely, she had taken on a radiance hard to miss. Why hadn't I noticed it before now? Too busy with my own concerns, that was why. For shame.

"When?" I managed to ask while I swiped a finger at the tears springing into my eyes.

"In December. Around Christmas."

"What a wonderful time to have a baby." Especially in southwest Florida. The days were cool, the nights cooler.

"We wanted you to be the first to know. And Paulo asked me to mention something else."

"Yes?"

"The bank has approved us for a mortgage."

"Wonderful!"

"Yes, we're thrilled." As if to prove it, her smile went from ear to ear. "So are you still willing to sell us your condo in Surfside?"

"Of course. I'd love for you to have it. That would be a perfect solution all around. Let me speak to Rossi. He won't be putting his place in Countryside on the market anytime soon, so I'm pretty sure I can move in with him until the new house is ready. Don't worry. We'll work something out."

I reached back into the desk drawer and lifted out the purse. "You're going to be a beautiful mother, Lee. And just for the record, I want to be called Aunt Deva."

She nodded. "I wouldn't have him call you anything else."

Him. This time I needed tissues to mop up my tears. "I'd like to have a baby too some day. A little boy maybe. I don't know if I'll ever be that lucky but I'm hoping so. I can see him now. He has red hair and a tough-sounding name. Rocco Rossi. What do you think of that?"

"I think you've picked out a daddy."

"I have. So maybe I better marry him and find out what life has in store."

"That's what my momma would say."

I hugged her again—more gently this time. For sure, her news had shaken up my thinking. Planning a house was one thing. A good thing. Planning a whole life was better, far better. After all, my doctor hadn't said I'd *never* have a child, just that the odds were greatly against it. Who knew? I might just beat those odds.

Humming "I Will Always Love You," I left the shop already making plans for the future—a baby shower for Lee and a small, intimate wedding for Rossi and me.

On the lanai of a brand-new house overlooking a Gulf inlet with an orange sunset gilding the water.

But those ideas were for a golden tomorrow. With an effort, I yanked myself back to today as I drove the loaner over to Whiskey Lane and a house with a more immediate wedding in its future. Usually calm in the face of any job-related glitches, Tom had sounded beyond harassed. I couldn't imagine what had gone so wrong he needed me there for immediate backup.

I found trucks clogging the driveway of 590. I'd expected to see Tom's vehicles parked there, but why Tony's Tiles? I shrugged and, with my stomach in a knot, parked on the street behind a gorgeous Honda Gold Wing.

Though not a biker, I stepped out of the car and gave the Honda an awestruck once-over. Lustrous and gleaming in the sun, the bike had every bell and whistle possible. It even had a helmet sitting on the seat as if the owner knew no one in the neighborhood would bother to touch it. Still, a motorcycle, no matter how glamorous, seemed out of place on hushed, elegant Whiskey Lane, and I wondered who owned it.

Inside, the house hummed with activity and looked as if it were peeling; wallpaper, loosened by hand-held steamers, hung in strips everywhere. What a beautiful sight! If the men removed all the paper in the public rooms today, the painting could begin in earnest tomorrow. Encouraged, I asked the same lanky young painter of the day before if he'd seen Tom.

"Earlier," he said, zapping a wall with a burst of steam. "He was talking to some lady. They might be out in back."

A lady? Kay might have dropped by to check on the

job. Dealing with her demands was probably what had Tom so agitated.

Wrong.

I found him in the kitchen on his cell phone. Eileen was there too, slumped in the breakfast nook, a cup of green tea sitting unnoticed on the table in front of her.

"He's not picking up," Tom said. "I got his voice mail again." He closed the phone and stashed it in his pants pocket. "I know the dog had to be walked, but this is an emergency. If we don't hear from him in five minutes, I'm calling the cops."

"What's going on, Tom?"

"I wish the hell I knew." *Hell? From Tom-who-never-swore?* He glanced over at Eileen. "You tell her," he said. "I've got wallpaper to strip off." He stomped across the kitchen toward the door. "Boy, you sure got us mixed up in a good one this time, Deva."

"Eileen?" I asked.

"She's not dead," Eileen said in a toneless voice.

"Who's not dead?"

"Marilyn Stahlman."

"James's *wife?* The one who was lost at sea?"

Eileen, the color of the tea in her forgotten cup, nodded. "She's come back. Like a ghost."

"Where's Mr. Stahlman?"

"That's the problem," Tom said, pausing in the doorway. "We can't reach him. He's out somewhere with that mutt of his."

Mutt. Charlotte with her impeccable ancestors would woof at that.

"Where is this woman? This Mrs. Stahlman?"

"She said she wanted to take a shower," Tom said, "and ordered me and the crew out of the house."

"Whoever she is, she has no right to do that."

"Understood. But just so you'll know, dealing with long-lost wives isn't part of my job."

Beyond agitated, Tom was positively angry. Having him walk off the project would be a full-blown disaster. So in the interest of damage control—and to satisfy my curiosity—I headed for the master suite and a look at this woman who had come back from the dead.

TWENTY-NINE

I KNOCKED AND, without waiting for an invitation, opened the bedroom door. Wrapped in a towel and nothing else, a woman stood in front of a mirror brushing her hair.

Letting the air whoosh out of my lungs in one big breath, I closed the door and leaned against it for support. "Who *are* you?" I asked.

She swung her long, damp hair over her shoulders. "No. I ask the questions. Who are *you?*"

"I'm Deva Dunne, James's interior designer." I stood up straight. "Now it's your turn."

For a second there, she looked as if she'd refuse to answer, then surprised me. "I'm Marilyn Stahlman. James's wife."

"He'll be interested to know you're back...Mrs. Stahlman."

She hung on to the brush but let the towel drop to the floor and strutted, butt naked, over to the bed. Though approaching forty, like Kay she had a great body, not an unnecessary curve anywhere and all the necessary ones in perfect position. Wherever she'd been for a year, she obviously had ample opportunity to work out. Radiating health and strength, she was a far cry from a ghost.

Unfazed at being naked in front of a virtual stranger, she unzipped a leather backpack and pulled out a pair of black jeans and a black T-shirt.

No underwear? I smiled, thinking of what Nana Kennedy would say about that.

"Where's Jimmy, anyway?" she asked, as she slid into the jeans. "I thought he might be at home when I arrived. It's not like he has to go to work or anything."

"I don't think he was expecting you, or I'm sure he'd be here," I said, wondering if she'd see the humor in my reply.

From the quick flash of her blue eyes, I think she did. She gave her hair a final brush—it was drying to a deep honey blond—and sans bra, sans panties, sans makeup, sans embellishment of any kind, she looked ravishing. Jimmy...I mean James...sure had polished taste in women. But whether or not he'd be happy to see Marilyn was anybody's guess. After all, with her reemergence he risked losing both Kay and the fortune he'd inherited from a supposedly dead wife. As for me, Marilyn's reappearance meant I risked losing an important client—no need now to rush getting the house ready for a wedding.

But there I went again, letting what I didn't know race ahead of what I did—until a moment later, when she flung down her brush and proved that sometimes suppositions were right on target.

"Well now, Deva, whoever you are," she said, "I want you to get the hell out of my bedroom and out of my house."

"Oh, really?" I squared my shoulders and raised my chin, Dorchester style. It had worked with bullies in grammar school, so why not here? "I happen to be in Mr. Stahlman's employ, and until your identity is confirmed, I have no intention of leaving."

Sheer bravado. Eileen had already identified her, and

having been with the family for years, Eileen would know. Furthermore, weird as the woman's sudden reappearance might be, my gut told me she really was the long-lost Mrs. Stahlman. All we needed was James's confirmation. He had been gone quite a while now. How long did it take a little thing like Charlotte to pee, anyway?

That question never got answered. Someone knocked on the door, and hoping it was the master of the house, I yanked it open.

Bingo! James Stahlman stood there with Charlotte in his arms. Staring past me, he gazed straight across the room at Marilyn, utter disbelief sagging his jaw to his chest.

"You," he said, and nothing else. His face the color of putty, he looked as if he could use a chair or a few fingers of cognac. Probably both.

Charlotte squirmed in his embrace. His arms must have gone limp, for he dropped her suddenly—dumped her really. She landed paws down, appeared dazed for a second, then, tail waggling, she scampered over to Marilyn, who promptly picked her up and kissed her. Which was a lot more than she'd done for James.

His arms free of dog, James clung to the open doorjamb. From the pale look of him, he'd be dropping to the floor next.

Marilyn glanced across at him, her face devoid of sympathy. "You're shocked. I guess I can't blame you."

He passed a hand over his eyes, as if trying to clear his vision. "Where have you been all this time?"

She shrugged. "Did you miss me?" When he didn't answer, she patted Charlotte and murmured in her ear, "I know *you* did."

"I asked where you've been? I thought you had drowned. The whole world thought you had drowned."

She placed Charlotte on the floor, rather carefully, and strode closer to her husband, though staying well out of arm range.

"What does it matter where I've been? That isn't important. Our marriage was over long before I left. And if you're wondering why I came back, blame the media. I read about your engagement." She laughed. "To Kay Hawkins of all people."

"Where have you *been?*"

"Hiding in plain sight."

He hadn't let go of the door frame, not for an instant, and he clung to it still, her non-answers plainly adding to his shock. "Why these months of hell? Why didn't you just divorce me?"

A strange, dreamlike expression floated across Marilyn's face, and she hesitated before answering. "That night when I swam from the yacht, I never intended to stay away, not in the beginning. It just…happened. The farther I went, the less and less I wanted to return— to you, to this house, to the life I was bored sick of. Without realizing it at first, I think I intended to die that night."

"Good God."

"Yes." She raised her arms then let them fall, like broken wings, to her sides. "But as you can see, I didn't."

"What happened? We were several miles out. You're a strong swimmer but—"

"I was rescued. Whether against my will or not, I still can't say. He was fishing for tarpon and caught me instead. I'm going to marry him. And since I have a reason to live after all, I'll need my money."

James bowed from the waist. "Of course, my dear."

Grace under pressure. I'd never seen such a display of consummate good manners and was totally impressed, if somewhat confused. Never mind clinging to the doorjamb, any other man would have had Marilyn by the throat demanding answers. How could he manage to be so calm, so courtly, in the face of such a profound insult?

A timid cough. James swiveled around. "Yes, Eileen."

"Sorry to bother you, sir, but I'm leaving for the grocery store, and there's a gentleman here to see you and Mrs. Stahlman. He's waiting in the kitchen."

"Who is it?"

"A Lieutenant Rossi of the Naples police."

"Please tell him we'll be right with him."

"Very good, sir," Eileen said and took her leave.

"Oh, heavens." Marilyn heaved a long sigh. "I suppose the inquisition is about to begin. Can't I just be left alone?"

Nope. Get ready, honey. The police, the Coast Guard and your investment bankers will all want to chat it up with you.

James swept a hand to one side and, ever the gallant, said, "After you, ladies."

What I wished he'd do, instead, was show some emotion. Yell, swear, punch a hole in the wall, cry, seize Marilyn in his arms and kiss her passionately. Act as if he were over the moon with happiness or ready to kill her with his bare hands. But no, flat as a tabletop, displaying no emotional highs or lows, he followed us from the master suite into the living room past Tom's crew who were ankle deep in damp wallpaper, and out to the kitchen.

As we walked in, single file, Rossi didn't seem surprised to see me. He'd probably spotted the loaner sitting out by the curb. All professional and noncommittal, he flashed his badge at the Stahlmans and gave me a brief nod.

"I'm Lieutenant Victor Rossi of the Naples Police Department," he said to James. "I've already met Mrs. Dunne, but you are?"

"James Stahlman." He gestured at Marilyn. "This is my wife, the reason you've been called here, I presume."

"That is my understanding."

"Please forgive the appearance of my home, Lieutenant. But I'm undergoing—"

Rossi held up a finger. Just one. "No need to explain. I'm well acquainted with Mrs. Dunne's work."

I'll say.

"I don't believe her testimony will be required," Rossi went on. "So if you wish, Mrs. Dunne, you may be excused."

Excused? Darn it. Rossi should know I wanted to hear every word. I shot him a quick, appalled glance. He knew, all right. He was smiling, the fox. We'd have to discuss this tonight—before bed.

But James came through for me. "I prefer that Deva stay. For the past year, in the court of public opinion, I've been tried and convicted of murder. I'm happy to have people know I never harmed my wife."

Ah, a show of bitterness. Not the jolliest of emotions, but proof that James had some steel in his spine. I treated Rossi to a triumphant grin, and we all sat cozy as four old friends in the breakfast nook.

While Eileen served coffee, and Rossi readied his tape recorder for Marilyn's testimony, I glanced out the kitchen windows. A slight breeze riffled the palm trees, a relief, no doubt, to Tony and Mike, who were on their knees replacing the stones on the slippery set of terrace stairs. A good move on James's part.

"I think we're ready," Rossi said, pulling my attention back inside.

Leaving out how bored she'd been with her marriage, but leaving in her death wish, Marilyn retold the tale of her disappearance, right down to the name of her rescuer. Showing little remorse for her husband's suffering, she was deeply concerned that her lover be spared any blame. When she finished, Rossi turned off the tape recorder.

"Disappearing is not a crime, per se, as long as no actual harm was done. Faking one's own death is another matter. However, if that wasn't your original intent, the circumstances may be considered somewhat extenuating. I can't guarantee that will be the finding, but from what you've told me, there's at least a chance this might be deemed a private matter between husband and wife."

"Oh good," Marilyn said.

"With one caveat." Rossi continued as if she hadn't interrupted. "The element of deception in your disappearance. My guess is that the Collier County taxpayers will have to be reimbursed for man hours spent investigating the case. And almost certainly the Coast Guard will expect compensation for its search at sea. If these charges are met, that may be the end of the matter. Again, no guarantees, of course. While the resolution of the case is underway, you may want to contact your lawyer. In fact, I recommend you do so."

Finished with his interview, he stood, pocketed the recorder and shook James's hand. He didn't take Marilyn's or nod farewell in her direction. Though what Rossi was thinking was always hard to psych out, this time I guessed he'd made a value judgment. He didn't quite care for a wife who, for an entire year, let her husband believe she was dead when the whole time she was alive and well. Not only that, she'd let him be ripped to shreds in the media.

Whatever he thought, without another word he turned on his heel and strode out of the kitchen. Marilyn cleared her throat, reached into her jeans pocket and withdrew a small slip of paper. "Here's my lawyer's number. And one where I can be reached." Careful not to touch James's hand, she placed it in front of him and stood. "I'll get my gear out of the bedroom and be off."

"Do you need a ride?" he asked.

My God, the man was unbelievable.

"No, thanks, my bike's outside." Halfway to the door, she swiveled around. "Any objection if I drop by mornings and use the pool?"

"Certainly not. I built it for you. Kay might object though."

She laughed and gave her hair a toss. "Not a problem. I can handle Kay."

James smiled, faintly, but still the edges of his lips did turn up. "You're well matched."

Ah, a flash of insight for James and for me. In that moment, we both understood that he liked tall, statuesque women with wills of iron.

Poor Jimmy.

THIRTY

BY NOON, EVERY scrap of wallpaper had been stripped off the public rooms of 590, which was a good thing. Condensation had been dripping down the inside of the windows all morning, and in the heat and humidity, even James's putty-colored face took on a pink glow. Truth be told, southwest Florida in July wasn't the best time to have an air-conditioning system fight a small army of hand-held steamers.

Tom's crew swept up the debris then left for lunch break. A couple of the men settled outside on the top terrace step to eat their sandwiches and swap tales with Mike and Tony. A quick peek out the living room sliders showed Mike doing most of the talking and Tony looking bored as if he'd heard it all before.

After the soggy paper had been stuffed into plastic utility bags and the floors swept clean, Tom and I toured the rooms. Rid of its dated wall coverings and ho-hum chairs, the bare, stripped interior reminded me once again of the reasons why I loved my work—transforming drab houses into beautiful ones and, not incidentally, making the people who lived in them happy. Or happier. I heaved a sigh. After what transpired here today, I wondered if this would ever again be a happy household.

"The walls are in better shape than I thought," Tom said, running a hand along the plaster. "I'll have the boys finish prepping this afternoon, and we'll start painting in the morning. It'll take three coats, but even so, we should finish up early next week." He glanced over his shoulder, and seeing we were alone, whispered, "That blonde. Is she the wife who disappeared?"

I nodded.

He let out a whistle. "It'll take more than three coats of paint to fix that mess."

"What mess?"

We both whirled around, as startled as if James had caught us doing something wrong. Well, in a way, he had. We were gossiping, pure and simple. Not a good thing ever, but especially bad at a time like this.

To cover my embarrassment—and my guilt— I quickly replied, "Tom was saying that when he's through here, he has another challenging job waiting for him."

James nodded, not bothering to ask anything about his own house, a subject that just a few hours ago had consumed him. As if he were a pricked balloon, all the air had whooshed out of his bubble, and I was sorry for his distress.

"I should get back to the shop," I said.

James peeked at his watch. "Please don't go, Deva. Kay's due home for lunch any minute now, and I'd love to have you join us. If you can…" His voice trailed off.

He hadn't said so, but I sensed that he needed me as a buffer, or for moral support…or perhaps to keep Kay's anger in check when he broke the news of Marilyn's return.

At the pleading in his brown puppy eyes, I didn't have the heart to refuse. So, tough as two cream puffs, we waited for the Iron Lady in the kitchen, the one comfortable room left in the torn-up house.

In the silence—even Charlotte had wisely scooted into her cage for a midday nap—we listened for Kay's arrival, and the minute a car door slammed, we both stiffened. As his fiancée's stilettos clicked across the bare floors, the pink in James's cheeks faded away.

Putty-faced again, he rose to greet her though he might have been wise to remain seated. Or better still, to stretch out flat on the breakfast nook bench.

With her long, leggy stride, Kay reached the kitchen quickly, pushed through the swinging door and careened to a stop when she saw me.

"Oh, you're here too." Obviously less than pleased, she rallied fast. "Well, I must say the painters have made wonderful progress. The house should be ready in plenty of time."

For the wedding.

She held out her arms to James—a far cry for sure from the way Marilyn had greeted him. He hurried to embrace her and placed a discreet peck on her cheek. "You look lovely," he murmured.

She did, in a black linen mini that showcased legs already highlighted by strappy spike heels. A lime-green bag tossed over a shoulder added a touch of colorful chic.

"But then, you are forever lovely," James added, running his hands along her arms.

"You always say the most marvelous things, darling. No wonder I love you."

She kissed him for real, and while they were enjoying it, I wished I were somewhere else, even outside talking about snakes with Mike and Tony.

The kiss ended, finally, and loosening his embrace a little, James cleared his throat. *Here comes the bombshell.*

"I wish I could say only wonderful things to you, darling, but that's not always possible. Do come and sit down."

Good move.

"You look positively grim, James. Is anything the matter?"

She suspects something.

I sat in a corner of the breakfast nook, quiet as dust, while he took her by the hand and led her to the table,

Once they were safely seated, he said, "There is something I have to tell you, darling."

Alarm swept across Kay's face. "Well, for God's sake, Jimmy, out with it."

He took a deep, bracing breath and expelled it slowly. "Marilyn didn't drown after all. She's come back. From the dead, so to speak."

Kay gasped and half rose from her seat, then fell back onto it as if she didn't trust her admittedly gorgeous legs to hold her.

James leaned across the table to retake her hands. "I have an appointment with my attorney at three today. I'm starting divorce proceedings immediately."

Well, well. No histrionics, but no wasting time either. Chalk one up for James.

"I knew that bitch wasn't dead." Her face rage red, Kay yanked her fingers out from under James's and sat up straight. "How dare she do this to us? Where has she been all this time?"

"It's a long story that—"

"The nerve of her. Showing up just before our wedding." Kay's hand flew to her mouth. "Ooooh." The realization had struck home, and she slumped against the back of the bench, stunned by the truth.

"Exactly," James said, a sardonic smile playing with his lips. "She's saving us from bigamy. Perhaps we should be grateful."

"Grateful?" Kay leaped to her feet. "I could kill her!"

THIRTY-ONE

So far I hadn't said a thing. All I'd done was witness James's kissing technique—which I have to admit was pretty darn good—and listened to Kay's outburst. Not that I blamed her for feeling the way she did or anything. Still, when James said, "Don't worry, dearest. We'll work this out together," I figured my career as a marriage counselor had ended before it began, so I eased off the breakfast nook bench.

As Kay slumped in her seat, I said, "If you'll both excuse me."

"Of course, Deva, thank you." James's earnest eyes telegraphed his gratitude, though he hadn't needed my help after all.

I paused. "Just one question before I go?"

His attention focused on Kay, he nodded briefly, eager now for me to leave.

"In light of what's happened, I assume there's no necessity to rush to completion."

A puzzled frown knitted his brows.

"The house?" I said.

"Oh. Yes. I mean no. No rush at all. Your original schedule will be fine."

That was when Kay astonished me. She laid her head on the tabletop and burst into tears.

As James murmured words of comfort and stroked her hair, I escaped out the back way through the living room sliders. Relieved to be in the open, I took a deep breath that gave my nose a thrill. Edging the property, gardenia plants the size of small trees perfumed the air with a magical scent. I loved it and inhaled again.

Though the exterior of the house wasn't something James had hired me to deal with, I was curious about those treacherous terrace stairs. The two painters were nowhere in sight, but Mike and Tony, on their hands and knees, were busy chipping away at the stone and didn't notice my approach.

"Hi, Tony," I said, bending over him for a closer look.

About to chisel out a tile, he missed it and hit his thumb instead. He dropped the chisel and jumped to his feet, waving his bonked thumb in the air. "Cripes, you scared the shit out of me. You can stop a guy's heart sneaking up on him like that."

I stepped back, out of reach of his flailing arm. "I'm sorry. I didn't mean to startle you."

"He's been pretty jumpy lately," Mike volunteered.

Tony shot him a why-don't-you-shut-up-for-a-change look, and for once Mike took the hint and went back to his task.

Tony stood sucking his thumb. The gesture made him look like a pouting child, but I hoped he wasn't badly injured. He needed those big, strong hands to make a living.

"Can you flex it?" I asked.

He took the finger out of his mouth and wiggled it up and down.

"Yeah, it's all right," he said, returning to his knees. Even the rubber knee pads he and Mike wore didn't relieve all the pressure. Laying tiles and stone all day every day was hard work. The relentless summer sun beating down on them didn't make it any easier. Neither did curious women.

Though I didn't stay to ask any more questions, I did notice that the new stones they were installing had a rougher surface than the old ones. No doubt, the stairs would be much safer now.

Beads of perspiration had popped out on my forehead. It was hot as Hades out here, and the sun wasn't helping my freckles any, but now that I'd gotten this far, I wanted to have a look at the pool behind the boxwood hedge. Avoiding the stairs, I started down the grassy slope.

Apparently not ready to give up talking, Mike called after me. "You're looking good, Mrs. Dunne. Real good." I half turned in time to catch him giving me an eye sweep. "Green's your color all right. Glad to see the accident didn't do any permanent damage."

"Are you?" I challenged. "So is Lieutenant Rossi." Let Mike chew on that for a while.

Undeterred, he said, "Any news for my boys at State?"

"You don't give up, do you?"

He shook his head. "Nope. That's not the road to success. At least not according to my philosophy. If you don't keep whittling at the problems life hands you, they never go away. My grandfather always—"

"Your grandfather isn't paying you," Tony said. "I am. How about whittling on the chatter? That jibe with your philosophy?"

I'd gone halfway down the slope when Mike yelled, "Well, Mrs. Dunne, what about it?"

I swiveled around, and hands akimbo, shrew style, yelled back, "I should have two installations for you by next week. But if you bring up the subject again, the deal's off."

"Not a problem," he yelled. He wiped the sweat off his forehead onto a tattooed arm and sent me a happy wave. As cheerful as if he were on vacation at St. Tropez, he acted as if he didn't have a care in the world. Or an enemy. Maybe that accident in my driveway had been just that—an accident, not a deliberate attack.

Still, Naomi's warning echoed in my mind. *His writing shows a felon's claw. Don't trust him.* He could be charming, she'd said, which made him doubly dangerous. I'd be wise to heed Rossi's advice and have nothing further to do with Mike Hammerjack, but a promise was a promise. That and my own stubborn nature stood in the way of prudence.

I continued down the slope and stepped behind the boxwoods.

Oh my.

A competition-size pool lay in the sun, its classic rectangle filled with blue lapis lazuli water so inviting I wanted to take a skinny-dip dive right then and there. But Tony and Mike's voices coming through the boxwoods quickly killed that impulse.

In the bottom of the pool, yellow tiles had been laid in the shape of five connected rings. A perfect practice pool for Marilyn, a former medal contender. Or a not-so-subtle reminder for her to keep on striving?

Whatever. Hidden back here, out of sight of the house and surrounded by a privacy hedge, the pool was a wonderful retreat for anyone and especially for a dedicated swimmer. Or it could be. James had obviously not spared any expense in building the pool but hadn't spent much on anything else. Two forlorn-looking plastic lounge chairs offered the only seating.

Too bad. Some padded recliners sheltered with umbrellas, and a few ceramic jardinières would make the whole area more inviting. A little pool house at the far end of the property would be delightful for patio parties, or for reading, or napping, or any other leisure activity. But this was a pool built with a serious purpose in mind, not for fun.

I stood staring at the brilliant blue water. Why had Marilyn faked her own drowning? Had her life really been too burdensome to endure? Even if it had been, why pretend you were dead? She had chosen a cruel solution, even if James, as she claimed, had bored her to death.

THIRTY-TWO

THAT EVENING OVER DINNER, I said, "You know something, Rossi, you're a very interesting man."

He'd finished his salad and moved the empty plate aside. Ready to start in on what he considered the good stuff, a slice of pepperoni pizza, he glanced over at me, a trifle surprised. "A compliment? What brought that on?"

"Why the surprise? It's not like I never compliment you or anything."

He stifled a smile. "True, but you don't fling them around lightly. The last one I recall was in bed immediately after—"

"Those don't count. That's the heat of passion talking."

This time he grinned ear to ear. "I'm disappointed to hear that. They've been some of your finest observations."

"Well, there have been others too," I retorted, hoping my face wasn't flaming. Warm cheeks made my freckles pop. To buy a little time to think, I took a sip of wine. *Ah!* "Remember last winter when you wore a tie and a white dress shirt? I definitely told you how handsome you looked that night."

"You really were saying I don't wear a tie often enough."

"Well, there is that, and also—"

He held up a hand for silence. "Wait! I remember another one. You once told me you liked standing beside me because we were on an even playing field. Eyeball to eyeball."

"Right."

"You were telling me I'm short."

"No way. I meant exactly what I said. I like your height."

"Or lack thereof. Now will you tell me something else?"

"Of course, anything."

"What the hell's this conversation all about anyway?" He washed down his pizza with a swig of Chianti and reached for another piece.

He was definitely finding his food more interesting than me. "Am I annoying you?" I asked, annoyed enough for two.

He looked up, mid-slice. "No, not at all. I'm curious. I really don't get the point of this discussion." He put down the pizza—rather reluctantly, I thought—and wiped his fingertips on his napkin. "So clue me in."

"Well, it's about Marilyn Stahlman. Her sudden return and all that. Why do you suppose she disappeared in the first place?"

"I'm a detective, not a mind reader."

"You're pretty good at that too."

He arched a brow. "Another compliment?"

"Yes."

Unimpressed, he went back to his pizza, but I wasn't ready to give up. "She had to have a reason for staying away a whole year."

"No doubt. A happy woman doesn't stage her own drowning."

"Go on." I moved in closer. Rossi had excellent insight, and I wanted to hear every word.

With a sigh, he leaned back in his chair. "Remember how at the beginning of my interview with the Stahlmans, I said you could be excused?"

"Yes. That was my next question. Why did you do that?"

"Because I knew if you stayed to listen—as you were panting to do—I'd be asked these very questions."

"I have a vested interest in James's house, so it's only natural that—"

He pushed his plate back from his place at the table. Not a good sign. A lecture was on the way.

"If Mrs. Stahlman pays the costs of investigating her disappearance, chances are good she won't be charged with a crime. Her crime, as it were, was in creating emotional anguish in those who knew and loved her. Especially in her husband. But now that he's engaged to remarry, I assume he's made a full recovery."

I wanted to comment, but Rossi was on a roll and wouldn't let me squeeze in a word.

"Mrs. Stahlman's motives for doing what she did are another story. Perhaps she's mentally unbalanced. Perhaps she's vindictive. Maybe she was suicidal the night she went for her famous swim and a fortunate quirk of fate saved her. In any event, once she pays up, the case—as they say—will most likely be closed."

"But her motives are the most fascinating aspect of what happened. *Why* did she do it?"

"Be satisfied with the answer she gave. It's simple enough. She wanted out of her life." His attention roamed back to his half-eaten pizza slice. "Why so curious, anyway?"

I shrugged. "Chalk it up to a benign form of voyeurism. Mentally peeking into people's lives. I guess what I do—my designing—is a form of that. I'm paid to look at how people live and then to change their surroundings. Maybe wondering why they do what they do is just going one step further."

He picked up the Chianti bottle and filled our glasses. "Excellent justification for snooping."

I didn't want to laugh but I had to. "You earn your living by snooping. In fact you've practically raised snooping to an art form. So what's *your* excuse, Lieutenant?"

"I don't need one. Art's only purpose is to be."

"Good, Rossi, very good. That's what I meant. You're fascinating, and you don't even have to work at it."

He leaned across the table to give me a pepperoni—and Chianti-laced kiss. "You know something, Deva? When it comes to being fascinating, you win the gold medal. You're the most fascinating woman in the entire world."

Now *that* was what I called a compliment. Rossi knew it too, the fox. It had me kissing him like crazy.

And so to bed. If not to sleep.

THIRTY-THREE

"DID YOU ASK HIM?" Lee said the next morning.

I looked up from my computer screen. "Ask him?"

"The lieutenant about, you know, selling your condo and all?"

In blue, which always became her, Lee was a vision, especially now with the glow of early pregnancy lighting her face. With all the crazy events of the past few days, I *had* forgotten, but I couldn't admit that and risk seeing her happy glow disappear.

"Rossi and I are meeting with the architect for lunch, so I thought I'd bring it up then."

Her face fell a little.

"I promise there won't be a problem," I added quickly. "Rossi will be delighted that I'm selling you the condo."

"We don't mean to rush y'all, but we're running out of time in our apartment. The landlord finally admitted his son's moving back home, and he wants us out of there like yesterday."

"Then consider it a done deal. The condo's yours whenever you and Paulo want it. Furniture included if you like."

Her eyes took on a shine and then the tears spilled over.

The rental apartment she and Paulo were squeezed into had come furnished, but only in a manner of speaking, so I'd suspected they would welcome the Surf-side things. Besides I wanted to furnish my new home slowly and carefully, one piece at a time. On heart of pine floors I envisioned tiger maple chests and canvas-covered couches and kilim toss pillows...

The Yarmouthport bells jangled. A woman stepped in, took one startled look at Lee and froze inside the door.

"Do come in," I said, giving Lee a handful of tissues. "My friend's crying with happiness."

"Oh, I've done that too," the woman said and with an understanding smile strolled around, browsing the table displays.

Turning my attention back to Lee, I said, "Plan on moving as soon as you need to. That way you'll be set-tled long before the baby comes."

Her eyes shining, she nodded.

"If you like, I can help you plan the nursery."

"I'd love that."

"Will it be a boy's room or a girl's?"

"I don't know. We want to be surprised."

Another surprise, a good one this time.

"I'm partial to white with touches of primary col-ors," Lee offered shyly.

"Me too! No insipid pinks and blues for this baby."

I retrieved my purse from the desk drawer, stood, and with a quick hug for Lee, hurried off. Online scouting for Stew's Western-themed furnishings would have to go on hold for a while.

WHEN I REACHED the Magnolia Café, they were both waiting. From the frown on Rossi's face, I could tell he was irritated. Well, five minutes alone with Harlan would do that to a saint.

We asked for a booth. As we were being seated, Rossi told the waiter we needed some time before ordering and slid in beside me. Across from us, Harlan unrolled the renderings he had downloaded and laid them out flat.

A single glance at the first one and my breath caught in my throat. He had captured it perfectly—my dream of a house.

A rectangle on stilts, its narrow side with high windows faced the street, its opposite side all glass, ending in a V-shaped teakwood deck that jutted over the water like the prow of a ship. With its tin roof, board-and-batten siding and Bermuda shutters tilting over the windows, it was exactly what I'd hoped for—an inspired combination of both the old and new Floridas. I loved it on sight.

"Brilliant! A marvelous use of the space."

I felt like high-fiving or jumping up and down until Harlan said, "You doubted I could pull off a simple design like this?"

"No, I never doubted your ability for an instant."

"That's why you're here," Rossi said, his voice gravelly with more than mere irritation.

I squeezed his knee under the table, a signal not to piss off the genius. "I was concerned though, Harlan, that your dreams and mine might not be the same." I tapped the drawing. "But in this we've come together in a perfect union."

"So to speak," Rossi added wryly. This time he squeezed *my* knee.

"I'm glad you're both pleased." Harlan flipped the

sheet to the next drawing. "Shall we have a look at the inside?"

"Can't wait."

Flanking the deck and open to the water view, a high-ceilinged great room dominated the interior. Behind it was a good-sized kitchen and ample area for dining. Two bedrooms, each with its own bath, he'd positioned farther back, on the side facing the rear lawn and driveway.

Harlan pointed to the deck. "Assuming you'll spend a good deal of time out here, I made it quite sizable. Notice how the point of the V is open to the sun, and the area adjoining the great room is roofed over for shade." He glanced across at me. "With your red hair and complexion—" *freckles*, "—I knew you'd want some shade."

"Good thinking." Rossi had forgotten his irritation and was studying the renderings with rapt attention. That he liked what he saw, I hadn't a doubt and knew I wouldn't have to squeeze his knee again anytime soon.

"For a hint of that old Florida reference you asked for, I see heart of pine floors and bead-board ceilings," Harlan said. "Their traditional look could be offset by the latest in kitchen and bath installations." He paused to throw me a bone. "That's where your…ah…expertise can come in."

"Yes, selecting the interior details will be my great pleasure. There are a few changes I'd like to make to the closets and some of the window placements, but overall, I'm delighted." I extended a hand across the tabletop. "My thanks to you, Harlan, for this wonderful vision. Rossi and I will be very happy living in it."

Harlan cleared his throat and nodded, though very slightly— he was obviously used to having his work praised—and flipped the sheet to show us a lateral elevation.

Happy with the plans, Rossi took a business card out of his pocket, scrawled his home address on the back and slid it across the table. "Send the bill to this address."

All was good. Better than good. Actually wonderful. Imagine, someone with Harlan's prickly personality creating so much joy. But he had. And we soon brought some joy to the hovering waiter by ordering a celebratory lunch.

After chicken quesadillas and iced tea, Harlan left for another appointment. Alone with Rossi, I snuggled up to him in the booth. "I'm so happy," I said.

He gave me a quick kiss. "Nothing could please me more. That's what I live for. Seeing how thrilled you were with the plans, I know you'll want to start building as soon as possible. So it's a good thing I put my house on the market this morning."

I nearly choked on the last of my iced tea. "What!"

He nodded. "No need to waste time. The realtor told me she thinks the house will sell fast. So as soon as it does, I'll be looking for a place to stay." He sent me an easy smile. "Any idea where I can bunk for a while?"

"No. I mean yes, but—"

He checked his watch and jumped up. "Sorry to run off on you, sweetheart, but I have to go. I'm late. The chief's waiting for me. We'll talk about the house later, okay?"

"But—"

"I'll call you as soon as I can."

He gave me a quick, distracted kiss and made a bee-line for the exit. And the waiter? Well, the waiter rushed over to the booth and handed me the bill.

THIRTY-FOUR

BACK AT THE SHOP, Lee was busy helping a client look for drapery fabric. I sent her a thumb and forefinger circle, indicating all was well—a little white lie—or maybe not so little. That was what I'd find out when I had a chance to talk with Rossi about our housing situation. Regardless, I'd promised Lee the condo and as far as I was concerned that was a sacred vow.

Needing to complete a search for the Hawkins house accessories, I went straight to the computer. My vision called for rugged Western-styled pieces but not cowboy clichés.

I was just getting into it when the shop phone rang. Lee usually answered, but she'd gone to the restroom. "We're back," a gravelly voice announced.

"Stew Hawkins?"

"The same. I told you to yank the guys out of here and lock up, but let's get the show on the road again."

"I'll have the crew there tomorrow morning," I said. "First thing."

"Sounds good. Not too early though, okay? My fiancée might want to sleep in. Me too."

"Fiancée? Wow! May I ask who the ah…lucky woman is?"

A short bark of a laugh burst through the line. "Who else? Teresa, of course. Bought her a rock in the diamond district. Figured I might as well. The price was right."

"Well, congratulations. Have you set a date yet?"

"No, no. No date," he said hastily. "I'm taking it one step at a time. Just keeping the household peaceful at the moment, you know what I mean."

"I see." *Interesting.*

I hung up wondering if he really intended to marry Teresa or was playing a waiting game—give her a ring and keep her dangling forever. Or until she gave up. If so, he was underestimating her. Badly.

THE NEXT DAY, Whiskey Lane went back to its new normal—two trucks, two crews, two houses undergoing renovation.

In my seasonal favorite, the mustard-yellow shift, I stopped in at the Hawkins place first. Teresa met me at the front door wearing red silk pajamas and The Ring. She waggled her left hand in front of my eyes.

"It's gorgeous," I said, meaning it.

Big, with baguettes, the center diamond sparkled all right but no more so than Teresa's big white grin. If I had doubts that Stew would actually marry her, she obviously didn't. I gave a mental shrug. I could be entirely wrong, and for Teresa's sake if for no other reason, I hoped I was.

Taking me by the arm, she drew me inside. "I told you I'd make him happy," she whispered. "And—"

"You did."

"Did what?" a deep voice asked.

"Researched some furniture for you," I said, whirling around to face Stew, who had stomped out of the bedroom wing in bare feet and a red silk robe that was an exact match to Teresa's pj's.

"Oh, Stew, you're wearing your new robe. I love it on you," she gushed. "Don't you, Deva?"

"Absolutely. Stew, you're enough to stop a car."

"Humph."

"I bought it at Macy's," Teresa said. "The real one on 34th Street. Isn't he handsome? Red's your color, Stew."

"Don't get carried away. I couldn't find another damn thing in the suitcase." He sniffed the air. "How about some of that coffee? Vacation's over. I have to get back to the plant."

"Coming right up," Teresa said. A dutiful fiancée or a dutiful housekeeper, I couldn't tell which, she hurried out to the kitchen after Stew.

I strolled into the living room and sniffed the air. The odor of fresh paint mingled with the coffee. A painter was already at work finishing up where he left off a few days ago. "Have you seen Tom?" I asked.

Without missing a stroke, he said, "He's setting up in the master bedroom."

The Snake Room.

Stop that, I told myself. There are no snakes in there. Not anymore.

"Desert sunset on the walls, Joe," Tom was saying as I walked in. "Classic white in semi on the woodwork and flat on the ceiling. When Pete's finished in the other room, he'll be in to help you."

With the situation at 595 under control, Tom and I crossed Whiskey Lane and rang the bell at 590. My pulse rate tangoed a bit as we waited for someone to open the door. But I needn't have worried. Eileen, in her white uniform, her hair tucked into its usual neat bun, let us in. All was calm.

In the living room, Tom's painters were applying the third coat of latex to the walls. That should do it. Even with two coats, the room looked fresh and bright.

Eileen went into the kitchen, returning with coffee and dainty homemade pastries for the men.

Nice.

James, Kay and even Marilyn were nowhere in sight.

"Is Mr. Stahlman at home?" I asked.

"No, ma'am," Eileen replied. "He's at a meeting with his attorney. He should be back soon though. Said he wouldn't be gone long."

I knew he hadn't taken his constant companion with him, for Miss Charlotte was outside in the rear garden, whimpering and barking and carrying on like an agitated tiger. She wasn't usually so noisy. Something had her all excited.

"Charlotte sure is having fun out there."

Busy pouring coffee, Eileen nodded.

Curious, I strolled over to the living room sliders and glanced outside. Tail wagging furiously, Charlotte scampered halfway up the slope, barking like a junkyard dog. Then, tail still wagging, she dashed back down and disappeared around the boxwood hedge.

Intrigued, I watched her performance a few more times. She was filled with energy today. The little devil. With James gone, the chance to misbehave must have been irresistible.

Woof, woof!

There she came again, running up the slope. I opened the sliders and stepped out into sunshine perfumed with gardenias.

"Come on, Charlotte, come on!"

She stopped, woofed a few more times and scooted away.

I tried temptation. "Be a good girl, and I'll take you for a walk."

But even that magic word didn't bring her running to me, eager for a stroll. Guess she knew it wasn't time for her cocktail dog walk. "Oh come on, Charlotte," I urged. "Be a sport. It's five o'clock somewhere."

She peeked out, barked, then disappeared behind the boxwood. God only knew what she was getting into back there. She'd probably found a squirrel or a dead bird and didn't want to leave it. For James's sake, I'd better make sure she was all right.

I hurried down the new terrace steps. Tony and Mike had done a super job. The rough-hewn stones had much more traction than the slick ones they'd replaced. Snake-man or not, Tony's name was one I intended to add to my growing list of good business contacts.

"Charlotte," I called from the bottom of the slope. "Where are you? Be nice. Say hello."

Woof. She scampered over, licked my ankles and let me pat her head. But when I bent down to pick her up, Miss Queen-of-the-Cuddle dashed out of reach and darted behind the hedge.

"You want to show me what you found? That it? Okay, but I hope it isn't gruesome." Feeling slightly apprehensive about encountering a mangled bird or something, I chased after her.

At the far end of the enclosure, the pool sparkled, beautiful and blue in the morning sunshine, and there she was by the deep end, her front paws on the very edge of the tiled apron.

Heavens, could she swim? If anything happened to Charlotte, James would die. A good thing I'd come to investigate.

For fear she'd run away, or worse, fall in, I didn't approach any nearer.

"Come on. Come on, girl," I coaxed.

No dice. She ignored me and stood her ground, her gaze riveted on the water.

What was so fascinating?

Curious, I stepped in closer and looked down into the pool. A scream ripped out of my throat. Then another. And another.

Submerged in eight feet of water, a woman was floating facedown, the stars on her bikini pointing to the bottom of the pool, the stripes to the sky.

Coming on the run, Tom reached me in no time, followed by an ashen-faced Eileen.

"It's Kay Hawkins," I said. "Call 9-1-1. Hurry."

Tom felt his pockets. "I don't have my cell with me."

Eileen grabbed Charlotte and ran up the slope toward the house. I kicked off my shoes, dove down and grasped Kay's lifeless body. When I raised her to the pool's edge, Tom grasped her under the shoulders, and together we lifted her out of the water and laid her on the tiled apron, her cold cheek pressed to the concrete.

"We have to resuscitate her," I said, but one look at Tom told me he was ready to pass out. Okay, I'd do it. Hiking the sodden shift up to my thighs, I straddled Kay and pressed on her back with both hands. Again and again, I pressed and let up. Pressed and let up. But she didn't move, or sigh, or flutter an eyelash.

Distraught, I asked, "Tom, can you do CPR?"

He shook his head, obviously alarmed at the suggestion.

I never had, either, but I'd seen it done. *What was keeping the EMS?*

"Help me turn her over. I'm going to try."

We rolled Kay onto her back, and kneeling beside her, I squeezed her cheeks until her lips parted. My face against hers, I blew air from my lungs into her mouth. I lifted off and breathed again. Off and on. Off and on. Over and over, I tried until a firm hand touched my back.

"That's enough, ma'am," someone said. "We'll take it from here."

The rescue squad. I hadn't even heard them arrive. With a sense of utter failure, I huddled by the pool in my wet dress while they struggled over Kay.

After a handful of minutes that felt like a lifetime, the medic said, "Sorry, ma'am. We did our best, but there was no pulse or heartbeat. She was gone before we got here."

I nodded and glanced over at Kay lying there so beautiful and cold in her stunning flag bikini. Then for the first time, I noticed the bruises on her neck.

THIRTY-FIVE

THE LIVING ROOM sliders slammed open, and heavy footfalls pounded down the stone stairs.

"Where is she?" Stew yelled. "Where is she?" He careened around the hedge, took one look at Kay and howled, "Omigod, noooooh!"

With a few long strides, he reached her and fell to his knees beside her. Big and strong and tough as nails—and as gentle as a mother with a child—he lifted her lifeless form to his chest and held her against him. Sobbing, he rocked her back and forth, keening in a hopeless, frenzied rhythm.

"I'm so sorry, Stew," I said.

Caught in a web of anguish, he didn't respond.

"Don't leave me, Kay. Don't leave me. There's never been anyone but you. There never will be. Never." He brushed her wet hair back from her forehead and kissed her cheek. "Say something, sweetheart. Talk to me. Say something. Anything. Give me hell like you used to. I miss that. I miss you. Please. I'm begging here, Kay. I'm begging."

Shivering in my wet clothes despite the relentless sun, I wanted to run from the scene or at least cover my ears and block out Stew's pain, but at that moment, I didn't have the energy to move a muscle.

More footsteps sounded on the terrace stairs, and the two medics reappeared with a gurney. The older of the two, the one with Matt embroidered on his shirt pocket, approached Stew.

"You can let go now, sir. We'll take care of her."

But Stew wasn't ready to relinquish Kay's body. Tears running down his face, he glanced up at Matt with dead eyes. "I'm her husband. Who the hell are you?"

"I'm part of the EMS team, sir. You can give her to us now."

Stew shook his head, sending tears flying off his face. "No, I can't." He clutched Kay tighter. "She's mine, not yours." He upped his chin. "Not his, either. She was never his."

She was never *whose?*

Startled, the medics and I swiveled around to see who Stew was glaring at. James Stahlman stood inside the hedge by the pool's shallow end, his face a rigid mask of disbelief. As though cast in stone, he remained motionless, staring in shock at what lay before him.

"What happened?" he asked Matt in a small whisper of a voice.

"It looks like a drowning, sir. We've notified the police. Are you Mr. Stahlman?"

James nodded.

"Can you identify the deceased?"

"Yes, she's my fiancée, Kay Hawkins." Spitting out "Hawkins" like an epithet, he pointed a trembling finger at Stew. "I want that man's hands off her body, and I want *him* off my property."

Matt swiveled his attention to Stew. "You heard the gentleman. Under the circumstances, would you please comply?"

"Gentleman, hah! He's just a stiff in a pair of linen pants. She's my wife, and I'm not letting her go. Not for the likes of him," he sneered. "She used to laugh at you, you know that, Stahlman? Said you were the most boring guy she ever met. Used to joke about what you'd be like in bed."

As if he'd been struck, James shrank back against the shrubbery but didn't reply. He wouldn't, not to a vulgar jibe like that, but he paled, alarmingly so. Matt glanced over at the other medic, Bill, according to his pocket. "A chair for the man. Quick."

James waved Bill off with an impatient flick of his wrist and strode over to where Stew sat cradling Kay's body. "Let her go," he said quietly.

"Like hell. I'm taking her with me. You've got no claim on her."

"We're engaged to be married. You're the one without a claim. You divorced her."

"That was the worst mistake of my life. Look what happened."

Out of the corner of my eye, I saw Matt talking into his cell phone. Asking the police to hurry, no doubt.

His chin trembling, James gazed down at Kay's inert form. "I loved her, and she loved me."

"You liar. You killed her!" Slowly, his every move deliberate, Stew laid Kay on the pool apron and, jumping to his feet, came at James with both fists up.

"Don't be ridiculous," James said, disdain clear in his patrician voice. Ignoring Stew, he gazed at Kay, tears welling in his eyes. "She said she was going for a swim...I kissed her goodbye. That was the last..." He bent down as if he, too, were about to kneel by her side and cradle her in his arms one final time.

Stew's beefy fist shot out. The right hook caught James on the jaw. The blow knocked him off his feet and sent him reeling. He swayed, shaking his head like a shaggy dog. A trickle of blood ran down his neck. He touched it with a finger, staring at the blood in disbelief. For a moment he stood stark still as if he didn't know what to do next. Not surprising. His careful code of behavior hadn't prepared him for a sock on the jaw.

A siren wailed in the distance. From the corner of my eye, I saw Matt run up the slope with Tom chasing after him.

"Come on, gentlemen," Bill pleaded. "The police are here. This is no way to act."

Whether James and Stew heard a thing—the police siren, the medic's warning or anything else—was doubtful. They hadn't taken their eyes off each other.

Then suddenly, his arms shooting out of his sleeves, his fists pumping, Stew lowered his head and roared at James like an enraged bull.

Legs apart, his bleeding jaw jutting forward, slender, elegant James watched him approach, and with a lightning fist sent a right hook slamming into his belly.

"Oof!" Stew clutched his gut. Stunned, he staggered away, recovered, and rushed forward. An uppercut caught him under the chin, setting him back on his heels. He teetered on the edge of the pool, flailing at the air for a second, then lost his balance and fell like a stone into the deep end.

As James flexed his bloody knuckles, the water closed over Stew's head.

Loud voices came from the direction of the terrace, and a moment later, my old friend Officer Batano rounded the boxwoods, followed by Matt and Tom.

"What's going on here?" Batano asked.

"Help, I can't swim!" Stew had bobbed up like a Halloween apple in a barrel, but as we watched, horrified, he sank below the surface again.

Since nobody made a move to rescue him, and I was wet anyway, I dove in. He had drifted to the bottom, his feet resting on one of the golden rings. I pulled on his shirt, hoping a strong scissor kick would buoy us both to the surface.

But at the pressure of my hand on his back, he twisted around and grasped me, pinning my arms to my sides in the mother of all bear hugs. I couldn't move. I couldn't speak. I couldn't do anything to save either one of us. Unless someone jumped in soon, we would both drown.

THIRTY-SIX

STROKING THROUGH THE turquoise water, a man in white pants and a Hawaiian shirt swam straight for us. In slow motion, like an old 1920s movie, he raised his right arm and smacked Stew on the jaw.

At the impact, Stew let go and groped for his chin. The instant he released me, Rossi thrust an arm around my waist and pulled me toward the surface. We shot up to the air and filled our starved lungs. Then, turning turtle, Rossi dove back down.

"Help!" I screamed. "They'll drown."

"It's okay, Deva," Tom yelled. "He's got him."

Treading water like mad, I glanced across the pool. With Stew splashing and panting and spitting all the way, Rossi towed him over to the shallow end. Dazed, Stew stood in water up to his knees, clutching the tiled apron with both hands. I had a feeling he'd just developed a mortal fear of bathtubs.

Rossi heaved himself up over the edge and stared down at him. "You all right?"

"Yeah. That was a close call. Thanks, Lieutenant." He choked out a wheezy cough and spit into the pool.

"Don't mention it."

Dripping water, Rossi strode over to James and said something I couldn't hear. Then he raised the sheet off Kay's body and studied her. I wondered if he noticed the bruises on her neck. Though little escaped Rossi, I'd be sure to mention them to him, just in case.

His examination finished, he lowered the sheet. The medics pushed the gurney up the slope and James followed. Stew, eyes lowered, made no attempt to stop them.

Rossi strode along the apron toward the deep end where I was alternating between paddling and floating.

"You staying in all day?"

Actually, now that I was out of danger, the water felt wonderful, but I extended a hand. Rossi helped me up and out, the sodden shift clinging to my body like a second skin.

He eyed me, head to toe. "You make quite a mermaid."

"Thank you, and thanks for rescuing me. You're my barefoot hero."

He looked down at his feet and smiled. Tom, standing to one side, shaken and pale, held Rossi's gun upside down in one hand and his loafers in the other.

"Too bad I forgot about the tape recorder," Rossi said, removing the ruined device from a pocket. He shrugged. "Oh well. Let's get up to the house. I have work to do."

He took the gun and his shoes from Tom and glanced over at Stew, who was still standing in the pool. "Help Mr. Hawkins out of there, will you, Tom? We don't need another drowning here today."

I retrieved my pumps, and together Rossi and I started up the slope. As soon as I had him alone, I whispered, "Kay didn't drown. She was murdered. Didn't you notice the bruises on her neck?"

He nodded. "I did, but that doesn't necessarily mean she was murdered."

I stopped mid-stride, arms akimbo, the stiletto heels in my hands jutting out left and right. "Why do you always do that, Rossi?"

His brow furrowing like a country road, he said, "Do what?"

"Tell me my tips are no good."

"I don't do that." He paused. "Not every time."

"Of course you do. Remember when I found the Monet everyone thought was lost forever? And what about the drug stash I discovered, and how that led you directly to the killer? And then there was the—"

"Stop," he said, using his no-nonsense cop voice. "You know the house we're building?"

"Yes, but what's that got to do with this?"

"I want, ah...orange...that's it, orange shag rugs in all the rooms, purple walls and a lime-green lounge chair, the kind with the footrest that goes up when you press a button."

"Those are lousy suggestions, and you know it. On the other hand, my tip is right on target."

"Only partly so." He resumed his trek up the slope. "What isn't on target is the conclusion that you—as usual—jumped to."

"But—"

"End of story, Deva. You're the decorator—"

"Designer."

"And I'm the detective."

I heaved a sigh and lowered the stilettos. No point in arguing further. The morning had been stressful, to say the least. James and Stew had suffered a tragic loss, and Rossi, in sopping wet clothes, had a crime to solve, whether he wanted to admit it to me or not.

We had nearly reached the top of the slope when Teresa came rushing past us. I glanced over a shoulder as she whizzed by. Moving slowly, with Tom following him, Stew trudged toward the house. Teresa ran to his side and put a hand on his arm. He shrugged it off and continued on alone, ignoring her as she fell into step behind him.

What Stew was going through at the moment, Teresa couldn't share. From her expression, she knew it and hung back without making another attempt to touch him. His reaction to Kay's death sure was a far cry from the detached emotion he'd shown when poor little Connie Rae died. Then what he'd seemed most upset about was the possibility that he'd be blamed for her death. This time he appeared to be genuinely grieving. Though appearances, I reminded myself, could be deceiving...

As we stepped onto the terrace, Eileen hurried over to me. "Would you like to get out of that wet dress? I have a dry uniform you can borrow."

Anxious to ditch the clammy shift, I accepted gratefully. In the powder room, I peeled off the shift and donned the uniform over my damp underwear. Not good, but better.

Rossi settled for a large beach towel, knotting it around his waist over his wet clothes, most likely hoping it would soak up most of the moisture from his wet pants.

Outside, slumped in a deck chair, Stew dripped pool water onto the terrace pavers. Alert to his every move, Teresa stood at attention behind him, but without the happy diamond-glow of earlier in the day.

While a fatigued-looking Tom sprawled on the top step and gazed toward the boxwoods, Eileen hovered near the sliders, wringing her hands on her apron.

"Would you please ask Mr. Stahlman to join us?" Rossi asked her.

"Yes, sir," she said and hurried inside.

A demoralized group, we waited for several tense minutes until, finally, James came out, holding Charlotte as if she were a lifeline. Which I guessed she well might have been. Avoiding eye contact with Stew, he sat as far across the terrace from him as possible, stroking Charlotte nonstop, his expression as controlled and rigid as ice. His quiet suffering was difficult to watch, and I longed for Rossi to finish his questioning so I could leave. How I could ever transform this house into a cheerful home with an air of carefree elegance loomed over my head like *Mission: Impossible*.

With his tape recorder rendered useless, Rossi asked Eileen for a pen and a pad of paper. When she brought them to him, he said, "Would everyone please write down your name, address and a number where you can be reached. Also I need to know where you were and what you were doing for the past few hours."

As the pad circulated among us, Rossi, with the towel still wrapped around his waist, glanced over at Stew. "How did you know your former wife had drowned?" He asked the question abruptly, hoping no doubt to catch him off guard.

His eyes lifeless, Stew raised his chin off his chest. "I saw the ambulance and was afraid something had happened to her. So I ran over here and one of the medics told me a woman had drowned. Who else would it be? The maid?" He cast a glance at plump, middle-aged Eileen in her white uniform and sensible oxfords. "I've seen you coming and going, ma'am, and you didn't look like you'd skinny-dip during your workday." He shook his head. "No, I knew it was Kay." His voice faltered. "I knew."

"Yeah, he knew," Teresa said, a hint of sarcasm coloring her tone. "I did too, that's why I came after him." She finished writing and passed the notepad to Tom. "Can we leave now? Stew needs to get out of those wet clothes before he gets sick."

"You're both free to go."

As if Stew were an invalid, Teresa took him by the arm and helped him out of his seat. She was behaving like a wife. Though this morning the odds seemed stacked against her ever becoming the next Mrs. Hawkins, the situation had changed since then, drastically so. Now that Stew had lost the woman he claimed was the love of his life, he might well turn to Teresa for consolation.

Before Rossi could ask him a single question, James said, "I was at my divorce attorney's office this morning. I put his name and number on the pad along with my own. He can verify my whereabouts." He cast a lethal glance at Stew's retreating back. "Should that be necessary."

Eileen swore she'd been in the kitchen all morning, except for a few minutes serving coffee to Tom's two painters. They, of course, had never left the living room, and Tom and I vouched for each other's whereabouts the entire time we were here.

Rossi collected the statements and slid them into the manila envelope that Eileen had thoughtfully provided. "Was anyone else on the property today?"

Still stroking Charlotte nonstop, James nodded. "My...wife...Marilyn came in for a swim. That was several hours ago."

"Did you speak to her?"

"No. I didn't see her. Eileen told me she'd stopped by."

"When was this, Eileen?" Rossi asked.

"About eight o'clock," she replied in a small, frightened voice, her hands wringing the life out of her uniform apron. "I remember because that's when Mr. Stahlman has his coffee, and I had just brewed a fresh pot."

"Did you talk to Mrs. Stahlman?"

Eileen nodded just once, in a scared, jackrabbit kind of way. I wondered what she was so frightened of.

"Yes," she said, "Mrs. Stahlman said she wanted to go for a swim. She hadn't been practicing much lately and was getting rusty. I offered her coffee, but she refused and went outside. I assumed she was going to the pool. She never came back in. So if she did have a swim, she must have left in a wet suit." A puzzled frown wrinkled Eileen's forehead. "Come to think of it, I didn't hear her motorcycle start up. Usually you can hear it all over the neighborhood. I must have been busy in the laundry and didn't pay attention."

"When did Kay Hawkins go for a swim?"

Eileen bit her lip as she struggled to remember. "I really have no idea. She must have slipped out quietly. I don't recall seeing her this morning."

"Mr. Stahlman, do you know?"

James shook his head. "No. I only know she wanted to go for a swim. That was about eight-fifteen." His voice faltered. "And then I kissed her goodbye."

"Were there any other visitors today?"

"Just the tile men," Eileen said. "They wanted to make sure the grout on the terrace stairs had dried properly."

"When was this?"

"Oh, later. Around ten o'clock. I think Mrs. Stahlman had already left. They were working two houses down and stopped by during their break."

"Were they here long?"

Eileen shook her head. "No, not long at all. I saw the rugged one, you know the one with the shaved head, leave a minute or so after they got here. And the other man, the tall thin one, followed him." She flushed. "He waved goodbye, that's how I remember."

"Thank you," Rossi said, and to James, "Do you have a number where your wife can be reached?"

James rose from his seat. "It's on the desk in my study."

Rossi whipped off the damp towel and laid it on the back of a deck chair. "I'll get that number from you then I'll be off. I'd like to have a word with the tile men—Tony and Mike I believe their names are—before they leave for the day."

When he said Mike's name, Rossi arched an eyebrow at me. He didn't need to say another thing. Sometimes body language said more than words. And this was one of those times.

THIRTY-SEVEN

AFTER CALLING LEE and asking her to manage the shop alone for the rest of the afternoon, I went straight home. I tossed Eileen's uniform, the shift and my underthings in the washer and stepped into the shower, letting the warm spray ease away the tensions of the day. *Kay was dead.* Hard to believe. She'd been such a vital, energetic woman with a lifetime of living left to enjoy.

Something evil had happened to her. I was sure of it, and proof or no proof, my mind began playing with the nasty possibilities.

Teresa's name popped up first. In love with Stew— or with what he could provide—she had a strong motive for wanting Kay out of the way. A shrewdy, Teresa would have recognized Stew's infatuation with his former wife…if that was the reality of it. Who knew for certain? Kay had said they'd had a battling marriage. Yet this morning he'd sobbed inconsolably, cradling her body in his arms and then fighting over her with James.

In short, Stew had acted like a broken-hearted lover. *Acted like?* Was that it? *Was* he simply acting? After all, love and hate were two sides of the same coin. And Kay was about to marry his arch rival. For a jealous lover, that alone might be a motive for murder. The If-I-Can't-Have-You-No-One-Else-Can Syndrome.

Perhaps. But according to that yardstick, bridegroom James was innocent. In love with Kay, too, and about to make her his own, he had no reason to kill her, at least none that I could think of.

I stepped out of the shower and toweled dry.

What about Marilyn? Maybe she hated having Kay replace her as Mrs. Stahlman. Technically, James was still her husband. Hmm. For an entire year, she'd let the whole world believe she was dead, and then on the brink of James's remarriage, she'd returned just as abruptly as she had left. Strange. But since she had a lover, chances were she didn't want James back. Certainly not enough to commit murder for him. On the other hand, I knew practically nothing about Marilyn…except that she had a mole on the left cheek of her butt. Halfway down.

I ran the towel over my hair, rubbing the curls until they rioted around my head. Black bra and panties, denim cutoffs and a loose BU T-shirt, and I was good to go. Actually I wouldn't be going anywhere in this outfit and with this wild hair, but the casualness was comforting, kind of like what mac and cheese were to dinner.

Mac and cheese. That would be perfect for tonight. With a salad…

That left only Eileen unaccounted for, but she was hardly the violent type. Besides, she had no motive for killing Kay.

I took some romaine from the fridge and separated the leaves.

But suppose, just suppose, that behind Eileen's placid exterior beat the heart of a passionate woman? If she were in love with her boss, she might have been tempted to bump off his fiancée and be the only female in the house. No. I shook my head. That was downright silly.

I dropped the romaine into a colander and ran cold

water over it. Or as cold as tap water ever got in Florida in July.

Yes, silly. For openers, Eileen wouldn't have the strength to strangle a fit woman like Kay.

The water dripped over the lettuce leaves and ran into the sink.

Or would she? Anger could give anyone abnormal strength. Look at how courtly, refined James had knocked hefty Stew right into the pool. Nobody would have believed *that* without seeing it. Much as I didn't want to, I had to face the uncomfortable truth that my work was bringing me into daily contact with a host of possible murder suspects. To deny it would be foolish, and, suddenly scared, I left the lettuce to drip dry and hurried into the living room. I needed a security blanket—the Cobra pistol locked in the lower drawer of my desk. I retrieved it and dropped it in my tote where it fell to the bottom with a satisfying *clunk*.

Feeling calmer, I returned to the kitchen where, with a little rummaging, I found a box of elbow macaroni in the pantry and Nana Kennedy's recipe for mac and cheese. It had been my favorite meal throughout childhood and beyond, though I hadn't made it in years. Not since my husband Jack died.

I stared at the pot of water I'd just placed on the stove. Days had gone by since I last thought of Jack. Once he'd been my first thought each morning and my last each night. A spurt of sadness shot through me as the loss of him came rushing back with all the ferocity of new grief. Unlike Kay, Jack hadn't died with bruises on his neck. He'd been killed by an icy highway. The foul play had been Mother Nature's, but he was gone just the same. I'd loved him and lost him.

Then, to my great joy, life had brought me a new love. And he'd be home soon. I shook off the sadness as I knew Jack would want me to, found a brick of cheddar cheese in the fridge and began cooking in earnest.

I was chopping the lettuce, so engrossed in my task I didn't hear Rossi come in, and suddenly there he was, standing in the kitchen doorway with a big white Chiclets grin on his face and his arms open wide.

I hurried to him and was rewarded by a kiss with a beginning and no end—the kind that segued from one into another and another. When we finally parted, leaving barely enough room to slide a piece of paper between us, I said, "You're still wearing your pool clothes. No time to get to Countryside and change?"

"No need. They dried on me. Florida in July. Nothing like it." He sniffed the air. "Something smells terrific."

"Yup. Comfort food. I thought I'd surprise you."

If anything, his grin widened. "And I have a surprise for you."

My heart skipped a beat. "The bruises on Kay's neck didn't mean a thing? She wasn't murdered, after all?"

A cold silence chilled the air. "No. That's not it."

"That's not what?"

"The surprise." His voice didn't warm things up a bit.

"Okay, I do want to hear the surprise, but first tell me about Kay. Was my theory correct? Was she murdered?"

He dropped his hands to his sides and gave me one of those long detective sighs he churned out whenever I prodded him for information. "If you must know, foul play is the probable cause."

"Officially? Did the ME verify it?" Now that I had him talking—sort of—I'd keep him going. With Rossi you never knew when he'd clam up, a trait I found both exasperating and endearing. *Exasperating.*

"Yes. She was dead before she hit the pool. There wasn't any water in her lungs. He's citing strangulation as cause of death."

Wow. I'd gone back to chopping lettuce, but stopped for a moment to digest what he'd just said. Believing the bruises meant bad news and knowing it for certain were two different things. Poor Kay. Like Connie Rae, she'd been a woman with so much to live for, and yet she'd come to an untimely end. A violent end. *They both had.*

The knife forgotten in my hand, I stiffened as the insight struck home. Connie Rae had been murdered too. Again I had no proof, nothing to go on. Just a sudden, soul-deep conviction that like Kay, someone's hatred had killed her. But *whose?* And *why?*

No question about it, a murderer was on the loose, and chances were good it was someone I knew, someone I saw every day. So it was a good thing I had the Cobra stashed in my tote.

Rossi's arm stole around me. "Deva, you okay? You kind of went pale just then."

"Sorry." I sagged against him for a moment. "The truth took my breath away, but I'm all right now." The last thing Rossi would want to hear was one of my hunches, or that from now until this case was solved, I'd be packing. So I stood straight, inhaled and changed the subject. "Tell me your surprise."

His grin returned, megawatt wide. "You're about to gain a star boarder."

"Meaning?"

"I sold my house."

Uh-oh. "Omigod, so fast?"

"Yeah. I can't get over it. The second couple who saw the place put down a deposit. Didn't even argue price. Isn't that great?"

"That's absolutely wonderful." I smooched him on the cheek before peering into the oven. The casserole was as bubbly as Mauna Loa. "Any idea when they plan to move in?"

"As soon as the ink dries on the sales agreement. They're paying in cash. No mortgage. No bank involvement. Just an inspection, a title search and the sale goes right through."

I cleared my throat. "We have a problem, Rossi."

His happy grin disappeared. "What's the matter? I thought you'd be pleased."

"Oh, I am. But everything's happened so fast, I haven't had a chance to tell you my news. I have a surprise too."

"Yeah?" His voice guarded, he waited for me to spring it on him.

"I sold the condo to Lee and Paulo. Guess when they're planning to move in?"

"Don't tell me next week or something."

"Bingo!"

THIRTY-EIGHT

WE SCARFED DOWN the mac and cheese. It was every bit as delicious as I remembered, and Rossi, to my delight, had thirds. *Thirds.*

Too busy enjoying our dinner, we didn't obsess over the fact that we'd soon be without a home. As Rossi pointed out, now we'd have more than sufficient construction money, and that was the important thing.

He leaned across the table to kiss me yet again. "Don't worry, sweetheart, we'll rent somewhere for a few months until our little dream palace is finished."

He had showered and changed. Fresh shorts and a Hawaiian with a view of Diamond Head repeated all over his chest.

After the day's juggernaut of events, we were finally beginning to relax when his cell phone rang. Darn it. *Trouble.* Too bad he hadn't been wearing the cell when he jumped in the pool.

He listened, said a few words then closed the phone. "I won't be watching that movie with you after all. Have to go." He quickly changed into long pants and a gun. "Be back as soon as I can. Dinner was fantastic."

A quick farewell kiss, the door closed behind him, and I was alone. Such was life with a homicide detective. I'd better get used to it. It wouldn't change, ever. He'd keep on dashing off to work at all kinds of hours with a Glock strapped to his body, and coming home in the wee hours. But complaining was futile. Rossi had chosen a dangerous career, and despite knowing that full well, I had chosen Rossi.

With a resigned sigh, I got up from the table and brought the dirty dishes out to the kitchen. Even with all the uncertainty and danger, I wouldn't ask for anything different. Rossi's job fulfilled him, and he fulfilled me. My cup runneth over.

Without a moment's hesitation, he had risked his own life today to save mine. I wanted to watch his back too, help him as best I could. My interference, as he called it, was my way of helping. My way of showing how much I loved him. Being the perceptive man that he was, he'd no doubt already figured that out. But no way in hell would he admit it, unless, say, in a moment of passion I forced the truth out of him. Or else. I had to smile. That probably would work, but it would mark a new low in the life of Devalera Agnes Kennedy Dunne.

I glanced at the kitchen clock. The movie would be on soon, and I hated missing the opening scenes. The table clear, the dishwasher stacked, I hurried out to the living room and switched on the lamps.

A manila envelope lay on a club chair. Rossi had left in such a rush he must have forgotten it. I picked it up, intending to put it on the desk, when my glance fell on his big bold handwriting. *The Kay Hawkins Case.*

Oh? I stood in the center of the living room, the envelope burning holes in my palms. I turned it over. Only a metal clasp held the flap closed. Would I or wouldn't I?

While I'm used to devils—after all, they're in the details of every project I tackle—this time a different kind of devil, demon curiosity, had me in its grip. Envelope in hand, pulse drumming out a guilty tango, I flopped down on the sofa and, forgetting all about a movie for one, I undid the clasp and slid out the contents.

The handwritten notes of everyone who had been at the Stahlman house that morning lay on my lap. The routine information—names, addresses, phone numbers—I perused quickly. The whereabouts of each person at the time Kay died were what captured my attention.

Naomi, my handwriting guru, would have a field day with the various ways these people wrote—left leaning, right leaning, large script, one so tiny it looked like cursive in miniature, a few flamboyant capitals and... wait a minute. I stopped riffling through the pages. One of these writing samples might belong to the murderer. As Naomi had explained when I brought Mike's letters to her, *what* a person wrote revealed the information he wanted known. *How* he wrote revealed his secret intent. I believed in the connection between handwriting and behavior but lacked the skill to get at the truth. I needed Naomi.

I checked my watch. Eight o'clock, still early. Rossi wouldn't be back until God knew when. He might even be gone all night. No time like the present.

I tucked the pages back in the envelope and went in search of my cell phone where I'd stored Naomi's phone number. If she were at home tonight and feeling well enough for a visitor, I'd ask if I could make a house call. With her expertise, no telling what she might uncover.

Her number rang three, four times.

"Come on, come on, come on," I urged and finally, on the fifth ring, someone picked up.

"Hello."

"Hi, this is Deva Dunne. May I speak to Naomi, please."

"Oh. I guess you haven't heard." At the sound of the young woman's lifeless voice, my heart sank. This wasn't going to be good news. "My mom died yesterday."

"No, I didn't know. I'm so sorry."

We spoke for a few minutes, and I learned that according to Naomi's wishes, there would be no funeral. No final farewell...and, of course, no handwriting analysis in an attempt to nail a murderer.

Poor Naomi. I sat still for a long while with the manila envelope forgotten on my lap. Yet another woman had died an untimely death, but there was a measure of comfort in remembering that while Naomi was alive, she'd done a lot of good for a lot of people. How I wished she were still here to do a good deed once again.

Now what? For sure, there were other handwriting analysts to be had, and with the resources of the Naples P.D. at his disposal, Rossi could undoubtedly find an expert graphologist somewhere. Providing, of course, he could be convinced to do so. If I suggested it, he'd probably think I was interfering again.

Well, I was... I sighed and slid the papers out of the envelope.

Naomi had told me about the writing differences between a truth-teller and a liar. What had she said? *Think. Think.*

Not knowing where to start, I flipped through the sheets. Rossi had had a busy afternoon. He'd gotten statements from Mike and Tony. And even one from Marilyn Stahlman. With my testimony and Tom's that made eleven in all.

I put the statements from the two painters and Tom's and mine back into the envelope—that left seven samples to consider.

Outside a dog's bark echoed in the quiet night. I smiled a little, thinking of Charlotte. Knowing something was wrong this morning, the tiny ball of fluff had tried to alert the household. I'd probably surprised her popping out of the sliders as I'd done. I stared past the pools of lamplight into the shadows. Something bothered me, but I couldn't put a finger on what it might be.

The dog barked again. Maybe he'd found a squirrel or a mouse to chase, or a passing car. Charlotte had been barking for James. Or Eileen. Not for me. Or the painters. Or Tom.

Tom. I bolted upright on the couch. He'd met me outside of 590 this morning. I'd never asked if he'd strolled around the property before I arrived. If he had, he might have encountered Kay in the bikini that had so entranced him the other day...but he hadn't said a word about seeing her. Not a word. Still, that didn't mean he hadn't.

Slowly, reluctantly, I removed his statement from the envelope and added it to the others.

Most familiar with Mike's writing, I'd begin with his. Wiping my damp palms on my T-shirt, I held his page under the lamplight, conscious suddenly of the danger that a graphology novice like me could falsely interpret what I saw—or believed I saw.

The only alternative was not to even try, and that would yield nothing. So I took a deep breath and plunged into what Mike had written. Despite the tension beading on my forehead, I exhaled a long, relieved sigh when I finished reading his report. He hadn't changed a bit since Naomi examined his prison letters. His signature was as flamboyant as ever, full of self-important swirls and flourishes, the rest of his writing small and crabbed. And there in a downstroke was the felon's claw again. Yup, Mike would lie like a rug and embezzle his grandmother out of food stamps, but I saw no signs of violence in his hand. No clubbed *t* bars, no dots looking like arrows over the i's, no stabbed ovals. He was a con man, not a killer.

I let the paper drop to my lap. Naomi's input had colored my thinking and skewed my observations. What about the other statements, the handwriting she hadn't seen?

Without her help, I had to figure out what these loops and lines and squiggles meant over and above what they actually said. I stared at the sheaf of papers. No way could I decipher their secrets. I didn't have the knowledge and no one and nothing to turn to for help. Not tonight anyway. And that was all the time I had. The statements were part of a police investigation. Rossi would be sure to look for them when he returned. If I were going to accomplish anything, it had to be now, but I had nothing to work with. Not a single tool.

And then, in a rush of adrenaline, I remembered. The book Naomi had given me. Of course! I'd put it in the guest room bookcase and then forgotten about it. Egads.

I leaped up and ran to the guest room. The bookcase was mostly filled with design texts I'd saved from BU, trade magazines and some glossy coffee table volumes. Where was it? Ah, there. Nestled between the iconic *Ralph Lauren Homes* and Mario Buattas's *Fifty Years of American Interior Decoration* lay M. N. Bunker's *The Science of Determining Personality by Grapho-*

analysis. Rossi would no doubt scoff at the word *science*, but I grabbed the book, a legal pad and pen, and hurried back to the living room.

Sitting on the sofa, I carefully compared each witness sample—one word, one line, one page at a time—with examples from Bunker's book. I was looking for signs of aberrant behavior and trying hard not to rush to judgment, or to be inventive and see what simply wasn't there to be seen.

I began with the men's handwriting, and found a lot of quirky stuff: tiny, uptight printing indicating anxiety; the left-hand slant of an introvert; the retraced upper loops of a cautious perfectionist; words with the unreadable middle zones that signaled unhappiness; and the high-flying *t* bars of a dreamer. In short, many fascinating traits, but nothing that revealed the potential for murder.

Hmm. Perhaps I wasn't concentrating on the right strokes. Since Kay's death appeared to be a crime of passion, maybe I should concentrate on the lower loops, the erogenous zone Naomi had called them.

I picked up a page. Stew's y's and g's swooped down then looped vigorously up to the baseline. No surprise at seeing his healthy libido. James wasn't outdone in that department either. That was a bit of a surprise, though it shouldn't have been. After all, he'd been about to embark on his third trip down the aisle. Tony's y's and g's were simply straight lines. Well, he did live with his mother, so not much of a sex life there. Tom and Mike's looked normal too, nothing deviant or weird that I could see.

Now for the women. While I didn't think a woman had killed Kay, on the theory that you never know until you know, I separated out their statements from the men's and took a good, hard look at their erogenous zones. Nothing. Nothing. Nothing. And then I got to Eileen's.

Omigod. Who would have believed it? The paper slid out of my hands and fluttered to the floor.

"Deva, what are you doing?"

His voice startled me so, I screamed. When my heartbeat went back to something less South American, I said, "Rossi, for Pete's sake. Why did you sneak in like that?"

"I didn't sneak in. I was trying to be quiet. I thought you might be asleep." He pointed to the papers scattered around me. "Are those what I think they are?"

Before I could answer, he stooped and picked up Eileen's statement, then began collecting the others.

"Rossi, I've just discovered something."

"No. *I've* just discovered something. You're interfering again."

"But this is important. It might have a bearing on the case."

He stuffed the papers into the envelope and placed it on the desk. "Let's turn in. We've both had a long day."

"But something's there in Eileen's handwriting."

"Deva, I appreciate your attempt to help. My right hand to God. But are you a skilled graphologist?"

"No, but—"

"It takes years to develop that skill. Years. Are you listening?"

I nodded.

"So not to be unkind but whatever you found is an amateur's insight, not a professional's. Got that?"

Another nod.

"I believe in graphology," he said. I tried to speak, but he held up a palm for silence. "The chief believes in graphology. And if he so decides, these writing samples may…may…be faxed to Miami to a professional analyst. Got that?"

When I didn't answer, he added, "No pun intended, but are we on the same page here?"

I treated him to a third nod, but somewhat annoyed by his lack of confidence in me, I didn't bother to tell him Eileen's handwriting showed that she was possibly the sexiest woman in Naples.

THIRTY-NINE

ROSSI LEFT FOR work the next morning without saying goodbye. I was asleep, but for him to leave without kissing me awake meant last night's mini argument still rankled. Maybe I'd been wrong. Maybe he didn't understand that my interference in the Kay Hawkins case—all right I'm admitting it—was an act of love. I guess he just saw it as the act of a non-professional pretending to be a pro.

Anyway, needing a morale boost, I dressed to kill in the black halter dress I usually reserved for dinner dates and sexy high-heeled sandals that really did kill. But that was all right. I planned to eat sitting down. To keep the look edgy, I carried a shocking-pink nylon tote.

My one new wardrobe purchase of the season, the mustard-yellow shift, hadn't survived the chlorine swim. Clothes shopping was definitely in my immediate future, but not today. Today I had house calls to make. A new client wanted me to take a look at what she called her blah family room. Blah rooms were mother's milk to me, but there were various shades of blah, and it would be interesting to see exactly how blah this one was. Actually, the worse the room, the more it needed my input. At least I was good at my job if not, in Rossi's view, at graphology.

After checking in with Lee and learning that everything was cool at the shop, I made Whiskey Lane my first call of the day.

With two clients in mourning, I didn't know what to expect when I arrived at the Lane, but everything seemed normal enough. Tom's vehicles clogged the driveways of both 590 and 595. Since no one could drive in or out of the garages, I assumed Stew and James had already left. Just as well.

I parked on the Stahlman drive behind Tom's SUV. Not wanting to bother the painters, I strolled around back to the kitchen entrance and rang the bell. No one answered, not even after several tries. Strange. Busy in the front rooms, the painters couldn't hear the bell over their blaring radios and probably wouldn't answer if they did. But where was Eileen?

After another futile attempt, I cupped my hands around my eyes and peered through the glass-paneled door at a kitchen long overdue for a revamp—a project I had a feeling was currently low on James's bucket list.

Though no one was moving around in the kitchen, a circular heating coil on the vintage electric stove glowed as red as a traffic light. Unattended, without a single pan on its top, the stove was a disaster in the making.

Without bothering with the bell, I grasped the door handle. To my relief, the door wasn't locked. I hurried in and turned off the burner. What on earth…? The refrigerator door gaped open. I slammed it shut. Food littered the countertops: flour and sugar, eggs, milk and spices were scattered everywhere.

A sudden soft moan scared me. I whirled around to face it, and there was Eileen, lying spread-eagled on the breakfast nook bench, her uniform skirt hiked to her thighs, her legs and mouth open wide.

Good heavens, what was wrong? I hurried across the room and bent over her. As I did, my foot struck something hard and sent it spinning. Like an aimless soccer ball, an empty Dewars scotch bottle rolled around under the nook before hitting the wall and coming to rest with a thump.

Eileen didn't hear a sound. She lay without moving, snoring softly and exhaling ripe, boozy breaths. No need to bend in any closer.

I was glad James wasn't home. He didn't need this on top of yesterday's tragedy. But what did Eileen need? Something obviously. According to her handwriting, I think I knew what that might be, but as Rossi had correctly pointed out, I was no graphology whiz.

What I could do well was make coffee. A brew pot sat on one of the littered countertops, its carafe empty. I tossed the basketful of soggy grounds in the trash and foraged in the pantry closet for a fresh supply. The hunt turned up only whole beans. *Figured.* With some difficulty I located the grinder, threw in a handful of Kona's Finest, and turned it on, hoping the loud pulsing would awaken Eileen. But she snored on, oblivious.

Well, maybe the aroma of brewing coffee would do it.

Nope.

Maybe actually drinking some would help. I carried a mug of strong black brew over to the breakfast nook and placed it on a corner of the tabletop out of harm's reach.

If I couldn't rouse her soon, I'd have to call 9-1-1. She might need to have her stomach pumped.

I leaned over her…phew…and shook her by the arm. She moaned in protest. I patted her cheeks and called her name, trying to coax her out of her stupor. In a way, I hated to. She'd tried to escape from some painful reality, and here I was insisting she return to it.

Poor thing. Life could be so damned difficult, but bottom line, it wasn't five o'clock anywhere in Eileen's world. She couldn't stay like this. The painters might barge in at any moment and see her lying there drunk, her skirt flying at high mast. Worse, no telling when James would be home expecting a lovely little lunch.

"Come on, Eileen. Come on. Wake up now."

She grunted and attempted to roll onto her side. I grabbed her shoulder and shook it. "No, you can't do that. You're not in bed. You'll fall off."

One of her eyes slit open.

Okay, a good sign.

It closed.

I patted her cheeks.

"No," she moaned. "No."

"Eileen, you have to wake up. Come on, open your eyes. I made some coffee for you. It'll make you feel better."

"Coffee? Nooo. Jimmy. Thash what I want. Jimmy."

Jimmy? Omigod. So her handwriting sample hadn't spoken with forked tongue after all.

"I want Jimmy."

"I'm sorry," I said, pretending not to understand her meaning, "but Mr. Stahlman isn't here right now."

Her eyes snapped open. Though slightly bloodshot, they were a gorgeous lapis lazuli blue. Funny, before now I'd never noticed how beautiful they were.

"Hesh never here. Not for me." *Hic.*

Lowering her legs off the bench she tried, and failed, to sit up. I sat next to her, put an arm around her shoulder and together we pulled her torso into an upright position. But not for long. Like a willow in the wind, she swayed several times then, abandoning the struggle, fell forward onto the tabletop, her head lolling on her arms.

One more try, and if that didn't work, I'd call for help. I shook her. Her arms slid back and forth on the polished wood, taking her head with them, but she didn't awaken.

I leaned over and whispered in her ear. Hissed really. "Eileen, listen up, girlfriend. We've got to get you out of here and into bed."

Not a muscle quivered.

In desperation, I went for the jugular, emotionally speaking. "If you don't wake up, I'll call an ambulance."

An eyelid fluttered.

"It'll come roaring down the street with the sirens blazing and haul you out of here on a stretcher. Is that what you want?"

Both eyes opened.

To keep them open, I upped the ante. "Think of what Jimmy will say then."

She lifted her head and ran both hands through her hair. A bemused expression flitted across her face as if she were surprised she still had a head. Peeking at me from the corner of one bloodshot lapis-blue eye, she said, "He woulden give a shit."

I nearly fell out of the breakfast nook. "Eileen, what are you saying? You're his most devoted…ah…employee."

"Thash the problem." She clutched at her left breast. "Ish this fuckin' uniform. I look like a refrigerator in it."

Who could argue with logic like that?

"He doshunt see me as a hic…woman."

"Be that as it may, you don't want him to see you as a lush, do you?"

"Yesh." She beamed her Dewars breath my way. I tried not to inhale. "At leasht he'll know I've got feeling-shs." She jabbed a finger on the tabletop. "Feelingsh."

"Eileen, I don't know what's bothering you, but whatever it is, you need to sleep it off. If Mr. Stahlman comes home, I'll tell him you're ill and went to bed. Okay? That way, he'll never know about this. But first you have to get off the bench."

She shook her head. "No I don't. I'll be out of here shoon enough."

"What does that mean?"

No answer. Her head was back on the table.

Okay, she hadn't vomited and she had been conscious, however briefly. Two pluses. I glanced down at her. Her thick dark hair, freed from its bun, lay spread across her arms like glossy black silk.

Between the bun and the uniform, Eileen clearly hadn't been able to shine.

I heaved a sigh. We were both working girls, and my heart went out to her. I couldn't just leave her where she was. Working girls in distress needed a helping hand from time to time. So my options were to call 9-1-1, or less drastically, to enlist the aid of one of the painters in getting her into bed.

While I stood there trying to decide what to do, the back door opened.

Oh, no.

"Well this is a first. A messy kitchen." Marilyn, a tall tanned goddess in sawed-off jeans and shit-kickers, strode into the kitchen as if she owned it. Well in a way, I guess she still did.

We nodded at each other, wary as two feral cats. Catching sight of Eileen, she gasped. "Omigod. What happened to her?" She hurried across the room and bent over Eileen's sleeping form. Straightening up fast, she said, "She's drunk."

"My conclusion exactly."

A moment of stunned silence, then Marilyn threw her head back and laughed, a deep, full-throated belly laugh.

"Glad you think it's funny," I said with a sniff.

"It's not funny. It's a riot. Good for her. High time she broke out of her shell. Waiting on James hand and foot. Yes-siring and no-siring him, and all the while madly in love with him."

Ah. "You're sure?"

"I lived here, remember? She'd die before admitting it but—"

"Actually she just did admit it."

"In vino veritas." Marilyn shrugged. "That coffee I smell?"

I nodded. "Help yourself."

She shot me an ironic glance and without any fumbling opened the cabinet containing the mugs.

Eileen, in LaLa Land, slept on.

"Will you help me get her to bed before James or somebody else finds her like this?" I asked.

"Yes, of course, but she's a sizable woman, and she's out cold. How are we going to lift her?"

"We need some old-fashioned smelling salts or something," I said. "Anything, to bring her to. I wonder if..." I got up from the breakfast nook bench and hurried over to the sink. As I'd hoped, underneath with the other cleaning supplies was a bottle of ammonia.

I opened it, inhaled and wished I hadn't. That should do it. Bottle in hand, I went back to Eileen and rubbed her back. When she stirred and moaned a little, I held the opened bottle near her face. Nothing. Did the woman never inhale?

I glanced back at Marilyn who was hovering nearby. "She might respond to your voice," I said.

Marilyn nodded and, leaning over Eileen, she shouted in her ear, "Eileen Bennett, this is Mrs. Stahlman. I insist you wake up immediately."

At the no-nonsense command, Eileen inhaled and came to with a start. I held the bottle under her nose, and with a shriek of protest, she bolted upright on her seat.

I capped the ammonia and put it down. "Now!" I said. Marilyn grabbed Eileen's arm and tugged her toward the end of the bench.

"Whash goin' on?"

Once we had her precariously perched on the edge, I slid an arm around her waist, and Marilyn, on the other side, did the same.

"One, two, three" and up she came. Sort of.

Lord, she was heavy, deadweight really. Sagging between us she more or less stood, and together we all stumbled forward a few steps.

"I'm gonna be sick."

Uh-oh. Across Eileen's slumping body, Marilyn shot me a horrified look. Now what? If we let go, she'd plunge to the floor. Helpless, Marilyn and I stood frozen in the middle of the kitchen while Mount Vesuvius erupted, spewing lava all over the place, including my best black dress and the ocelot slides.

This was definitely not part of my job description, but I hung in there, retching, as did Marilyn, until the spasms ceased, then we soldiered on down the narrow back hall into Eileen's modest room.

"Thash my bed," she said. With a sigh of satisfaction, she lurched forward a step and fell onto the mattress.

"She stinks," Marilyn said with a laugh. "We all do."

"What do you say we strip off her uniform and wash her face and hands? She can shower when she comes to. And we can't leave the kitchen reeking like that."

Marilyn wrinkled her nose at my suggestion. "Yuk," she said, giving her shorts a hike. "But okay. You're right. I'll start out there, and you take care of Sleeping Beauty. No point in getting cleaned up ourselves until after we've dealt with the mess."

"Sounds like a plan."

"Yup."

With no further ado, Marilyn strode out of the bedroom and headed into a tough mission in besmirched shorts and vomity shit-kickers.

FORTY

SOMETIMES WOMEN BONDED at spas while they were being pampered with facials and massages or munching on body-sculpting food out by the pool. As for Marilyn and me, we bonded without any frills back in the breakfast nook of recent memory.

Eileen was peacefully sleeping it off in her red lace bra and panties—who would have guessed? I had showered and, for the second day in a row, borrowed one of her uniforms. Then I bundled up the black dress and slides and threw them in the trash. After Marilyn showered, she put on an old flannel robe while her shorts and T-shirt whirled around in the washer.

Needing an energy jolt, we sat sipping the rest of the coffee as the clock on the wall ticked peacefully and, in the distance, a radio belted out an old Elvis hit.

"I wonder what made her break down like that?" Marilyn asked. "It's so unlike her."

I shook my head. "I don't know, but she did say something about leaving. That might explain it."

"Oh?" Marilyn was all ears.

"Yeah, she said she'd be gone soon. I asked her why but she passed out before she could answer."

"I know one thing," Marilyn said. "She'd rather die than leave James. He's her life. He doesn't see it of course." She picked up her mug and took a sip. "He sees only what he wants to see. What suits him. And what suits him best is a woman of means." She shrugged. "I guess I fit that description…and so did Kay. Poor Kay. She should be alive today, not lying on a slab in some morgue."

I hardly dared breathe. Did she suspect Kay had been murdered?

She set down her mug so hard a little of the coffee slopped over the edge. "Bottom line, I don't trust James…I mentioned that to the sexy lieutenant when he questioned me yesterday. What's his name? Rossi?"

I nodded. *Sexy.*

"I told him to check out both Kay's will and James's. I think he played the same game with Kay that he tried on me—and on his first wife."

"Game?"

Marilyn nodded. "He's clever and so very polite and correct that you don't suspect a thing. At least not at first. It's an old con. I found that out a little late, but not too late, thank God."

"Marilyn, you've lost me."

Cradling her mug in both hands, she glanced across at me. Her eyes narrowed. "You don't believe me, do you?"

"Honestly, I don't know what to think."

"Well, let me tell you how James worked his con on me. He began by saying he wanted to change his will. Leave everything he had to me—the woman he loved. Everything, got that? So if anything should happen to him, I'd be protected financially.

"We were engaged at the time, and I was in love with him. Ha! What a mistake.

"Anyway I swallowed the bait and said I wanted to do the same for him—in case anything happened to me.

Oh, he protested very effectively, but I insisted. Wasn't my love and concern as strong as his? I'd be hurt and insulted if he refused, etcetera, etcetera."

"If you were both sincere, I see no problem."

"*If* is the operative word. I married him, and the rest as they say is history. Or maybe not. When I found out he had the same arrangement with his first wife, I never trusted him the same way again. Like Kay, Number One died unexpectedly. OD'd on sleeping pills. There was gossip when it happened, but nothing was ever proven."

She looked up from the coffee, straight into my eyes. "The night...when I dove off the boat...he upped anchor and sailed off." She let go of her mug and shoved it aside. "He left me to die. He wanted me to drown."

Wow. "Maybe he was sailing around, looking for you. Worried sick that he couldn't find you in the dark. That something had happened...it's understandable," I finished somewhat lamely, my voice conveying anything but conviction.

She shook her head so hard her hair whipped around her face. "No way. The only reason I come here to use the pool is to rub in the fact that I'm still alive. Still swimming."

"Did you tell the lieutenant about your suspicions?"

"Yes, I told him everything."

And he told me nothing. I tried not to be hurt, but a lump rose into my throat. Rossi knew all this last night and had kept silent about it. That was the right thing to do, I told myself, the professional thing. My face flushed as I recalled nattering on about graphology. No wonder he hadn't wanted to reveal any more about the case.

"Anyway," Marilyn was saying, "that moonlight

swim was the best one of my life, even better than when I qualified for the U.S. team."

"You were rescued."

She smiled, remembering. "In more ways than one. Who knows? I may never have returned. There was no one left to miss me. Not really. My parents passed away several years ago, and I have no family. But when I read of James's engagement in the Palm Beach paper, I couldn't let him trap another woman without trying to warn her."

"Did you?"

"I tried. She wouldn't listen. And now look at what's happened."

I was stunned speechless, and that doesn't happen very often. James a con man? A serial killer? Either Marilyn was paranoid or she had hit on the truth. My hot cheeks turned icy cold, and in my heart of hearts, I was glad Rossi knew all this—even if he hadn't breathed a word of it to me.

But Marilyn's surprises weren't at an end. "I don't want to be a total hypocrite," she added. "I came back for another reason too. My money. It's a good thing I did. I thought since my death hadn't been proven, and I was technically a missing person, James couldn't touch my estate for several years. But I was mistaken. He had his lawyer working on a loophole in the law. By proving I had been exposed to a specific peril—drowning—he was about to have me declared legally dead. That meant my will could be probated and James would inherit my estate without further delay. He was only weeks away from doing exactly that when I…" her lip curled up, "…miraculously reappeared."

The swinging door to the dining room creaked open, startling both of us.

James, with Charlotte in his arms, walked quietly into the kitchen, coming to a dead stop at the sight of Marilyn. His jaw hardened. "I'm unpleasantly surprised to see you here. You have permission to use the pool, but I don't want you in the house. Please leave immediately."

"Can't do it, Jimmy, not till my clothes are dry."

Deva to the rescue. "Eileen is ill. She's has a bad stomach upset. We had to put her to bed and—"

"She was sick all over us," Marilyn said. "I think she's down for the day. Nerves, no doubt. And you home for lunch, Jimmy. What a shame. Want me to make you a peanut butter sandwich?" A little smile flirted with her mouth. "I'll cut off the crusts."

Without uttering a word, he turned on his heel and strode off as quietly as he had entered. The swinging door creaked behind him and bumped to a close.

"Weren't you a little rough on him, Marilyn?" I asked. "It's possible he truly loved Kay. Not only her money. If so, he's just suffered a tragic loss."

Marilyn slugged down the last of her coffee and slammed her mug on the tabletop. "He's had a loss, no doubt about that, but not a financial one. I'd stake my life on it."

These days, on Whiskey Lane, those sure were dangerous odds.

FORTY-ONE

"I HAVE SOME NEWS, but I warn you it isn't good," Rossi said as we were finishing dinner.

My pulse revved up a notch. He was going to talk about his problems with the Hawkins case. "Whatever you say, I promise I won't tell a soul."

He stared at me, puzzled. "It's not exactly a secret."

"Public knowledge, so soon? That's a surprise." My enthusiasm dimmed a little. If everyone knew already, telling me wasn't such a big deal. "Well, bad news or not, I'd like to hear it."

"Harlan Conway called me this morning."

"Harlan? What's he got to do with Kay's murder?"

"Nothing. And let me remind you that no one has been arrested for the Hawkins woman's death. In short, no one's been accused of murder. At least not yet."

"But—"

He pushed his empty dinner plate back from the edge of the table. "You did it again, Deva."

"I don't mean to be a pain. I'm just concerned about—"

A flash of humor flitted across his face. "What do you say we start this conversation over? First, dinner was delicious. I love leftover mac and cheese."

I'd let that one go by. It had been a long day.

"Second, the news from Harlan—which is what I was referring to—is somewhat disappointing."

"Oh?" My revved-up pulse soared into alarm mode. The last couple of days had been so traumatic, I'd actually forgotten about the house. "What's wrong?"

"Harlan had some test holes bored to see how deep the foundation supports should go."

"And?"

"There's no hardpan for over forty feet."

"Which means?"

"The foundation will be way over budget and take twice as long to build as estimated."

I sagged against the back of my chair. "But it can be done?"

"Yes. With time and money."

"And while all this is going on, we don't have a place to live."

"Correct."

For the short term, six months or so, renting a place wasn't a problem, but Naples was a resort mecca, and rental properties were at a premium. We couldn't afford to spend a hefty part of our construction money on expensive digs while we waited God knew how long for the house to be finished.

I blew out a breath. "We're in trouble."

He treated me to one of his dazzling white smiles. "On the same page at last."

"I'm serious, Rossi."

"I know." He leaned across the table to take my hand and rub his thumb across my palm. "In the morning I'll call a few realtors, and I'll put out feelers at the station. Some of the boys may know of a few reasonable rentals." He wiggled his thumb. "Don't worry, sweetheart, we'll work this out. Every problem has a solution."

True. Even if it was one you didn't like. Rossi knew

that full well; he was trying to reassure me, and I loved him for it. But bottom line, we needed an affordable place to stay for maybe a year or more, and we needed it within a few weeks. So I wouldn't leave all the searching up to him. I'd simply have to find some time to go apartment hunting too.

I squeezed his hand before getting up to remove the dinner dishes. "Your news surprised me," I said. "I thought you were going to tell me something about the Hawkins case." He arched a brow but didn't nibble at the bait. "Anyway," I continued, "just so you'll know, I saw Marilyn Stahlman today. She told me all about her James theory."

"That right?"

"Yup. She said she'd told you everything too."

"Whatever everything means. All I know is she had a lot to say. All of it unsubstantiated suspicions."

"Maybe, but have you checked out Kay's will?"

"Yes." He held up a warning finger. "Don't go jumping to conclusions now…she left everything to Stahlman."

I nearly dropped the plates. "Aha! Marilyn was right. I *knew* it."

"What did I just say? There's nothing illegal about Kay Hawkins's will."

"Perhaps not, but have you checked out James's as well?"

"No."

"No? Why not?"

Rossi frowned. "I could take the Fifth here, but I'll answer you just to end this discussion. There was no need. He told me what it contains. Kay was his sole beneficiary."

"Doesn't that shoot off flares in your head?"

"Not necessarily." Rossi's voice had gotten all clipped and terse. I was pushing and knew it, so I blew out a breath and stomped out to the kitchen carrying the dishes and feeling as low as a garage sale reject. I'd spent the past two days in a white nylon uniform five sizes too large, I'd just served leftovers for dinner, and my dream house—which at the moment was only a couple of bore holes in the ground—was already way over budget. Worse, my beloved fiancé wasn't confiding in me, not fully anyway, even though I had been on what I was convinced was the murder scene from the get-go.

In cargo shorts and bare feet, Rossi padded into the kitchen. I was rinsing the plates in the sink when he came up behind me and put a hand on my arm.

"Deva, turn around," he said. "Please."

The "please" did it. I whirled around and snugged my arms around his waist. Resting my head on his chest, I inhaled his aftershave as if it were oxygen.

"I want to ask you something," he said.

"Anything. Shoot."

"If I suggested that you and I make each other the beneficiaries of our wills, would you agree to do so?"

I pulled away a little so I could look into his eyes. "Of course. I trust you completely."

"Ergo."

"Oh no, you don't. You're no James Stahlman."

"And just who and what is a James Stahlman? A con artist? A killer?"

"According to his wife, yes."

"A wife who disappeared for an entire year, letting rumors and innuendo swirl around her husband. Her grieving husband, I might add. The same woman who after mysteriously disappearing, suddenly reappeared out of the blue." His hands dropped down my back, way down. "Now I ask you, is the word of a woman like that to be believed without question?"

"Naturally you have questions. That's only logical."

"Thank you." Just a trace of sarcasm colored his tone.

But I wasn't ready to concede yet. "I like her. She cleaned up after Eileen yesterday without hesitating a moment. Trust me, that wasn't easy, and she did it willingly. You could at least consider the possibility that she's a decent woman who's telling the truth."

"I have considered it. I am still considering it, but so far I've found no evidence to support her theory. When I do—"

"I'll be the first to know."

"Absolutely not. And now what do you say we continue this conversation somewhere else? Like in bed."

"How can I carry on a conversation, Rossi? I can't think straight with your hands all over me this way."

"Now *that's* an interesting bit of news. So let me ask you something else."

Busy nibbling on his earlobe, I just murmured, "Umm."

"If one part of you shuts down, does another part open up?"

I bit his lobe. "That question's not worthy of an answer, Detective. Is your interrogation technique slipping?"

"Apparently," he said with mock despair. "I need to lie down."

And so I played a love game with Rossi and adored every moment of it. But my brain hadn't shut down, not for a second. Whether it was true or not that James was a con man and possibly a murderer, I didn't know. But Marilyn had planted seeds of suspicion in my mind and removed any lingering doubts I had that he was too polite to be real. Until now, I'd been hesitating about introducing prison-made furniture into his superficially flawless world, but no longer. The Help-a-Con Program needed a boost, so why not begin at the house of someone who might…might…be a con artist himself?

FORTY-TWO

THE BEST-LAID PLANS of mice and men often go belly up. No surprise there, and this time not even a hint of trouble. Actually, the morning was glorious, filled with sunshine and the scent of the sea. The breeze blew humid, of course, but that was no reason not to smile in a world that was so beautiful. Worry would do no good—it never did—and besides, I had work waiting and calls to make. Particularly one to Mike Hammerjack.

At the door to the shop, our postal delivery woman handed me a stack of envelopes, probably all bills and ads, though on the top of the pile sat a lavender envelope addressed to me in a small, neat hand.

I carried the mail inside, dropped it on my desk and picked up the letter. The postmark was too smudged to be legible, and there was no return address on the back. *Hmm.* Curious, I slit the envelope open and removed a sheet of lilac-scented paper written in the same neat handwriting as on the envelope.

Dear Mrs. Dunne,
Thank you so much for sending me the notebook of my beloved lost daughter, Connie Rae Hawkins. She was the dearest thing in my life and having her words to read over and over is a priceless gift. How sad that her new husband couldn't get her

to a heart surgeon in time to save her life. I know
he intended to. He told me so himself...

The rest of the words were a blur. In my hands, on
this piece of lavender paper, was a written testimony
that Stew had known about Connie Rae's condition.

When my initial shock ebbed, I read the letter a second time. Connie Rae's mother sounded like a thoughtful, giving person. Despite her grief, she had reached
out to thank me for a very pathetic little gift.

Trying to remember everything Naomi had told me
about graphology, I studied the handwriting. All I could
see was sweetness in the rounded letters and sincerity
in the lack of flourishes, and yes, sorrow in the droop
of the final strokes. Though I'd be the first to admit my
graphology skills were limited, I believed the woman
was telling the truth about Stew. He'd known all along
about his wife's life-threatening condition and had denied knowing it both to the police and to me. The question was why?

I slid the letter back in its envelope and placed it in
my desk drawer for safekeeping. Straight ahead through
the front window, a bougainvillea the color of heart's
blood cascaded over the facing wall. Basking in the
sun's warmth, full of life and energy, it lifted its petals
to the sky. The sight made me want to weep.

Kay's death had been tragic, no question about that,
but in the chaos that ensued, little Connie Rae had been
all but forgotten. Though the shop was warm—I needed
to turn down the air conditioning—a chill shot through
me. Two women living mere yards apart had died within
days of each other. And at one point in both their lives,
Stew Hawkins had been their husband.

Hmm. I jabbed the letter opener under the flap on one of the bills...so James wasn't the only husband whose recent behavior raised questions. Maybe Rossi's investigation should expand to include Stew. True, Connie Rae's death had been declared the result of natural causes, but somehow Stew's lie continued to raise hackles of doubt in my mind.

I glanced at the electric bill—too high—and tossed it on the desk.

Two women, two prime suspects, two unrelated deaths.

I pitched the phone bill on top of the electric bill.

Or were the deaths related in some way?

The Yarmouthport bells jangled and, head spinning, I rose to greet Lee. Fresh and lovely in a snug blue top with a white accordion-pleated skirt fluttering around her legs, she was bubbling over with anticipation. "Only four more days till moving day, Deva."

"I know," I said, smiling, trying to match her mood.

As she stowed her bag behind the sales desk, she said, "Hasn't everything worked out perfectly for us all? Paulo and I get to buy your beautiful condo. And until your dream house is finished, you and the lieutenant have his place to live in. Things couldn't be better if we'd planned them this way."

"Right." I loved seeing her happiness and knowing I'd played a small part in creating it. What did sleeping in my car matter compared to that? At least that was what I told myself. Not helping Rossi with the apartment hunt hadn't helped the situation. And in fairness, I needed to. Trouble was, every day lately had been chewed up with one crisis after another. Well, today I'd make a point of checking out the listings in the *Naples Daily News*, and this afternoon I'd…

Our first walk-in customer of the day rattled the bells on the door. Lee strolled over to greet her, and I hit the phone.

First Mike Hammerjack. Then I'd confirm today's meeting with the "blah" family room client, and after that call Rossi. No, on second thought I'd wait until we were together to tell him about the lavender letter. He had enough to deal with for now, what with the demands of his job and contacting realtors all over town.

Mike's phone rang and rang, but he didn't pick up. Either he was too busy to answer or was having trouble fishing his cell out of the tight shorts he wore on the job.

Finally, as I was about to hang up, a gruff, "Yeah," barked across the line.

"Mike, this is Deva Dunne."

"Hey, designer lady," he said, his voice changing so much it was as if he'd handed his phone to somebody else.

"I'm ready to place a furniture order and need a contact name and number at State."

"For you, anything," he said, his voice dropping into a lower, sexier register. "I've got that info out in the truck."

A crash loud enough to jar my eardrum rocketed through the line. "What was *that?*"

"That was Tony. We're into demolition over here. Getting rid of the pink tile you wanted out. Look, can I call you back? I've gotta go."

Another crash and the phone went dead.

Pink tile. That had to be Stew's place.

Twenty minutes later, I found the girly pink tiles in a

shattered heap on the master bathroom floor and Tony and Mike covered in plaster dust.

"Whoa!" Mike said when I walked in unannounced.

"Did I startle you?" I asked.

"My heart's flipping over is all."

"Sorry. The housekeep...ah, Teresa...didn't answer the doorbell."

"That'd be tough," Mike said with a grin. "She's in Puerto Rico."

My jaw dropped open. "For good?"

"Nah. Mr. Hawkins said she went to show her family a rock. Whatever that means."

Mike sounded like he really didn't know. I guess the education at State wasn't too thorough.

I looked around the torn-up room. "As long as you're into demolition, you want to complete the job? Take out the vanity, the mirrors, the toilet, the tub? Everything down to the studs?"

Seeing Tony's question coming, I quickly said, "Add the extra cost to your total."

He glanced around the space, frowning. "The tub's a problem. We'll have to break it up to get it out of here. That'll chew up another day."

"Whatever it takes, Tony."

He gave his jeans a hitch and nodded. "Okay. You're the boss."

"Have the new tiles arrived?"

"Yeah, they're out in the truck."

"I'd like to take a look at them. Make sure they're the warm sand color I ordered. I need to see that decorative frieze too...and how about that number, Mike?"

"Come out to the truck and—"

Mike got no further. The wail of a siren shattered

the neighborhood's calm. Louder and louder, the siren screeched along Whiskey Lane, then came to a halt right outside the house.

"No one's at home here, right?" I asked.

"Nobody," Mike said.

I ran for the front entrance as fast as my high-heeled slides would allow and yanked the door open.

An EMS vehicle, lights flashing, rear doors open, was parked in front of 590.

Omigod. What now?

I dashed across the street. The front door of the Stahlman house stood ajar. I pushed it open and walked into the foyer. Low-pitched male voices and lighter female tones came from the direction of the master suite. The woman was most likely Eileen. So chances were she wasn't the one needing emergency treatment. That left only James then, but what on earth had happened to him?

A nervous wreck, but not wanting to interrupt the medics, I paced the living room, trying to work off my tension. As I strode back and forth, heels clicking on the bare hardwood floor, it finally dawned on me that the room looked beautiful. Tom's painters had done a wonderful job. Like a crisp bright day washed clean by rain, the empty room stood clean and bright waiting for its new furnishings, waiting to be enjoyed. I sighed, wondering what the odds were of that ever happening.

I wandered into the dining room. Yesterday when Marilyn and I were dealing with Eileen's crisis, the men had finished the papering. I lit the crystal chandelier suspended from the center of the ceiling. In its light, the coral-toned wallpaper glowed soft and warm. At night, punctuated here and there with silvery birds of paradise, it would flatter every woman seated for dinner. Add James's collection of silver hollowware and the room would be a...

Voices coming closer drew me back to the foyer. Eileen in her signature white uniform, her hair pulled back in its usual tidy bun, led the way. Behind her, the same medics I remembered from two days ago pushed a gurney toward the front door. Stretched out on top was none other than James, his face deathly white, his lips blue.

When Eileen saw me, a moment of confused surprise crossed her face.

"Mrs. Dunne? We didn't expect you today. We have a problem. We..." Her voice trailed off.

"What happened?" I whispered.

"James...Mr. Stahlman has had—"

One of the medics nodded at me and said to Eileen, "We're taking him to the Naples Community Hospital. If you go to the emergency room, they'll direct you from there."

"Is he...is he..." Eileen couldn't bring herself to ask the question.

"We've stabilized him, ma'am. He'll be in good hands."

We followed the medics to the front door and watched as they wheeled James out to the waiting ambulance. I glanced across the street. Tony and Mike must have gone back to their demolition. The tile truck still sat in the driveway at 595, but they were nowhere in sight.

"I have to get to the hospital," Eileen said, tears wetting her blue eyes. If anything happens to him..." Her voice broke, and she covered her face with her hands.

"You heard the medic, Eileen. James is in good hands. That sounds very positive to me."

She nodded, found a tissue in her uniform pocket and dabbed at her eyes. "I owe you an apology for yesterday. I'm so sorry. And so ashamed."

"You've been through a lot, Eileen. If you were upset, that's understandable. Anybody would be."

"I wasn't upset, I was drunk."

"Well…"

"It's the truth." Her chin quivering, she glanced over at me. "I don't remember how much I said, but whatever it was, I hope you'll ignore it."

"Don't worry about a thing, Eileen. My lips are sealed."

"Oooh." Her voice rose into a wail. "Then I *did* say too much."

"No, no," I said, hurrying to reassure her. "Only that you were leaving. So I'm glad to see you're still here."

"*Leaving?*" Her brow furrowed. "I would never leave James. He needs me."

"Absolutely. He won't want to come home to an empty house."

"No." Eileen's soft, plump jaw hardened. "The minute that woman walked in this morning, I knew she meant trouble."

"What woman?"

"Marilyn, of course. She gave James a heart attack."

"But that's not—"

"You should have heard her. It was awful. Do you know what she accused him of?"

I had a pretty good idea, but I shook my head.

"She told him he was a thief. That he wanted Kay dead so he could steal her money. Imagine, accusing James…Mr. Stahlman…of something like that." Eileen sniffled, but her eyes were dry. "She didn't even have the decency to wait for the ambulance to get here. The nerve of her. She's a vicious woman." Eileen straightened her shoulders. "A…a…bitch."

I guess she found swearing tougher when she was sober.

She glanced out the front entrance, but the ambulance was long gone. "I have to follow them."

Moving faster than I thought she could— chalk one up for sensible oxfords—she dashed through the house, returning with a tan leatherette purse slung across her body and a key chain in her hand.

"Will you lock up, Mrs. Dunne?" she asked. Without waiting for a reply she was out the door and on her way to the garage.

My "Certainly" drifted unheard on the warm summer air. Eileen had already disappeared around the front of the house.

A moment later a car roared to life, backed out of the driveway, braked, straightened, and with a screech that made my teeth clench, laid rubber halfway down Whiskey Lane.

Good grief. I hoped there wouldn't be another death in the family, so to speak.

The family, such as it was, had had a full measure of sorrow…and now to think that James had been stricken. Was Eileen right? Had Marilyn's accusation caused his collapse? If so, there had to be a reason. Outrage at the injustice of what she said, or guilt at its truth. Either way, James was fighting for his life, and at least one person in the world wanted him to survive. For her sake above all, I prayed he would too.

Alone in the house, I wandered out to the kitchen, every step echoing in the empty rooms. The kitchen was as neat as ever, all evidence of yesterday's debauch erased as if it had never occurred.

I shot the bolt on the back door, the sharp noise in the silence of the house an eerie reminder that I was alone. A pang of unease slid through me. Despite its lovely potential, the house had been witness to strange happenings recently, including a murder. Goosebumps erupted on my skin; I suddenly needed to get out of there and fast.

Woof.

Charlotte's rough little tongue licked my ankles. So I wasn't alone after all.

"Hi, girlfriend," I said, scooping her up. Glad to see her, I smooched the top of her head next to her red, white and blue bow. The bow was either a homage to the Fourth of July or part of a mother and daughter outfit. Since neither one was timely any longer, I plucked the bow from her topknot and kissed her again.

"You slept through all the excitement, didn't you? James is gone, but don't worry. He'll be back to take you for a walk."

Woof. Woof.

"Just not today, okay?"

Today? What about today? I couldn't leave her alone to roam through the house unattended. And no telling when Eileen would return. A woman on a mission, she'd raced away with the urgency of a NASCAR driver. I didn't think she'd be back anytime soon.

"What am I going to do with you?"

Bowless but beautiful even with her fuzzy white topknot held upright by a bare elastic band, Charlotte gazed at me with melting brown eyes. No, I couldn't leave her alone.

"You want to come with me?"

No answer.

"You want to go for a ride?"

Woof. Woof! She wriggled in my arms to be put down and get going.

"Okay, let's find your leash."

Tail up, she hurried over to a wall rack that held a rainbow of leather leashes. Pink, blue, green, red, black, ocelot—ocelot?

I hitched her up to the feminine-looking pink one and let her pull me through the house to the front door. As she tugged on the leash impatient for an adventure, I locked up.

"Come on, we're going to see the tile boys for a few minutes, and then we're going to take a look at a blah family room. But no matter how bad it is, we have to be polite. Understood?"

No answer. Charlotte ignored my warning. Rightly so. She knew how to behave on social occasions. As long as she didn't pee on the woman's floor, we'd be fine.

FORTY-THREE

LOCATED IN PELICAN MARSH, a North Naples gated community, the home of the blah family room turned out to be a faux Tuscan mini-mansion. The peach stucco façade, all turrets and angles, featured a baronial door set into a recessed entryway. To get to it, Charlotte and I had to pass between a row of sago palms and through a wrought iron gate, kind of like storming a castle. On the wall by the door, a gargoyle's glowing mouth was the only thing remotely resembling a bell, so I pressed it.

No one answered. I pressed again, then again. Finally, a plump-cheeked woman in a purple leotard yanked open the door.

"Hi," she said, gasping for a breath. "You must be Deva Dunne."

"Yes, I am. Are you Dorothy Kindall?"

"In the flesh. Sorry to keep you waiting, but when I'm into my Jazzercise routine the world fades away." She slapped a hand on one ample hip. "But not my flab. No matter what I do." She sighed. "It's a struggle."

Woof!

Dorothy Kindall laughed. "For you too, sweetie? What's your name?"

"This is Charlotte. I'm sorry, but I'm dog-sitting and—"

"Oh, I love doggies. Bring her right in."

"It's paws on the floor, Charlotte," I said, putting her down. "So be a good girl."

Happy to sniff out a new place, she scampered ahead of me as I followed Dorothy through a mind-blowing great room in Madagascar red. New Guinea artifacts, mostly ebony nudes and spears, stood alongside oil paintings of Venice canals. A brass étagère held a riotous collection of Chihuly glass and...that's when I screamed. A gorilla the size of King Kong loomed straight ahead. Even Charlotte skidded to a stop.

"Oh, don't let old Maxwell scare you," Dorothy said. "He's stuffed. A souvenir from our safari in Kenya. Ever been there?"

"Not till today."

Dorothy laughed. "I like you." She gave Charlotte's topknot a pat. "I like you too, sweetie. Here it is, girls, the family room. Tada!" She flung open double doors and gave us a sweeping view—of chaos.

Painted charcoal gray with a chrome-yellow stripe up near the ceiling, the family room was crammed with objects: a universal, a stationary bike, a treadmill, a rack of weights in various sizes and a sixty-inch flat-screen TV. Opposite the TV was a chrome-yellow sofa and a pair of fifties lava lamps that immediately fascinated Charlotte.

Woof!

I was beginning to question her taste in lamps when she abandoned them to play with a beach ball.

As I glanced around, Dorothy looked at me with expectation in her eyes.

I took a deep breath and sank onto the sofa. "Someone obviously took great pains to coordinate the colors in here. The yellow and charcoal carpeting goes well with the sofa," I said, wondering how to press on from there.

A dimple appeared in Dorothy's cheek. She nodded, pleased. "I put it all together, colors and everything. The problem is my husband hates this room." The dimple disappeared. "Says he can't relax in here, and our great room is too formal."

Formal?

She raised her arms and waved them around. "So I need to do something. But *what?*" She plopped down next to me and lowered her voice. "Just between the two of us, I don't really like charcoal all that much. It's kind of blah, you know, but I thought George would find it restful." A deep sigh. "He's done nothing but complain."

"Then our priority is to make George happy."

The dimple made a cameo appearance. "You understand."

"Of course I do. As my Nana Kennedy used to say, 'If the husband is happy, the wife is happy too.'"

Dorothy leaned forward to give my hand a squeeze. "It's so nice dealing with a married woman. I don't need to explain what a husband can be like. You already know what I'm up against, Mrs. Dunne."

"Deva, please," I said, hoping she wouldn't ask me any questions about my husband. To this very day, I found talking about Jack difficult…but she didn't.

"So what would you suggest we do?" she asked.

We, a good sign for Deva Dunne Interiors. Time for a little show biz, a little psychology. I studied the room as if contemplating a difficult problem, although the answer was painfully obvious.

"Well, Mrs. Kindall…"

"Dorothy."

"Yes, thank you. Well, Dorothy, the truth is, exercise equipment makes some people feel guilty. Instead of watching TV, they think they should be pounding away on the treadmill. Maybe that's how George feels. When he comes home at the end of a long day, he's tired and needs to sit down and well…relax. Not be faced with exercise equipment."

She sighed. "That's exactly what he told me."

"Can you move the equipment somewhere else?"

She thought about it for a moment. "The master bedroom maybe. It's large enough."

I shook my head. "You'll turn George into an insomniac."

"We do have three guest bedrooms."

"Is any not needed, or seldom used?"

"Let me see…there's the Caribbean Room, the African Room and the Aztec Room… George has never been too crazy about the Aztec Room. That might do, though everything would have to be moved out first. What a shame. I have the most gorgeous Ecuadorian textiles in there…but for the sake of my marriage, I guess I don't have much choice."

"Sight unseen, the Aztec Room sounds perfect. As for this room, my instinct tells me that for George's sake, we need to act fast."

"The sooner the better. He was pretty cranky last night…didn't even want to watch TV in here."

"Then we need to have a renovation that's simple and quick."

Perching on the edge of the couch, Dorothy gave me her rapt attention.

"First we'll hire a moving crew and have them switch out the exercise equipment. Next we'll lighten the color

of the walls but stay within the same palette. Soften it
from charcoal to, let's say, Whisper Gray. One coat
should do it, and I can recommend an excellent painting contractor." I pointed toward the ceiling. "We'll
keep the chrome stripe. It ties the decor together, and
besides it's out of eye range. I doubt George will find
it a problem.

"So to sum up, we retain the sofa, the TV, your wonderful stainless steel bar…and to make George supremely happy, how about adding a lounger? One of
those big ones in black leather."

"The kind that looks like an ocean liner?" Dorothy asked.

"That's exactly what I mean. Men love them. The
Clive-Daniel showroom has a huge collection. I'm sure
we can find one there and a roomy table to stand alongside it. One large enough to hold George's remote, and
a glass and maybe a snack."

"Oh, I have a darling monkey table we can use."

"A what?" I asked, my heart sinking a little, for I
feared I knew what she meant.

"One of those small tables with a monkey dressed
in a tuxedo holding up a tray."

"I've seen them," I said, smiling as if agreeing with
her suggestion. "They're very colorful and interesting."
I wasn't lying, I told myself. They *were* colorful and
interesting. And god-awful. "But rather too small for
George's needs, don't you think?"

"Oh. Right."

"And let's change out the lava lamps too."

"Are you sure?" I was beginning to think the dimple
was gone for good.

"I really am. The way the oil in those see-through

bases moves up and down probably makes George nervous."

"I see." She really didn't, but she was being a good sport as her creation was verbally torn apart.

"The lamps would be perfect in your exercise room," I said, offering her a consolation prize, wanting to see her smile. "You know, for energy."

She grinned across at me. "Perfect. I can watch the oil move around in the bases while I'm on the treadmill. It'll keep me going."

Not knowing what else to do, I nodded. "A good choice for lamps in here would be—"

"This is so exciting I've forgotten my manners. Before we go on, may I offer you a cold drink? An iced tea, or a soda or something?"

"None for me, thanks, but Charlotte might enjoy a little water."

"Oh certainly." Dorothy jumped up and went over to the stainless steel sink nestled in the well-stocked bar. She filled a small bowl with water and placed it on the floor. As we looked on, Charlotte noisily lapped up her drink, splashing it around on the carpet in the process.

"She's adorable," Dorothy said.

"Yes, she is. She belongs to one of my clients. Unfortunately he had a heart attack this morning and in the confusion I'm afraid Charlotte was overlooked. I couldn't leave her alone for the day, so here she is."

"How thoughtful of you. You must be close to this client."

"You could say that. When you design someone's living space, sometimes you become almost like family."

"That's nice, so warm and caring. Families are the most important thing in life. That's why I worry about

George…and not just about him either. There's my mother too."

"Oh? Does she live here as well?"

"No, but I wish she did. We have a mother-in-law apartment all ready and waiting for her. That's one of the reasons we bought this house, but she refuses to step foot in it."

"Why?"

"Says it sets her teeth on edge." Dorothy put a hand on each generous hip. "And to think I decorated that apartment just for her. When we finish in here, do you want to take a look at it?"

FORTY-FOUR

"ROSSI," I SAID, hurrying to the door the instant he got home. "You're not going to believe this."

"Probably not." Planning on viewing some rentals today, he'd worn a shirt and tie and a pair of chinos. He loosened the tie as soon as he walked in and ripped it off. After catching me in a distracted bear hug, he sank onto a club chair, looking as tired and frustrated as I'd ever seen him.

"Tough day?"

"You could say that." He held out his arms. "How about coming over here and letting me give you some TLC?" He patted his knees. "Come on. Come on."

"You're sure you're up to it?"

"For you, always." He grinned, only briefly, but still a good sign. I sat on his lap and laid my head on his chest.

"Aah," he said, "This is what makes life worth living."

"What happened today? You seem discouraged."

"No, I'm not discouraged. Once in a while the negatives get to me is all."

"Anything you want to talk about?"

"Well for openers, the chief agrees Kay Hawkins was murdered." He heaved a sigh. "As luck would have it, the man we want to interview underwent heart surgery and can't be questioned. Nor can his wife. The Stahlman woman's disappeared again."

I lifted my head from his chest. "Marilyn?"

"The same. No forwarding address. No active telephone number. Gone."

"So now what?"

"We hope Stahlman will recover and shed some light on her whereabouts and on a few other issues as well. Until he does, we wait…and we search for his wife. Chances are she's floating around somewhere with the boat guy she calls her fiancé. The Coast Guard's working on it, but that's like looking for a needle in a haystack. Especially if he's tied up in some remote cove with the radio shut down." He stroked my arm. "Do you know you have the softest skin in the world?"

"Thanks but you're changing the subject…so are James and Marilyn your two prime suspects?"

He ran his fingers along my other arm. "Um, so nice…"

"Rossi."

"At the present time, they're persons of interest. So is everyone who was present the day Kay Hawkins died."

I stared into his eyes. "Me too?"

"Technically. You found the victim, so you're implicated. The same for the workmen and the other two women, the housekeeper Eileen and the one across the street—" a faint smile played with his lips, "—Teresa of the tight red pants."

"You noticed."

"I'm in love, I'm not dead." His smile disappeared. "Judging from the bruises on the victim's neck, I doubt a woman strangled her. That takes a lot of strength." He shrugged. "On the other hand, anger can lend strength to someone who doesn't ordinarily have it. Make that passionate anger and who knows?"

As if trying to put the pieces together in his mind, he stared past me at the opposite wall—at nothing, really. "Practically speaking though, our culprit is mostly likely a man. What I'm hoping is that one of the women might know something that would help us." His glance refocused on me. "That includes you. So if you can think of anything you haven't mentioned yet, now is the time. The chlorine and the water washed off any forensic evidence that might have been left on the remains. All we have to go on are the bruises and the lack of water in the lungs."

He shifted me from one knee to the other.

"Am I getting heavy?"

"No not at all. I love having you just where you are."

I sat up straight. "There is one other thing."

He had leaned his head on the chair back and closed his eyes. "Go on."

He was actually seeking my advice. I couldn't believe it. "What about the written statements? The ones you collected from everybody the day Kay died?"

An eye, just one, slit open.

"Have you sent them to a graphologist yet? It's sad that we've lost Naomi, but there must be other handwriting analysts out there you can call on."

Both eyes opened and stared into mine. "Copies of the original samples have been faxed to Miami. We're awaiting the outcome."

"Wonderful."

"Maybe yes, maybe no. Graphology's an inexact science. I'm not even sure the word *science* applies. But at the moment, we have little else to go on, so we're giving it a shot. Tomorrow I'll question the witnesses in depth. Think I'll start with Teresa. Get another look at those red pants." He wiggled his brows up and down, Groucho Marx style.

Red pants. "Sorry, you're out of luck. Marilyn's not the only person of interest who left town. Teresa's on a trip too."

"I know. Puerto Rico. She's due back tomorrow night."

"Oh, rats. You set me up for that one, Rossi. Not nice. Not nice at all. Besides, your knees are getting bony." I went to get off his lap, but he was too fast. His arms encircled me, trapping me right where I really wanted to be.

"Just so you'll know, among other things today, I searched for a rental. Didn't find a thing I liked. At least not in our price range. So yeah, I guess you could say it's been quite a day all told." His arms tightened around me. "But any day that ends with you in it is wonderful. You're the best thing that ever happened to me, you know that?"

I raised my face for a kiss as a spurt of guilt snaked through me for not returning his lovely compliment. Rossi was and always would be the best thing in my life. But truth be told, he wasn't the first man I'd ever loved, or the first best thing that ever happened to me. That had been Jack. How could I tell the truth without wounding my now and forever love? Better not to say a word, so I didn't even try. Instead I dropped some good news on him. "I have a surprise for you."

"That right? Did I ever tell you detectives don't like surprises?"

"You're going to love this one."

"Uh-oh. One of those."

"You ready for this?"

"No, but go ahead anyway. The suspense is killing me."

"I found us an apartment."

His jaw dropped open. "You *did?*"

"Yes. It's perfect in every way except that it's horrible, but—"

"Wait, wait, wait. That's an oxymoron."

"I know. What I mean is it's completely furnished—hi-def TV, large sofa, kitchen appliances and every utensil we could possibly use, plus a king-sized bed. With a feather duvet. Best of all, Rossi, I got it for us by bartering."

He heaved a sigh. "Since I'm feeling mentally challenged tonight, would you please explain in simple terms?"

"I redo the décor free of charge and in return it's ours free for a year."

"There has to be a hitch. What's the horrible part?"

"The colors."

His eyes widened in disbelief. "That's a hitch?"

"You haven't seen them. Purple, lime green and orange. Everywhere. On everything. So while we're living there, I'll have to make some changes, but Tom Kruse's men will be minimally invasive. You'll see."

"Where is this perfect, horrible place?"

"Pelican Marsh. It's a mother-in-law apartment."

"Interesting. Very interesting. Actually fantastic."

"You're impressed, I can tell."

"Good sleuthing, Deva. Can you also tell I'm chagrined."

I stood up from his lap and stared down at him,

all of him—tieless shirt, five o'clock shadow...frown. "No...why?"

"You expect me to live free of charge in a place that you'll pay for with your labor?"

"Oh, for God's sake, it isn't like that."

"It's exactly like that. Remember how you wanted to pay for our Hawaiian trip with money from the sale of Jack's antiques?"

"Ye-e-e-s."

"Then you may recall that was a no. How could I have gone on a vacation your late husband paid for? Much the same principle applies now. I can't live there."

"That's ridiculous. Three more days and we have to be out of here. Then what? Are you going to let your male pride stand in the way?"

"Without my pride—" he grinned, "—yeah it's male all right—you wouldn't want to have anything to do with me. No lioness wants a wimpy lion roaming around the lair. Isn't that right?"

Refusing to be baited, and a little hurt that my wonderful solution was being scorned, I folded my arms and waited in silence for him to go on.

"Our imminent housing problem is not lost on me, and I very much appreciate your clever solution."

"Well, then..."

He waggled a finger. "There's more. So I propose an alternate solution."

"There is none."

"One that will make us both happy."

"Which is?"

"The money I'd spend on renting temporary digs, I give to you instead."

"You don't need to do—"

The finger waggled again. "Not so fast. There's a string attached. I want you to take the money and buy yourself a new car, another Audi if you wish, brand-new with all the bells and whistles."

"Green with tan leather seats?"

"If that turns you on."

"Well, actually only you do, but a new car would be wonderful. I am in the image business, and my car *is* getting shabby."

"It's settled then. We move into a mother-in-law apartment and you get a new Audi."

He looked pleased and not the least bit tired anymore. I hated to dampen his mood but felt I had to remind him of the visual onslaught he faced.

"Remember now, the colors in the apartment are beyond bad."

He stood, ripped off his tie and headed for the bedroom, probably for some shorts and a Hawaiian shirt. "I happen to like purple and orange and what was the other one? Oh yeah, lime green."

And he had the shirts to prove it. But I wasn't finished with my news yet. "By the way, we're going to have a ménage à trois, at least for a while."

Halfway to the bedroom, Rossi whirled around to face me. "Explain."

"No need," I said, "there's your answer."

Awake after sleeping off an exciting afternoon, Charlotte had hopped off the bed and was padding out to the living room to greet him.

"She's just in time for her cocktail dog walk. Want to come with us?"

FORTY-FIVE

WITH THREE MAJOR projects to complete, a move to orchestrate, new home construction to check on and Charlotte to babysit, I had my work cut out for me. So after Rossi left for a day of sleuthing, I began in earnest with James's empty house. Superior Home Cleaners was due at nine to wash the windows and polish the hardwood floors in the refurbished rooms. Though not strictly part of an interior designer's service, I wanted to be there. Such attention to the final details made a renovation shine…and helped enhance the reputation of Deva Dunne Interiors.

I reached Whiskey Lane just as the cleaners were arriving, but Eileen had already left for the hospital. She'd propped a sweet note in quickly scribbled handwriting on the kitchen table, thanking me for taking care of Charlotte.

Poor Eileen, she was stressed beyond belief. If anything happened to James, she would lose the man she loved and her livelihood as well. I wondered what would happen to her if Chez Stahlman were no more.

Anyway, while the cleaning crew did their thing, I sat in the breakfast nook with Charlotte and called my workroom. James's reupholstered chairs and sofas were ready—*yes!*—so I arranged for a noon delivery. As a special favor for all the business I'd sent them, they agreed to move the rest of the furniture from safe-keeping in the guest bedroom and arrange it in place.

The house redo was coming together nicely but was far from complete. While James recovered in the hospital, workmen tramping through the house wouldn't be a problem...but redoing the master suite when an invalid might need it soon wasn't a good idea.

I glanced around the kitchen. It too was badly in need of remodeling. But not now. If and when Eileen's beloved boss returned home, she would want a functioning kitchen to prepare special delicacies for him. So as far as Deva Dunne Interiors was concerned, the Stahlman project had largely ground to a standstill.

I assumed that even without Kay to please, James would live up to the terms of our contract, but—to stare reality in the face—if he died, all bets were off. I couldn't pretend I'd be as distraught as Eileen if that were to happen, but Deva Dunne Interiors would definitely be affected. No arguing with fate, I told myself, and besides, James had already paid me generously for work rendered. The upholstery bill and today's cleaning fee, I'd send to his financial advisor and hope for the best...

Woof!

I lowered my hand and let Charlotte lick my fingertips. "Hi, darling, you want something?" Her tail wagged. "I don't read wags well. What would you like? A dish of water?"

The wagging stopped.

"You need to go out?"

The tail turned into a metronome.

"Okay, let's get some fresh air."

Despite the glorious morning, all golden sunshine

and salty sea breezes, a shiver of unease slid along my spine when I stepped onto the terrace. I hadn't been out there since Kay died, and an eerie silence pervaded the lush garden.

Charlotte ran down the stone stairs and headed for her favorite spot, the pool area. *Darn.* I should have put her on a leash. Now I'd have to chase after her, and I had no desire to go anywhere near that pool.

"Where are you girl?" I called. To let me know she'd heard, she popped out from behind the hedge, then disappeared from view again. The little devil.

I jogged down the stairs, calling her name all the way. Heart pounding, and not from the exercise, I rounded the hedge. There she was, digging divots in the grass. The pool, empty of all but water, sparkled aqua blue and beautiful in the sun. Relieved, I turned my back on it and concentrated on Miss Charlotte.

"You having fun, honey?"

She ignored me and kept on clawing at the grass, sending up tufts of the immaculate lawn.

"What would James say if he saw you doing that?"

At "James" she paused, but not for long. She was enjoying herself too much to stop. I bent over to scoop her up, hoping she had accomplished the reason for coming out in the first place. If not, another one of my outfits was doomed. As I reached for her, something shiny caught my eye. A brass button with red threads still clinging to it. *Hmm.* I picked it up and turned it over. The threads looked strong, as if they'd been forcibly snapped off, maybe from the strain of a too-tight pair of pants.

I pocketed the button, and with Her Nibs in my arms, climbed the slope back to the house. The cleaning crew had left the windows sparkling and the washed and waxed floors ready for the next step—staging.

Promptly at noon, the workroom truck pulled onto the drive. I gave Charlotte a doggie treat and left her in the kitchen while I directed furniture traffic. First the rugs. The beautifully faded Tabrizes, with ivory backgrounds and random patches of faded blue and coral, went down first. Then the sofas. Their blue damask repeated the blue of the rugs with the understated echo I'd hoped for. Not insistent. Not overwhelming. Perfect.

In the dining room, we centered the heirloom table under the crystal chandelier and placed the new mirrored sideboard against a long wall where it shimmered like the showstopper it was. Along with the blue-and-ivory-striped host and hostess chairs, the mirrored sideboard dispelled the curse of the average dining room—drab brown furniture.

So far, so good. After the movers left, I sprung Charlotte and let her explore the furniture and sniff out the interesting new scents. While she played, I took notes. The bones were in place; now to flesh out the skeleton—I needed to have the windows measured for draperies, shop at Clive-Daniel Home for lamps, design custom pillows, look for Limoges boxes and tabletop bronzes, and check James's preferences in oil paintings.

Before we left, I wrote a note to Eileen. When she found time, the mahogany pieces needed waxing and the sterling hollowware should be polished before going on display. My mouth fairly watered at the thought of how the silver would glow on that mirrored buffet—each piece adding luster to the other. I signed the note and propped it on the breakfast nook table where she'd be sure to find it.

I attached Charlotte's collar to her pink leash. "Come on, girlfriend, we're going across the street. I have another client to take care of, and some tight red pants to check out."

I hoped Teresa hadn't taken the pants to Puerto Rico. If not, they should be hanging in her clothes closet. I was dying to see if the button I found belonged on them. If so, what was it doing down by James's pool? To my knowledge, the only time Teresa had stepped foot on the Stahlman property was the morning Kay died. But she hadn't gone anywhere near the pool that day. Or had she?

FORTY-SIX

"HIGH TIME YOU got here," Stew said, yanking open the door to 595. He stood in the entryway and upped his chin at 590. "You've been camped out over there for hours." He pointed the lit end of his stubby cigar at Charlotte. "What's that mutt doing in my house?"

"She's no mutt. She came in second at the Westminster Dog Show."

"A second-rater huh? Make sure she doesn't—"

"She won't," I said, cutting him off at the pass. "I'm sorry I haven't been here for you. But with Mr. Stahlman gravely ill, I needed to finish what I could before he's discharged from the hospital. I hope you understand."

"What's to understand? My wife died over there."

"Actually your ex-wife, Stew," I said as gently as possible.

"A technicality. She was mine. He should have taken better care of her." *As you should have of Connie Rae.* "So no, I don't give a damn about his place. Or him. Come in, come in," he urged, waving his cigar around. The moment I stepped inside, he slammed the front door so hard the whole house shook.

"Concentrate in here now," he said, barging ahead of me into the great room. "So far all I've got is a half-done paint job."

"Three-quarters done. As soon as your master bedroom is completed, the painters will be back to tackle the other bedrooms."

He took a few puffs but wasn't ready to give up. "Where are those leather couches you ordered and the big chairs?"

"Your great room furniture is being custom designed, and that takes time. I know the wait's frustrating, but it'll be worth it in the end, you'll see."

He mulled that over as he sucked on the stogie, then, "What about all that Western-themed crap you mentioned?"

I stifled a sigh. "No point in bringing in accessories before the major pieces are in place. Have a little faith, Stew. You'll like the finished product. Guaranteed."

"I hope the hell so."

"There is one bit of good news. Your bedroom furniture is due for delivery tomorrow. And didn't the color in there turn out well?" A dangerous question. In his current mood, Stew wasn't likely to be positive about anything, but I couched my query in a way that almost forced him to agree.

Almost. "I've seen brown before."

"What?" Client or no client, I couldn't let him get away with that. "The color's not brown, it's terracotta, a warm version of the hallway tone. Haven't you noticed how the shade deepens from the great room, to the hall to your bedroom? Kind of like an escalating scale with the bedroom as the…ah…climax."

His eyes narrowed, but a little amusement flickered around his mouth. To my relief, he ground out his smoke in an ashtray. "That's flowery B.S. You're good at it, you know that? So yeah, the bedroom color's okay. Anything in there would be better than pink. Keep on the job, you hear? I don't want to hire somebody else to step in. Not now that you've gotten this far. Just finish up ASAP."

He arched a thumb in the direction of the master bath. "I need those guys out of the house before Teresa comes back. So make sure they don't leave until they're finished." He stuck a fresh cigar in his shirt pocket, yanked out his keys and stomped toward the front door. "I have to get to work. My business is going down the tubes while I babysit the damn house. That's your job, not mine. So do it."

"Wait a New York minute," I said, but too late. With a bang, the front door slammed shut and he was gone.

The nerve of him. I should abandon the project, let somebody else put up with his attitude. I heaved a sigh. What about the contract I'd signed? If I walked off the job, Stew was just the type who would sue me. Hoist on my own petard. Damn.

Charlotte was looking up at me with those big browns of hers. "You're smart, aren't you? You know something's amiss. Well, we won't let it bother us, will we?" I dropped my tote on the sofa and unclasped her leash. "Go ahead, run around, have fun. Pee on the floor if you want to."

Dim scraping sounds and the muted voices of Tony and Mike came from the direction of the master bath. Since Stew was anxious that they finish up today, I wouldn't bother them, though I was curious to see the decorative tile frieze. I was also curious about those red pants.

The pants won out.

"Want to come with me?" I asked Charlotte. "I think

you should. You might not get another chance to see Teresa's wardrobe."

No *woof* of agreement? As I went to reach for my tote, tiny nails clicked along the tiled floor. I glanced over a shoulder.

"Hey, what've you got?"

She scampered past me, but I grabbed her en route and lifted her into my arms. "Come on, let it go. Be a good girl. Open your mouth. Come on." With a lot of coaxing and more than a little tugging, I finally convinced her to open up and release the billfold. I kissed her topknot. "Good girl. This is your day, isn't it? One treasure after another." I put her down but held onto the wallet. Stew must have dropped it on his way out. I'd leave it on his dresser for him to find.

I only planned to take a quick look at Teresa's clothes, but for some reason, guilt at snooping maybe, I tiptoed along the hall to the master bedroom. If I were quiet enough, I could be in and out in a minute or two without the tile guys even knowing I'd been there. As silent as if she were a cat, my new friend padded along beside me. No doubt about it, she had an adventurous streak.

I cracked open the master bedroom door. We slipped in, and I closed it behind us. The odor of new paint filled the empty room, pleasantly so. I knew I was weird that way but to me the aroma of latex paint was right up there with Chanel No. 5 and Prada Candy—providing the wall color had been well chosen. And despite Stew's nasty crack, the terracotta would be a great foil for the platform bed I'd ordered in a he-man rough-hewn pine.

With her paws on the French doors, Charlotte stared outside at a squirrel romping up and down a palm tree. I hurried over to the walk-in closet and, pulse revving up a bit at what I might find, swung open the double shutter doors.

Oh, I'd forgotten. The closet was empty. After the python nearly scared her to death, Teresa had transferred her clothes and Stew's to the guest room across the hall. I should have remembered.

"Come on, girl, we're hitting the road," I said to Charlotte.

As we strolled along the hall, I could hear loud voices coming from the bathroom. Or mostly one voice, Mike's. Didn't he ever keep quiet? Apparently not. All incensed about something or other, he was rattling on nonstop. We went into the larger of the two guest bedrooms. I closed the door, surprised that the room's hideous, snaky vine wallpaper hadn't given Teresa nightmares. Tomorrow after the master bedroom was complete, we'd start in here.

Charlotte hopped up on the unmade bed and settled down on the duvet with a contented little sigh. I laid the wallet on the dresser and opened the closet doors, hoping I had the right ones this time.

Bingo.

Stew's clothes filled the left side and Teresa's colorful duds hung on the right like a rainbow about to explode. Of all the people I knew, only Rossi had a closet as full of color as this one.

Red. Look for red. I riffled through the hangers. Blue, purple, cerise, chrome, floral, stripes, black. Black? How did that get in there? And then I found them, Three pairs of bright red pants.

I placed them on the bed next to a dozing Charlotte and looked them over carefully. Not one pair was missing a single button, brass or otherwise. So there went my theory about Teresa's guilt.

Pleased she'd been saved by a button and yet a little deflated that my sleuthing had been so far off the mark, I hung the pants back in the closet. Charlotte seemed so comfy nestled into the duvet, that on an impulse I kicked off my shoes and stretched out next to her. Just for a minute, I told myself.

A LOUD THUD brought me to with a start. Where was I? Oh God, I'd fallen asleep on Stew Hawkins's bed. Unbelievable. Long shadows fell through the French doors, the light softer than at midday. What time was it anyway? I glanced at my watch. Egads. Late afternoon. I leaped off the bed and gave Lazy Bones a little pat. "Come on, girlfriend, let's go see what the tile job looks like. I've got that decorative frieze on my mind."

Charlotte stood on the duvet and shook herself awake. Then she leaped off the bed and scampered straight for the French doors.

"You need to go out?"

A rhetorical question. She didn't even bother to answer, the urgency of the moment all that mattered. I'd left her leash in the great room, but the yard was enclosed by a six-foot-tall fence, so she wouldn't be able to scamper away.

"Okay, I'll leave the door open so you can come back in. Be good now."

She ignored me and, tail high, ran outside.

I finger-combed my hair and slid into my shoes. My skirt was hopelessly wrinkled but nothing to be done about that. So much for literally sleeping on the job. A peek in the mirror told me I could use some lip gloss, but I'd left my tote in the great room. Only Stew's bill-fold sat on top of the dresser. Brown and beat-up, it didn't strike me as the kind of accessory you'd expect a wealthy man like Stew to keep in his pocket. Well, he was a one-of-a-kind type of guy. Still...I picked the wallet up and flipped it open. Ah, it wasn't Stew's at all. The wallet belonged to a Tony Pavlich——the same Tony Pavlich who was installing tile in the bathroom down the hall. And in a plastic sleeve next to his ID was a photograph. My heart thrumming in my ears, I stared at a smiling image of Connie Rae in her high school graduation cap and gown.

Whoa!

The snapshot looked to be at least three or four years old. I slid it out of the sleeve and turned it over. In purple ink, in a broad, childish hand, I read, *To Tony with love. C.R.*

Omigod. Tony had known Connie Rae all along and never said a word to anyone. Why not? Whatever the reason, somehow I doubted it was a good one. What good reason could there be in shrouding their relationship in secrecy? None that my stunned mind could come up with. Only fear of being implicated, somehow, in her death. Or...because he had caused it.

A door opened and banged against a wall. I dropped the wallet in a dresser drawer and stood there, too scared to move, too upset to think.

"Hey, watch it. Don't bust up the place." *That was Tony.*

"You know something? I'm sick of you telling me what to do. No more orders. Got that?" *Mike.*

My hand on the bedroom doorknob, I stood frozen, listening.

"If that's your attitude, take a hike. You do more talking than working anyway. Who needs it? Go find another job. If anybody'll hire you." Tony guffawed, an ugly, throaty sound.

"You can't fire me. I'm yours for life, buddy. Or until I walk. Or decide to talk."

"Don't threaten me, you punk."

Something heavy hit the floor. Or the bathroom wall. I couldn't be sure. Another thump and a muffled shout. Or was it a groan? Whatever it was, it wasn't good.

They were closer now, in the hallway right outside the bedroom door, scuffling and banging against the walls.

"Get your hands off me." That was Mike, gasping out the words. "Save the rough stuff for your women."

Tony's women? What did that mean? I thought he lived with his mother.

A loud crack, like a fist against bone, then a thud that sent the walls shuddering.

"You got a glass jaw?" Mike yelled. "One sucker punch and you're down? Hell, you're no challenge."

A groan. *That must be Tony.*

"Wake up, Tone. You can't be out after that. I hardly touched you."

Oh yeah? The walls were shaking. I hoped the new paint job hadn't been wrecked. That's all Stew would need.

"You son of a bitch." *Ah, Tony was coming to.*

"Nah. I'm your pal, Tone. Your only one. You have to learn not to dis me."

A muffled moan. "Why don't you shut up once in a while? Your yammering is driving me nuts."

"Aw, you don't mean that. Come on, let me help you

up. We'll call it a day. Stop off someplace for a couple of beers and relax. Forget all about this."

"No, we have to finish the job first. I want my money, and Hawkins is getting antsy."

Somebody, maybe Mike, whistled through his front teeth. "He wouldn't be so tear-assed if you hadn't put that python in the bedroom."

What! I pressed my ear to the door, anxious to catch every word. Mike had said *he* accidentally released the snake, not Tony.

"I had to do it." *Tony again.*

"No, you didn't. There's women everywhere. You can't have one, you find another."

What did women have to do with this?

A deep, loud sigh. "You don't get it, do you? Connie Rae and me, we were talking marriage, then Hawkins waved his money in her face. That's all it took. A few bucks."

"Tone, she told you the reason. You couldn't afford that operation she needed so—"

"She was sleeping with him!"

"What did you expect?" Mike asked. "They were married. You shouldn't have done it." *Done what?* "A hell of a way to go if you ask me. Scared to death by a monster snake."

"Who's asking you?" *Omigod, Tony had deliberately released the snake while Connie Rae was alive. He had caused her death, and Mike had covered up for him.* "The case is closed. She died from natural causes. Nobody can prove otherwise."

"You got lucky that time, but killing the second one was dumb." Mike barked out a short laugh. "That flag bikini was too good to die."

"If it wasn't for you, nothing would've happened."

"My fault, huh? You've got a helluva nerve. I never laid a finger on her."

"Blame your big mouth. Talk, talk, talk, that's you. Bringing up Connie Rae while we were working on those stone steps. After the broad in the bikini heard you shooting your mouth off about the python, how could I let her go? Next thing you knew, the cops would've been swarming all over me."

"It would've been her word against yours."

"Yeah, you're good with the advice. Shut up for a change. Give my ears a break. And help me up. We got to get back to that grout."

"You're the boss. But let's hurry. I'm nursing a hell of a thirst."

Omigod. I'd just heard Tony confess to double murder. I felt like sliding down the bedroom door and melting into a puddle on the floor, but that wasn't an option. I had to get out of there and fast. Get word to Rossi. But how? My cell was in the tote. It might as well have been in Alaska. A house phone then? I glanced over at the bedside table. No, only a lamp.

A trickle of sweat trailed down my spine as I tried to think…*think*…okay, I'd sneak out the French doors, grab Charlotte…and then? My thoughts skidded to a halt. I couldn't scale a six-foot-high fence, and there were no gates. Maybe the opening to the great room was unlocked. Stew was pretty casual about locking up…or maybe we could tiptoe back down the hall to the front entrance.

I pressed my ear against the door again. No voices but the scraping was louder than earlier. They'd re-

turned to their task but left the bathroom door open.
No way could I sneak past them.

Woof, woof, woof!

Back inside again, Charlotte wanted attention. I put
a finger to my lips. "Shh," I whispered. "Not now. Be
a good girl."

Woooof!

Excited by her outing, Charlotte was in a party mood
and not about to be quiet.

"I scooped her up. "Shh."

Woof, woof, woof!

"What the hell was that?" Tony asked.

"Sounded like a dog."

"What's a dog doing in here? I thought we were
alone. Hawkins left for work hours ago."

"Beats me."

"We've been talking. What if someone heard us?"

"Oh. Yeah."

Something metal hit the floor. A trowel?

Heart pumping as fast as Charlotte's tail, I raced
for the closet and shut it behind us. *Uh-oh.* I'd left the
French door open. A dead giveaway. In Florida in July
no one went out and left a door open, not while an air-
conditioning system was pumping full blast.

Footsteps pounded along the hall. Too late. We were
trapped.

I hugged Charlotte tight. Sensing something wrong,
she nestled into my arms and tucked her head under a
paw.

The bedroom door opened. Through the slats on the
closet door, I saw Mike stride in.

"Hey, Tone, somebody forgot to close a door in here.

That dog we heard must have been out in a yard somewhere."

Tony strode in and glanced around. "Funny, I don't hear no dog now."

Mike poked his head outside. "We did a good job fixing those pool tiles, you know that? It's looking terrific out there."

"Right now, I'm not thinking of tiles. Something's off. I can feel it."

With that, Tony strode over to the closet and threw open the doors.

FORTY-SEVEN

"Hi, Tony."

"What are you doing in here?"

"Oh, um, Teresa, Mr. Hawkins's fiancée—"

"Ha!"

"—asked me to send some of her things to the dry cleaners."

"How long you been here?"

"Just a minute or so. You were so busy in the bathroom I didn't want to disturb you. Though I'm dying to see the frieze. Is it all right if I go in and take a look?"

He squared his big shoulders. "Nah, it's not okay."

"What's going on?" Mike said, crowding into the closet with us.

"The spatial planner didn't allow for parties in here," I said, trying to keep the atmosphere light.

"That's a wiseass comment," Tony said.

"Hey, take it easy." Mike put a hand on his arm.

Tony shrugged it off and gave his low-flying cargo shorts a hitch.

No wonder his shorts rode so low on his hips. I had his top button in my pocket.

With a bravado I really didn't feel, I said, "If you'll excuse me, gentlemen, I'd like to get out of the closet."

"Ha, ha, you're a riot, you know that?" Mike said, his voice rising as he glanced quickly from me to Tony.

"First, I want to know what you heard," Tony said.

"Mike and me, we were talkin'. You must have heard something."

"No...I—"

"Leave her be, Tone."

"Shut up for once."

Without warning, Tony reached out and snatched Charlotte from my arms. "Python food," he muttered, flinging her out of the closet.

She sailed through the air, landing with a yip on the bed. Unhurt but furious, she stood knee-deep on the duvet, growling like a grizzly.

"Hey!" was all I had a chance to say when Tony shoved me up against Stew's collection of polyester pants.

"Get off her," Mike said.

Tony looked over a shoulder at him. "You shut up, and I'm not telling you again."

He swiveled back to me. "You picked the wrong bedroom to decorate." He poked a finger against my chest. "Understood?"

I nodded. Of course I understood.

"Why you roughing her up like that?" Mike asked. "You stupid or something? She'll have you up on assault charges." He shook his head but didn't try to step between us. "I don't understand your thinking, buddy."

"No," Tony said, "you don't. At least you got that right. But you're wrong about charges. She's not leaving here." His lip curled up. "Not on her own. I can't take the chance. We don't know what she heard. So we take her with us and head for the swamp."

"No way! I'm not leaving with you." I struggled to get away from Stew's pants, but Tony's fingernails cutting into my throat kept me from moving.

"You're leaving, all right. Count on it. You know too much."

He jerked a couple of silk ties off Stew's rack. "Tie her hands and feet together and gag her. I'll get the mutt. She goes too." Giving his cargoes another hitch, he stomped out of the closet.

"Are you okay, Mrs. Dunne?" Mike asked in a whisper as soon as we were alone.

I shook my head, too terrified to speak. But Charlotte wasn't scared. As Tony rounded the bed determined to grab her, she leaped, a bundle of fury, and sank her teeth into his hairy calf. He howled and limped around the room, careening into the hall as he tried to shake her off. No dice. Charlotte was pissed.

I grabbed Mike's shirtfront. "Call the police. Tell them what he did."

Mike's face stiffened. "I'm an ex-con. I can't go to the cops with that."

"Ow, ow, ow! Mike! Mike!"

"You want to be up for murder one?"

He stared at me—without speaking for once— his worried expression telling me he'd had the same thought.

"Help me get out of here before he changes his mind. I know the truth. I'm your insurance policy."

He hesitated, for a split second only. "I'll get him in the bathroom and shut the door. You can run down the hall."

"Hammerjack! She's killing me."

"Take it easy," Mike yelled. "I'm tying up the woman, like you said. Besides, the mutt's real small."

Poor Charlotte, she wasn't getting any respect lately.

I slumped against Stew's pants, my heart pounding against my ribs.

Woof, woof wooff!

Charlotte had let go.

"Look at my leg, will you? It's bleeding like a pig. I ought to wring her neck."

What! Halfway out of the closet, I was ready to pounce on Tony myself when Mike said, "Nah, don't bother. We'll find some stuff in the bathroom to put on it."

"Yeah. The mutt could have rabies or something."

Rabies. As if Princess Charlotte, the darling of her vet's office, would have rabies. I wanted to shout, "What's a little rabies to a tough guy like you?" But I didn't, and when Charlotte, drunk with triumph, ran into the closet looking for me, I picked her up. "Good girl," I whispered into her ear, "but now be quiet, okay?"

I needn't have worried. Battle fatigue had taken its toll. Worn-out, she cuddled in my arms and closed her eyes.

I wished my heartbeat and pulse would slow down, but nothing doing. Like out of control trip hammers, they kept pounding away. No wonder. I was trapped in a house with a double murderer, dependent for escape on the word of an ex-con who, on top of everything else, wrote with a felon's claw. I gulped a deep breath of air and exhaled slowly. It didn't do a bit of good. No way would my heartbeat go back to normal until I got out of there. Holding onto Charlotte, I tiptoed over to the bedroom door and opened it a sliver. The bathroom door was closed.

"Ouch, that stings," Tony yelled.

"The wuss," I said to Charlotte who didn't open her

eyes to reply. I slipped off my heels and, hugging Charlotte tight, I ran barefoot down the hall, grabbed my tote off the sofa and fled out the front entrance.

In my rush to escape, I didn't bother to close the door carefully. A gust of wind caught it and banged it shut.

So much for leaving unannounced. I glanced up at the sky. No wonder the door had slammed. Rain clouds had replaced the sun, and a sudden chill in the air had sent the palm fronds into a frenzy. We were in for one of Florida's violent summer showers.

I yanked my keys out of the bag, unlocked the Audi and hurried Charlotte into the backseat. No sooner had I slipped behind the wheel and reset the locks when the front door opened and the two men burst out onto the lawn.

Tony ran over to my car and rapped on the passenger side window. "Open up!"

Was he crazy?

"I didn't mean it," he said. "I won't hurt you."

"That's right," I replied, inserting the key in the ignition.

"Keep your mouth shut. Or else."

"Or else what, you creep?"

I turned on the engine.

"Let her be, Tone."

"No. She'll blab. I can tell. Why didn't you tie her up, asshole?"

Tony reached into one of the side pockets of his cargos and pulled out a hammer. Startled, I went to shove the car into reverse but not in time.

With one powerful blow, he smashed open the passenger side window and snatched at the lock. He jerked the door open and, flinging the hammer aside, reached in and grabbed me, ripping the sleeve out of my shirt and raking his nails along my arm.

I screamed and stomped on the gas, backing down the driveway so fast the open door knocked him to the ground. An instant only and he was up and running toward his truck. At the end of the drive, I jammed on the brakes, shook the glass shards off the tote and dumped its contents on the passenger seat. I grabbed the Cobra, released the safety and stepped out of the Audi. The truck's rear lights flared on. I took careful aim, shot out one back tire, aimed again and shot out the other one.

"Whoa!" Mike yelled as the tires sagged onto their metal rims.

Tony came leaping out of the truck and ran around to check out his wheels. I jumped back in the car. *He might have a gun.* I rocketed out to the street in reverse, braked, slammed into drive and sped around the corner. Only then did I glance out the rearview mirror. No need to speed. Tony might have one spare tire in the trunk, but not two. He'd have to come after me on foot through the now-pelting rain.

On the next street, I spotted a driveway that wrapped around the side of the house. I pulled into it, parking in back where I couldn't be seen from the street. Leaving the motor running, I fumbled among my things strewn over the wet passenger seat, grabbed the cell and glanced around at Charlotte.

Recognizing a crisis for what it was, she lay quietly stretched out on the backseat with her head on her paws, studying me with her big brown eyes.

"Girlfriend, you sure know how to sic a guy. Now it's my turn," I told her as I punched in 9-1-1.

FORTY-EIGHT

THE AUDI'S INTOXICATING new car aroma wafted around us as Rossi and I sat side-by-side enjoying the view of our future home. Which right now was only a series of pylons sticking out of the earth. Beyond them lay the water and the peach glow of the sun as it slowly descended into the Gulf.

Though tired, I hadn't felt so relaxed in days, and leaning back on the tan leather headrest, I murmured, "I'm so glad the killer's been arrested, and the whole thing's all over."

"Your celebration's a little premature, sweetheart," Rossi said. "Nothing's over. It's only just begun. There's a trial to get through, and it's going to be your word against Tony's."

"I know."

His glance scoured me. "You know too much for your own safety."

"Don't be mad, Rossi. I'm sorry that I was in the wrong place at the—"

"I suppose you're going to say right time."

I nodded.

He took my hand and stroked my palm with his thumb. "I'm not mad, but I have been scared sick—for you. When the call came in, I was already on my way over there and hoping to God you weren't involved." He heaved a sigh.

"I'm sorry."

"No need to apologize. I love you, and I can't stand the thought of anything happening to you."

"The feeling is mutual, Rossi. So think of how I feel when you leave for work every day with that Glock strapped to your body."

"I've been trained for this kind of work. You have not."

"Well, let's look on the bright side," I said, anxious to change the subject. "Justice has prevailed. The murderer of two women has been arrested, and—"

"Now our job is to make that arrest stick." *Our job, that's a first.* "You'll be up against a tough cross-examination in court. Tony's lawyer will use every trick in the book to discredit your testimony." He peered at me with those dark, silky eyes. "That said, I think your word will prevail. You'll have Hammerjack's testimony as backup. Though it's anybody's guess how a jury will react to the word of an ex-con."

"Doesn't it count that Mike was sitting on Tony when Batano got there?"

"Of course it does." A smile lifted Rossi's lips. "Sitting on the killer and trying to get his cell phone out of his pocket at the same time. He never did get to the phone. I guess he isn't a multitasker."

"No wonder. His pants are so tight I don't know how he ever squeezes in a phone."

"Oh?" Rossi arched a brow. "You've noticed."

"To steal your line, I'm in love, I'm not dead."

He wrapped his arms around me and pulled me close. "Thank God."

"There's also that wallet I found. And the missing button."

"Sorry to be a spoiler, Deva, but as evidence, the button's of questionable value."

"Why questionable? I'm sure it came off Tony's cargo shorts."

"Probably, but no telling whether he lost it the day Mrs. Hawkins was killed or earlier. He and Hammerjack were working on the property for several days. Still I suspect the prosecution will point it out to the jury. More important is the way Tony bashed in the window of your old car. Uncontrolled anger like that is lethal when you're fighting a murder rap."

The setting sun finally completed its descent and disappeared below the horizon. A faint orange afterglow lingered in the sky. Then that too faded and we were left sitting in our car in the dark like a couple of teenaged lovers. Rossi, a firm believer in *carpe diem*, seized me in a searing kiss. Then his lips blazed a trail along my neck. When he reached my earlobe, I said, "Will you stop nibbling for a moment and tell me something?"

"Umm."

"The day my call came in? Why were you on your way to Whiskey Lane?"

"Okay," he said with a groan. "I guess you won't be at peace until all your questions are answered."

"Correct."

"Remember the handwritten statements I took the morning Kay Hawkins died? The graphologist in Miami targeted Tony."

I sat up straight, my fatigue forgotten. "Oh, really?" I had examined those samples and hadn't noticed anything incriminating in Tony's handwriting. "What did she see?"

"She said the left side of the page represents the past,

the right side the future. The normal tendency is to leave a space on the left—as if the writer were pulling away from the past—and to write close to the edge on the right side—as if eager for the future. Tony's handwriting reversed that normal tendency."

"Proving?"

"His obsession with the past."

"That's it?"

"That's it."

I slumped against the seat back. "I missed that completely."

"Don't beat yourself up. You'd have to be a pro to notice such a minor point. As things turned out, it was irrelevant anyway. Thanks to you, we already had his confession. When we showed him that picture of Connie Rae Freitas, he broke down. Blubbered like a baby."

"I'm glad I helped. For a while there I sure was headed down the wrong road. I thought Stew had something to do with Connie Rae's death, but all the while he was innocent."

"Your thinking wasn't so off base. When a spouse dies unexpectedly, the survivor is often a person of interest."

"But why did Stew lie like that? If he hadn't denied knowing about her heart condition, I wouldn't have suspected a thing."

"My guess is his priors for domestic violence had him nervous. He was probably afraid he'd be accused of killing her."

"That makes sense, but to think I also believed James might have killed Kay. Just like Marilyn said, for her money. Courtly, courteous James who adored Kay and loves Charlotte too. Treats her like a queen. I'm glad they're back together again. He needs his doggie. He needs Eileen too, but he certainly doesn't need Marilyn. I wonder where she's off to this time."

Rossi shrugged. "We'll leave that up to the Coast Guard." His hand found my knee. Then my thigh. "Maybe we should get a room."

"We have a room. An orange, purple and green one."

"When the lights go out, the colors don't matter."

"Ha! I can see them in the dark."

"I can't see a thing in the dark. Lucky I have fingers."

Concentrating on the case wasn't easy, but I managed to say, "Mike Hammerjack will likely go to prison, right?"

"With his record, I doubt he'll get off scot-free. He aided and abetted a murderer. He might not have known about the python in time to save Connie Rae, but if he'd told the truth in the first place, Kay might be alive today. On the other hand, he did apprehend Tony and helped you live to tell the tale. No doubt his attorney will plead to the court for leniency."

"Whatever happens, I'm going ahead with the Help-a-Con Program. It's a good cause, and the furniture is great for the price. And you know something else? The day he rammed my car with Tony's truck? I really think he told the truth. It *was* an accident. Anyway, my knee's fine now, and I'm more than willing to give him the benefit of the doubt."

In the dark, I couldn't read Rossi's expression, but he didn't protest as he put the car in gear.

I closed my eyes while we drove toward our rental apartment in Pelican Marsh. "I hope Lee and Paulo are enjoying their first night in Surfside. I sent them flowers, and I'll be happy to design a nursery, but I haven't done a thing about it yet."

"Not to worry. You have how long…five more months to plan."

He was trying to be comforting, and I loved him for it. Lately so much had come rushing at me I hadn't had time to concentrate on what was most important in life—the people I loved. There was such a thing as being too busy. Starting tomorrow, I intended…without warning, Rossi pulled off Tamiami Trail onto the lighted parking lot of a strip mall.

"What on—"

He switched off the ignition and turned to me. "As soon as the house is finished, I want us to set a wedding date. I was going to save this till then, but the suspense is killing me. I can't wait any longer." He leaned across the front seat and reached into the glove compartment. He withdrew a sheet of paper, unfolded it and held it out. "For you. My wedding vows."

"*Really?* I haven't written mine yet, Rossi. I didn't have ti—"

"Shh. Just read."

I glanced at the paper he'd placed in my hands. It was covered in big bold handwriting with long, enthusiastic *t* bars and fabulous, sexy lower loops. I read it all, and then again, as tears formed in my eyes.

To my bride, Devalera Agnes Kennedy Dunne,
   I vow to love and honor you. To cherish and protect you.
   To adore you body and soul for the rest of our days on earth.
   However long that may be, however rocky or

smooth our path in life, you are now, and always will be, my beloved partner in crime.

This I swear to you,
Victor Giuseppe Rossi

* * * * *

REQUEST YOUR FREE BOOKS!
2 FREE NOVELS PLUS 2 FREE GIFTS!

Ⓗ HARLEQUIN®

INTRIGUE

BREATHTAKING ROMANTIC SUSPENSE

YES! Please send me 2 FREE Harlequin® Intrigue novels and my 2 FREE gifts (gifts are worth about $10). After receiving them, if I don't wish to receive any more books, I can return the shipping statement marked "cancel." If I don't cancel, I will receive 6 brand-new novels every month and be billed just $4.74 per book in the U.S. or $5.49 per book in Canada. That's a savings of at least 12% off the cover price! It's quite a bargain! Shipping and handling is just 50¢ per book in the U.S. and 75¢ per book in Canada.* I understand that accepting the 2 free books and gifts places me under no obligation to buy anything. I can always return a shipment and cancel at any time. Even if I never buy another book, the two free books and gifts are mine to keep forever.

182/382 HDN GH3D

Name	(PLEASE PRINT)
Address	Apt. #
City	State/Prov. Zip/Postal Code

Signature (if under 18, a parent or guardian must sign)

Mail to the **Reader Service:**
IN U.S.A.: P.O. Box 1867, Buffalo, NY 14240-1867
IN CANADA: P.O. Box 609, Fort Erie, Ontario L2A 5X3
**Are you a subscriber to Harlequin® Intrigue books
and want to receive the larger-print edition?
Call 1-800-873-8635 or visit www.ReaderService.com.**

* Terms and prices subject to change without notice. Prices do not include applicable taxes. Sales tax applicable in N.Y. Canadian residents will be charged applicable taxes. Offer not valid in Quebec. This offer is limited to one order per household. Not valid for current subscribers to Harlequin Intrigue books. All orders subject to credit approval. Credit or debit balances in a customer's account(s) may be offset by any other outstanding balance owed by or to the customer. Please allow 4 to 6 weeks for delivery. Offer available while quantities last.

Your Privacy—The Reader Service is committed to protecting your privacy. Our Privacy Policy is available online at www.ReaderService.com or upon request from the Reader Service.

We make a portion of our mailing list available to reputable third parties that offer products we believe may interest you. If you prefer that we not exchange your name with third parties, or if you wish to clarify or modify your communication preferences, please visit us at www.ReaderService.com/consumerschoice or write to us at Reader Service Preference Service, P.O. Box 9062, Buffalo, NY 14240-9062. Include your complete name and address.

REQUEST YOUR FREE BOOKS!
2 FREE NOVELS PLUS 2 FREE GIFTS!

ROMANTIC suspense

Sparked by danger, fueled by passion

YES! Please send me 2 FREE Harlequin® Romantic Suspense novels and my 2 FREE gifts (gifts are worth about $10). After receiving them, if I don't wish to receive any more books, I can return the shipping statement marked "cancel." If I don't cancel, I will receive 4 brand-new novels every month and be billed just $4.74 per book in the U.S. or $5.49 per book in Canada. That's a savings of at least 12% off the cover price! It's quite a bargain! Shipping and handling is just 50¢ per book in the U.S. and 75¢ per book in Canada.* I understand that accepting the 2 free books and gifts places me under no obligation to buy anything. I can always return a shipment and cancel at any time. Even if I never buy another book, the two free books and gifts are mine to keep forever.

240/340 HDN GH3P

Name	(PLEASE PRINT)
Address	Apt. #
City	State/Prov. Zip/Postal Code

Signature (if under 18, a parent or guardian must sign)

Mail to the **Reader Service:**

IN U.S.A.: P.O. Box 1867, Buffalo, NY 14240-1867
IN CANADA: P.O. Box 609, Fort Erie, Ontario L2A 5X3

Want to try two free books from another line?
Call 1-800-873-8635 or visit www.ReaderService.com.

* Terms and prices subject to change without notice. Prices do not include applicable taxes. Sales tax applicable in N.Y. Canadian residents will be charged applicable taxes. Offer not valid in Quebec. This offer is limited to one order per household. Not valid for current subscribers to Harlequin Romantic Suspense books. All orders subject to credit approval. Credit or debit balances in a customer's account(s) may be offset by any other outstanding balance owed by or to the customer. Please allow 4 to 6 weeks for delivery. Offer available while quantities last.

Your Privacy—The Reader Service is committed to protecting your privacy. Our Privacy Policy is available online at www.ReaderService.com or upon request from the Reader Service.

We make a portion of our mailing list available to reputable third parties that offer products we believe may interest you. If you prefer that we not exchange your name with third parties, or if you wish to clarify or modify your communication preferences, please visit us at www.ReaderService.com/consumerschoice or write to us at Reader Service Preference Service, P.O. Box 9062, Buffalo, NY 14240-9062. Include your complete name and address.

HRS15

REQUEST YOUR FREE BOOKS!

2 FREE NOVELS
FROM THE SUSPENSE COLLECTION
PLUS 2 FREE GIFTS!